continued on next page...

TO KISS A TEXAN

"Compelling . . . fans will appreciate Thomas's subtle humor and her deft handling of sensitive topics."
— *Booklist*

"[A] poignant, exciting, emotional story . . . Jodi Thomas understands the workings of a woman's heart and a man's mind."
— *Romantic Times*

"A shootout, a treasure map, and a love that was meant to be—this book has all that and more. Ms. Thomas also brings back past characters to add texture to this well-told story."
— *Rendezvous*

THE TEXAN'S TOUCH

"A warm-hearted tale of a different sort. Fans of Ms. Thomas will long remember this book. Readers are in for a treat!"
— *Rendezvous*

"A terrific tale."
— Harriet Klausner

"Delightful and memorable characters and a roller-coaster pace . . . Another wonderful read from a true shining star."
— *Romantic Times*

TWO TEXAS HEARTS

"Thoroughly delightful . . . Ms. Thomas shows her extra-special talent as a first-class author." —*Rendezvous*

"A welcome gift . . . filled with sensitive, sometimes funny, romance." —*Affaire de Coeur*

"Jodi Thomas is at her remarkable best in *Two Texas Hearts*." —Debbie Macomber

"Jodi Thomas writes with a true love of Texas and her characters. What makes *Two Texas Hearts* special is the unique twist on the marriage of convenience plot created by her special brand of humor and characters who stay in your heart." —*Romantic Times*

"A wonderful book, destined for my keeper shelf simply because I felt happy while I read it." —*The Romance Reader*

"Provocative, sensual . . . clever and captivating. A tale that keeps you riveted from start to finish. Her characters are the kind of folks you'd want to have in your own family tree." —*Times Record News* (Wichita Falls, Texas)

FOREVER IN TEXAS

"A winner from an author who knows how to make the West tough but tender. Jodi Thomas's earthy characters, feisty dialogue and sweet love story will steal your heart." —*Romantic Times*

"A great western romance filled with suspense and plenty of action . . . will have the audience forever reading *Forever in Texas*." —*Affaire de Coeur*

continued on next page . . .

TEXAS LOVE SONG

"A warm and touching read full of intrigue and suspense that will keep the reader on the edge of her seat."

—*Rendezvous*

TO TAME A TEXAN'S HEART

*Winner of the Romance Writers of America
Best Historical Series Romance Award*

"Earthy, vibrant, funny, and poignant . . . a wonderful, colorful love story." —*Romantic Times*

"Breathtaking . . . heart-stopping romance and rip-roaring action." —*Affaire de Coeur*

THE TEXAN AND THE LADY

"Jodi Thomas shows us hard-living men with grit and guts, and the determined young women who soften their hearts."
—Pamela Morsi, bestselling author of
Something Shady and *Wild Oats*

PRAIRIE SONG

"A thoroughly entertaining romance." —*Gothic Journal*

THE TENDER TEXAN

*Winner of the Romance Writers of America
Best Historical Series Romance Award*

"Excellent . . . Have the tissues ready; this tender story will tug at your heart. Memorable reading." —*Rendezvous*

"This marvelous, sensitive, emotional romance is destined to be cherished by readers . . . a spellbinding story . . . filled with the special magic that makes a book a treasure."
—*Romantic Times*

Twilight
in Texas

Jodi Thomas

JOVE BOOKS, NEW YORK

TWILIGHT IN TEXAS

The Penguin Putnam Inc. World Wide Web site address is
http://www.penguinputnam.com

ISBN: 0-7394-1576-X

A JOVE BOOK®
Jove Books are published by The Berkley Publishing Group,
a division of Penguin Putnam Inc.,
375 Hudson Street, New York, New York 10014.
JOVE and the "J" design
are trademarks belonging to Penguin Putnam Inc.

PRINTED IN THE UNITED STATES OF AMERICA

ONE

THE AIR ON A WINDY JULY DAY IN AUSTIN, TEXAS, had a way of weighing down against a man's skin, heavy as a river made of sand. Wolf Hayward felt the thin layer of grit around his eyes crease as he squinted into the sun.

"Tuesday," he mumbled, pulling his handcuffed prisoner off a horse. If possible the man was dirtier than he. "I think it's Tuesday, Francis, but I can't be sure."

The prisoner shook like a long-haired dog, creating his own personal dust cloud. "Call me Francis again, Captain, and I'll have to escape just to kill you. Ain't no one but my mother ever called me that, and I let her live 'cause she could cook. Can't say the same for you, Hayward."

"I haven't heard you complain about the grub all week." Wolf checked the wrist chains one last time before they started down the street and into civilization. Francis Digger might be congenial enough right now, but Wolf had seen the man turn to killer in the blink of an eye. Francis and his brother had been in Texas since before the war. For years, they'd stuck to robbing their own kind. But with the state's new growth, they'd taken to bothering respectable folks. Their last stagecoach robbery left two passengers dead and the driver without the use of one arm.

"It weren't that your cooking's so bad." Francis followed behind Wolf, the chains allowing him little freedom. "It was just monotonous. Beans and sourdough twice a day for a week kind of makes a man long for a little variety. Ever' night I fell asleep knowing what I didn't finish for supper, I'd face at breakfast."

"Well, they'll give you whatever you want to eat before they hang you." Wolf watched the street. If Francis's brother planned to free him, there were only a few minutes left. In a hundred feet, the cold-blooded killer would be safely locked away in jail, and there were enough Texas Rangers in Austin to make sure that's where he stayed.

The buckskin-clad prisoner swore as he raised his nose like a wild animal smelling trouble. "Tuesday, you say. Hell, it don't matter to me, but you oughta know the day you're going to die, Captain Hayward."

Wolf chuckled. "I got you this far, didn't I? In a few steps you'll be in jail, and I'll be having my first drink in a month. If your brother planned to save you, he would have done it long before now."

Wolf pulled the prisoner along the covered walk. Signs advertising each business hung so low Wolf had to bend his huge frame slightly as they moved toward the jail. He glanced into the new mercantile as they passed. Austin was growing so fast, he couldn't keep up with the stores. At the end of the war, cattle grazed in the streets; now stores popped up fast as weeds once had.

Two ladies strolled by. They stared at him, from his hairy face to his knee-high leather moccasins, and giggled as they quickly moved along. Wolf realized he no longer fit in. He hadn't reached thirty, but he felt like an old man. He now looked more like a drifter than an officer of the law. Four years ago when he landed here in Texas, this had been the place for him. Wild, and rough. A state where a man's history didn't matter as much as his strength and skill with a gun.

But now there were new businesses and respectable ladies. Austin had more permanent buildings than he could count. Curtains even framed the drugstore they moved past.

He glanced in the window at the line of bottles circling a mortar and pestle. For a moment he stared at the sun glistening off the display. Then, like a vision from an old nightmare, Wolf saw the reflection of Francis's brother, Carrell Digger, in the window. The older Digger was crouched in the shadows between two buildings across the street.

As the wavy vision raised a rifle, Wolf reacted with lightning movements. With a mighty heave, he swung Francis by his handcuffs into the glass storefront and twisted to face Carrell with his Colt already springing to action.

Gunfire shattered the air. The women and Francis screamed. Glass fell like crystal rain into the sunlight.

The ambusher crumpled, his second shot striking metal just above Wolf's head.

Wolf had no time to exhale with relief or see if Francis was all right. A shingle flew from above and struck him hard across the forehead.

As the huge lawman folded to his knees, the remaining chain holding the pharmacy sign snapped. The sign hit the walk only seconds before he did.

The last thing Wolf Hayward saw before his world went black was Molly Donivan's name carved on the sign with the word *alchemist* below it.

Molly Donivan, the one name he'd spent a war and what seemed like half his life trying to forget.

Memories danced in the blackness of his consciousness, drowning out the hard thud of his head against the walk.

First only as shadows, then clearer in his mind's eye, came a vision from the past.

"Pardon me, miss," he whispered to an angel dressed in Union blue. Hundreds moved around them at the crowded Philadelphia train station. New recruits anxious to go to war, returning heroes, families whispering tearful good-byes and crying heartfelt greetings.

She met his stare with shy green eyes.

He couldn't tell her he'd watched her all morning as she moved among the arriving wounded. He'd never be able to explain how each time she touched a soldier in comfort, he'd felt a longing grow within him. Or how the sight of her warmed his heart as though he'd known he'd always find her.

"You don't know me. . . ." He stumbled over words. "There's no time, and I don't know if you'll believe me." He loved the way she faced him so directly. The intelligence in her gaze shook him to the core. He rushed ahead. "But my name is Benjamin and I know I've been looking for you all my life."

A train whistle sounded, rippling the air with impatience. Smoke swirled around them. He felt suddenly uncomfortable in his blue uniform with the shiny lieutenant's bars on the collar. Strangers rushed in streams on either side.

"I have to board. This is my train." He smiled down at her, memorizing her face. "But I must have your name before I go. I'll carry it with me until this war is over. Then I'll find you. I swear, I'll find you." He knew he sounded desperate, but he didn't care. She wasn't someone he could see once and forget.

"Molly," she whispered, then shouted above the crowd. "Molly Donivan."

A soldier running to board pushed him closer to her. "Molly," he whispered only an inch from her cheek. "Do you believe in love at first sight?"

Young, innocent eyes studied his face. "I'm starting to," she answered as her fingers lightly brushed across his heart.

Before he could stop himself, he kissed her boldly, wildly, in front of hundreds of people. Heaven exploded in his mind as she moved into his embrace, and he realized she was kissing him back.

She was tall, willow thin, and made for his arms.

The whistle sounded again. Urgent now. Steam

poured from the train as the mighty iron horse began to move. There was no time. He had to go. But for a second he wasn't sure he could release her.

She slowly stepped back without a word, her eyes sparkling with tears. There was no need, no time for words. Somehow in a moment they both knew what they'd found . . . what they were about to lose.

He ran frantically, catching the last steps of the now moving train. "Wait for me, Molly Donivan," he yelled above all the noise. "For I'll love you until my heart beats no more."

She touched her fingers to her lips as tears bubbled onto her cheeks.

He patted the side of the train as though it were a horse that had waited for him and now had to run. Just before he lost sight of her, a general stepped to her side. It took him a moment to place the older man. General Donivan! One of a handful of Union doctors he'd been watching. She had to be the general's daughter!

The realization slammed against his heart with the impact of a fully powered locomotive.

She was a general's daughter, and he . . . he was a Southern spy deep behind enemy lines, dressed in Union blue. For a moment, he'd forgotten the war and his mission.

Wolf fought the memory from eight years ago as voices intruded into his brain. He could have gone back and found her somehow—if it had only been time and space that stood between them. But a war separated them. He'd known as she disappeared from his sight he could never return to her. Not to Molly Donivan. Not to a general's daughter.

Shouts grew louder, pulling Wolf back fully to the present.

"Move him out of the way while I see to the man in chains," a woman proclaimed.

Wolf opened his eyes slowly as a skirt brushed the side of his face. A tall lady in black stood above him, issuing orders to everyone.

"We'll see to the prisoner, ma'am!" someone shouted. "You see what you can do for our captain."

The skirt tickled his face again. "This mountain of mud and hair is a Texas Ranger?" the woman asked.

Josh Weston leaned down. "Yes, ma'am, Captain Wolf Hayward. One of the best, but unfortunately he don't clean up much prettier." Josh laughed and stepped over Wolf. "I doubt a board hitting him over the head could do much damage, but you might want to see to it before he bleeds all over your porch."

Before Wolf could stand and put the young ranger in his place, the woman knelt beside him.

Intelligent green eyes locked with his.

"Molly," he whispered, matching a memory with reality.

"That's right," she answered. "I'm Molly Donivan. Dr. Molly Donivan. If you'll lie still, I'll see what I can do about that cut."

Her fingers brushed his forehead, pushing hair away from the wound.

Wolf closed his eyes and reached for her as he'd

tried to reach for a memory for eight years.

Molly screamed as she tumbled atop him. He held fast until her punches hurt enough to register that maybe she didn't want his hug. Groaning like an animal, he released her.

She wiggled to a sitting position atop him. "Stop that!" she ordered as she shoved his arm to the walk beside his head.

He made no effort to move.

"Be still and behave yourself, or I'll hit you with the board across the other side of your head, Captain."

He stared into her angry green eyes and fought down a laugh. His Molly had matured into one headstrong woman, full of fight and fire.

"Nice job." Josh Weston squatted beside them, his clean-shaven face dimpling with his wide smile. "You always sit on your patients, Doc?"

Molly quickly scooted off Wolf. "When they don't cooperate."

Wolf didn't miss the way she lifted her chin. She was not a woman given to apology or explanation.

Josh tipped his hat respectfully. "Well, you'd better climb back on the captain, 'cause I've never known him to cooperate. He's worse than a wild mustang about being doctored. Last year when a doc over in El Paso had to dig a bullet out of his leg, it took four of us to hold him down."

The young ranger patted Wolf's shoulder as he gave Molly an apologetic look. "Just rest easy, Captain Hayward. We got the Digger boys on their way to jail.

Neither one is hurt bad enough to miss the hanging tomorrow."

Wolf nodded and raised up, forgetting that Molly thought her grip held his arm down.

He watched her stiffen with anger. "If you're able"—she tried to gain control once more—"I can treat you in my store easier." Despite what Josh had just told her, there was no fear in her stare.

Standing, Wolf followed her inside as the last of the rangers headed toward the jail. Watching her move, he tried to believe she was really before him. If this was his Molly, she'd changed, he thought. The willow-thin body he remembered had matured into a woman with gentle curves. But the eyes were the same. The voice only slightly lower.

It couldn't be her, he reasoned as he moved through the small store. The same name, the same hair, the same eyes didn't matter. If she was his Molly, she'd remember him.

Wolf glanced past the counter to a wall covered in mirrored shelves filled with all sizes of bottles. A hundred reflections looked back at him.

Hell, he thought, I don't even recognize myself. He'd gained fifty pounds, at least, from the slender man of years ago. His face had been clean-shaven, his hair short. A hundred battles had scarred not only his body, but his soul. No wonder she didn't know him. Even his speech had slipped back into his natural Southern drawl, losing the practiced Northern tone he'd worked so hard on.

She pointed him toward a stool as she disappeared

behind a curtain at the back. "I'll get water. You stay put," she ordered.

Wolf let the blood drip down his face and onto his shirt. He didn't own a scrap of material clean enough to wipe an open wound.

His eyes followed her when she returned. Questions came to mind, but he held his tongue. The war might be over, but nothing had changed. If she even remembered that day at the train station, she still wouldn't want to see him. He'd heard her father died a hero for the North, fighting disease and operating conditions in field hospitals until a stray bullet from a nearby battle found him.

She rolled up her sleeves. "Hold still. I have to wash enough dirt off you to see the wound before I can treat it."

Wolf frowned. "Are you a real doctor?"

She winked as if thinking of lying. "As real as you're going to get in this town. I can promise you I went to med school as long as any practitioner in Austin. My studies were mostly in pharmacy. Much to my father's disappointment, I prefer to work making prescriptions rather than with patients."

"Like the snake-oil doctors with the wagons going from town to town?" He watched her reaction, almost hoping to make her angry again so he could see those green eyes sparkle.

To his surprise, she nodded calmly. "That's me." She leaned forward and began cleaning the wound. "I did go to college for two years and my father was a doctor, but today, basically I mix potions."

"Over at Fort Mojave in Arizona, the Apache killed six medicine men last year for failing to cure the fever infecting the tribe."

"I assure you, Captain, you'll live. I'm in no fear of my life."

She was so close he could smell her, an intoxicating blend of medicines and perfume and woman. He was afraid to breathe for fear he'd lose himself in the smell of her. "You married?" The question was out before he thought to stop it.

"No," she answered as she worked.

"Widowed?" He glanced the length of her sober dress. Black was the color many women her age wore. But his Molly belonged in blue.

She paused. "Not that it's any of your business, Captain, but the man I loved died in the war."

Wolf didn't know if he was happy or sad to hear that she'd loved someone. Happy, maybe, that she'd gone on with her life and not pined away for him. Sad that she'd known loss.

"Want to go to dinner with me?"

She continued to wipe blood from his forehead. "No," she answered simply.

"If I take a bath and clean up?" he tried again. In his life he could never remember asking a woman to step out with him, but he figured the direct way had to work.

"No, thank you," she answered as she dabbed ointment on his cut.

Wolf shrugged. "Then I guess marrying me is out, Doc?"

A smile brushed her lips. "This is going to hurt, Captain. Try not to jerk."

Wolf's stare never left her face as fire brushed across his torn skin. She leaned close, blowing softly along the cut.

He fought the urge to reach for her. "Thanks," he whispered. "What do I owe you?" He didn't want to think that she'd treated him for money, but after all, it was what she did for a living.

"A new window." She replaced the cap on her bottle of medicine. "I don't charge for the doctoring."

"A window and dinner. I insist on evening the score. I'll not be beholden."

"All right. If you can clean up before sundown, I'll share a meal with you. But understand clearly, Captain, we're not walking out with one another, only having dinner. I'm far too old and have no time in my life for such foolishness as courting."

Wolf replaced his mud-caked hat. "I understand." He knew she couldn't be much past her mid-twenties. "I'm obliged you've agreed to share a meal with me. Until sundown."

"Until sundown, Captain." She turned without another word and disappeared behind the curtain at the back of the store.

It took Wolf several breaths to make himself move away. "Until sundown, Molly," he whispered as he walked outside.

TWO

THE SUN DISAPPEARED BEHIND GRAY CLOUDS BY MID-afternoon, making Austin seem drab and colorless. Molly Donivan tried to work through the rest of her day with little thought of the dust-covered ranger who'd destroyed the front of her store. But the dinner she'd promised to have with him kept drifting through her mind, no more beckoned than the clouds.

Every day since she'd arrived in Austin had been unpredictable. Why should a chained prisoner flying through her storefront be a surprise? She'd already encountered salesmen as slimy as snakes and town folks who didn't believe an unmarried woman should have a business of any kind. Then there were the people of the back streets who resented her voicing her opinions on the sale of opium.

For the hundredth time, she wondered why she'd left the safety of Philadelphia. Had the need to be her own person, not just Gen. Patrick Donivan's daughter, been so important? Or was it more the feeling that she'd always been at the starting gate and never really entered the race called life?

Her father's two old-maid sisters had begged her not to leave, yet drove her away with their constant smothering. They didn't understand why a life with books and tea parties wasn't enough for Molly. They thought her interest in being an alchemist would fade, not land her in the wilds of Texas.

Molly almost laughed out loud thinking of what they'd say about this morning's events.

Miller, the undertaker/cabinetmaker from next door, poked his balding head through the opening where glass had been. "Got here as soon as I could, Miss Donivan." He looked disappointed when she only answered with a nod and continued working. "This spot seems the unluckiest place for a window. You haven't been here a month and it's been shattered twice."

"Only, I know who did it this morning. Not some coward in the middle of the night, but a ranger. This time it was just an accident."

The little carpenter grunted as he moved his toolbox inside.

Miller was nice enough, but something about him bothered Molly. Maybe it was the way he stared at her. She couldn't tell if he was flirting, or visually measuring her for a coffin. He always seemed a little anxious when asking about everyone's health, and he called her Miss more as a label than out of any respect.

Molly glanced at herself in the mirrored wall. No, she thought, he wouldn't be flirting. She was not the kind of woman men made eyes at. Molly knew she was too tall, too thin, and too outspoken.

Only once in her life had a man been swept away with her beauty. When he didn't come back from the war, she made up her mind that once was enough. She carried the memory of a perfect moment and all the dreams of what might have been to keep her warm. She'd not lower her standards or hide her intelligence to draw men. Her father taught her to stand alone. And her aunts had often reminded her that that was exactly what she'd do if she didn't change her ways.

She gazed once more at the reflection of a woman dressed in black and wondered if the ranger had any idea that he was the first man in years brave enough to ask her out. She'd stopped others before they could finish the question.

But Captain Hayward had asked directly, without plying her with compliments or poorly hidden innu-endoes. He was nothing like the fortune hunters back home. Hayward could know nothing of her finances, for all he saw was a tiny shop smaller than her bedroom in Philadelphia.

"I can have the glass delivered in a few hours if they've a piece the right size," the undertaker said, interrupting her thoughts.

"Fine," Molly answered, noticing as Miller lowered his gaze to her shoes then slowly returned it to her face.

"I could come over tonight and install it for you."

"That would be fine." Molly kept her voice even, polite. "Ephraim will be here."

The undertaker glared at the old man sweeping up

glass near the door. In frustration Miller opened his mouth round and wide like a fish, but nothing came out. He didn't know her well enough to ask questions. He never would.

Tension eased in Molly's shoulders when Miller finally left—after having made several comments about how much easier life would be for her if she had a man around.

By noon, Ephraim had cleaned up the last of the broken glass. He'd taken on the project with his usual slow steadiness, which somehow always managed to get everything done. He might be old and frail, but he seemed his happiest when he knew he was helping Molly.

She'd inherited Ephraim after her father died. He'd been her father's assistant for twenty years at the hospital in Philadelphia. When the war broke out, Ephraim had been too old to enlist, so he'd followed Dr. Donivan from hospital to hospital.

He'd always been in the background, taking care of things. When the general was shot in a medical tent pitched too close to the fighting, Ephraim caught him before Molly's father hit the ground. He'd kept the general alive for two days, then brought the body home for burial.

Now, at almost seventy, he had no duties but was always around, ready to help Molly. He lived in a room at the back of the store; Molly occupied one of the rooms above. As he had done when she was a child, he looked after her.

When he passed with the last dustpan of broken

glass, she looked up from a cream she was mixing. "Quite a mess. Thanks for cleaning it up."

Ephraim nodded. "Shall I save you a bowl of soup tonight?"

"No, thank you. I'm having dinner with the hairy giant who wrecked the shop." She couldn't help but smile.

Ephraim looked like she'd just promised to mud-wrestle in the street. "Shall I accompany you?" He straightened his bony frame, but he looked tired.

"I don't think that will be necessary," Molly answered as calmly as she could. The thought of Ephraim chaperoning her and Captain Hayward was hilarious. The man could probably blow Ephraim over with a deep breath. "We're only going down the street to dinner, nothing more. You need to rest."

Ephraim didn't say another word all afternoon, but she knew he was as flustered as a mother hen who'd misplaced her one chick. In the four years since her father's death, he'd hardly let her out of his sight during waking hours. When she'd decided to move to Texas, he hadn't said a word. He just packed. He would never have allowed her to make the trip if he'd known part of her reason was to move him to a warmer climate.

Molly wished there were some way to put his mind at ease. She had a feeling that Captain Hayward, despite his appearance, was gentleman enough for her to dine with.

While she concentrated on her mixture, needed for a toothache, shadows darkened the store. The oil of cloves she used flavored the air, drifting from her marble workstation and in and out of the hundreds of bottles and boxes surrounding her. The smells of the mixtures always made Molly feel at home, for they were the aromas of her father's office.

"Smells good." Captain Hayward's deep voice startled her.

Molly glanced up. His huge frame blocked the door, closing out any remaining sunlight. He stood tall and proud, but, as predicted, the man didn't clean up much prettier. His clothes were freshly washed, but he was still the odd mixture of gunfighter and mountain man. His hair had been cut several inches, but remained touching his wide shoulders. The beard was shorter, but so thick it looked like dark underbrush threatening to take over the few inches left clear on his face.

"Sorry, it's not food." She closed the mixture into a tin. "It's for old Mrs. Hollard's toothache. I can make a potion or powder to cure everything from a headache to head lice, but I can't cook anything worth eating."

Molly marked the tin and looked up at her company when he didn't reply. He was a man whose presence would frighten most folks into becoming law-abiding. Wide shoulders, well armed. And, to her disbelief, nervous.

"Captain Hayward." She removed her work apron. "My, don't you look nice." The lie in her words made her grin.

Wolf breathed as though he'd been waiting for permission. "Thanks, ma'am. I soaked through three tubs of water hoping I'd get clean enough to be seen with you at dinner."

"And the weapons?" Molly looked down at the twin Colts strapped to his powerful legs.

Wolf misunderstood. "Oh, I left most of them in the hotel room. But I'll go back for them if you think we might run into trouble."

"No." She lifted her shawl from the hook, wishing she'd taken time to change. "We should be safe enough crossing the street."

Wolf started out the door, then stopped and backtracked. When he reached her side, he offered his arm. "Shall we go?" he said with a slight bow.

Molly fought down the first urge she'd had to giggle in years. She couldn't believe she was stepping out with Captain Hayward. Her father, if he were still alive, would surely think she'd lost her mind. The general never allowed even a button to tarnish. He would have a hard time understanding someone who looked more like his nickname than a law officer.

She took Wolf's arm and let him lead her past the undertaker. Miller stared at them with his open fishmouth. Molly may have insisted earlier that they were just going to dinner, nothing more, but she knew it would appear as more to all in town.

"If it's all right with you, Doc, I thought we'd eat at Noma's." Wolf didn't look at her as they moved down the street, but stared straight ahead as though marching in formation. The muscles of his arm were tight as iron beneath her touch and the slight scent of lye soap surrounded him.

"Noma's is fine." Molly relaxed and wished he would. She was glad he'd picked a cafe and not a fancy restaurant in one of the hotels.

He didn't say a word as they entered the cafe. A waitress showed them to a table in the middle of the crowd while a young girl hurried to the kitchen. As Molly unfolded her napkin, the girl set two slices of pie in front of Wolf.

"Heard you were in town, Captain. Have your pie ready." The waitress nodded politely and hurried away, not expecting an answer.

He looked at Molly, and she almost believed he blushed beneath all that hair. "I haven't had a meal that wasn't cooked on an open fire for over a month." He watched the desserts. "Noma knows I like pie."

Molly saw him stare at the pie once more, but he didn't lift his fork. His glance was as transparent as a child's. "Go ahead. Have your dessert first, Captain. I wouldn't want to upset your pattern."

Wolf winked at her and forked a third of one of the slices in his mouth.

Noma's place looked like several others she'd seen in the West. The menu was posted on a slate at the front door. Everyone who entered was served the same meal within minutes after taking a seat.

Slowly, as they talked and ate, Wolf relaxed. He asked questions about her business, and Molly found herself telling him details and problems she'd never talked over with anyone. He was easy to talk to. A man more interested in knowing than telling. She found herself wondering if he'd used such a skill all his life, but she didn't ask.

He ate everything on his plate except the beans. Each time he finished a slice of pie, another appeared on the table. All kinds, creams, chocolates, fruit, chess. He cut each in thirds then inhaled it along with the rest of the meal.

Finally, Molly could remain quiet no longer. "I'm sorry. I know it's impolite to comment, but to my count you've eaten two pies."

Wolf wiped his beard. "I know. I'm saving the third one for dessert."

She laughed so hard several heads turned in her direction.

She couldn't remember when she'd had such a good time. Wolf proved a perfect gentleman beneath the layers of hair and leather. They talked of Austin, the weather, and her world. If she'd expected him to brag of the men he'd captured or killed, she would have been disappointed. Like many men in Texas, he avoided discussing his past. A few years ago, the thought that he might have fought for the South would have bothered her, but she'd finally let the prejudice of war go. After all, she lived in Texas, where men from both sides tried to start over.

As they walked back to her store, Molly leaned naturally against his arm, feeling his strength along her side.

"Thank you for having dinner with me," he said as his huge hand covered her fingers where they rested on his arm.

"You're welcome," she answered. "I enjoyed it."

He slowed his pace. For the first time all evening, neither knew what to say.

Finally, Wolf cleared his throat and faced her. "I don't know what to call you. Doc? Miss Donivan? Molly?"

The way he said her name sounded like an endearment, as if he'd said it millions of times in a prayer. She couldn't hide a smile. "What would you like to call me, Captain?"

"Molly," he whispered, "if we are to be friends."

She offered her hand. "I'd like that. And what should I call you?"

He took her hand in his but didn't shake it. "I've been called Wolf for so long I probably wouldn't answer to anything else."

He moved his thumb slowly over her palm. Molly felt the warmth all the way to her toes. Beneath his rough exterior, Molly guessed, dwelled a man who knew how to please a woman. Yet his hesitance made her wonder how many women he'd taken the time to know.

"I'll be here for three more days." His warm dark eyes captured her. "Then I'll be back to eating my own cooking. Will you have dinner with me again before I have to go?"

"As friends, Captain? I'm not looking for anything more."

"Friends it will be then," he answered.

She tried to pull together her feelings for him. He was not the kind of man she'd ever thought she'd talk to, much less have dinner with. She'd learned a long time ago to depend only on herself and no one else. She never fit in with women. She'd never known a mother to tell her how to act.

Ephraim and her father had brought her up and taught her much but they'd also forgotten to warn her. When she'd been a child, men treated her kindly, thinking it entertaining that she knew so much about medicine. When she was a young girl, they'd flirted and teased her as if her interests were a joke. As she'd matured, the men around her saw her as a threat. Something unnatural to be dealt with.

But this ranger fit none of the categories. He seemed to see her as a real person.

"You've told me nothing of you." His face was in shadows now, but she sensed his nervousness once more.

"Nothing I could tell you would be of any importance."

She liked the way his low voice had an easiness about it. Sometimes she thought she could hear the Mississippi in his slow words.

She also felt a strength about him that had nothing to do with the size of his body or the hardness of his muscles. This man's character had been fired in more than one blaze of courage.

As they walked on, she decided she wanted to know more about Wolf Hayward. She doubted his suggestion that there was nothing to tell.

When they neared her store, Molly saw movement

through the new glass. Her fingers tightened slightly along his arm.

"What is it?" Wolf whispered, sensing trouble.

"Someone's in my store." She could see the shadows of several men moving around inside the tiny space.

Wolf slowly released her hand and pulled his jacket back to clear the path of his Colts if needed. "What about the old man I saw with you?"

"Ephraim? He turns down the lamps at sundown and goes to bed. He's never up this late."

Wolf met her stare in the lamplight. "Would I be wasting my breath asking you to stay here?"

"You would." She appreciated the fact that he made no attempt to order her.

"Stay behind me, then, Molly? It's probably nothing, but just in case there's trouble, I'd like to have your word."

She thought of arguing but reconsidered. "It may be some of the businessmen who swore I'd be gone by now. Maybe they only want to talk again. They've stopped by a few times to inform me my space is needed for more important businesses."

Wolf slipped his revolver from its cradle. "Then they should have come during business hours."

She nodded, knowing he was right. She hadn't told even Ephraim about the veiled threats. She'd noticed open hatred in a few eyes when she'd promised to clear the town of opium dens at the first town meeting she'd attended.

Wolf walked across the street, staying well within

the shadows. He took one quick glance into the window and let the tension ease.

"It's all right," he said as he slipped his Colt back in place. "They're rangers."

Slowly, Molly moved past him and opened the door to her store. Rangers lined the counters.

"What's going on?" Wolf asked as he followed Molly inside.

"Shhhh!" Josh Weston ordered in none too soft a tone. "We finally got her asleep."

As Molly twisted the light higher, a chorus of groans sounded. All eyes turned toward one of the counters, where a bundle began to squirm.

"What is it?" Wolf neared.

"It's yours, Captain. The judge said so."

Before Wolf could ask more, the bundle began to cry. A tiny girl with golden ringlets sat up, rubbing her eyes. She was dressed in a tailored wool navy coat with stockings to match. She was so small, she looked more doll than human.

"This isn't mine." Wolf took a step backward.

Josh shrugged, as if feeling sorry for his captain. "Judge said you're the one who brought in her uncles, so she's your problem."

"Uncles?" Wolf mumbled as a ranger helped the tiny thing to the floor. He was surprised she was old enough to stand.

"Francis and Carrell Digger," Josh replied. "It seems her folks died back in Savannah, and the only kin she has are two uncles. Someone must have thought Francis or Carrell was a female to have sent her all this way. Her ticket was for one direction. No one wants her back."

"Yeah, Captain," another ranger offered. "Her uncles hang tomorrow, so she's all yours."

Wolf looked like he'd just been handed his own death warrant. "What am I going to do with her?"

The little princess walked straight over to the huge captain and kicked him hard in the shin. "Feed me," she ordered, rearing her foot back for another blow. "Feed me, now!"

Molly pulled Wolf out of harm's way. "Maybe you'd better stand behind *me,* Captain."

THREE

Wolf stared at the tiny child dancing around the Ranger office and frowned. This wasn't the way he'd planned to end the first evening he'd ever spent with his Molly.

If possible, the years had made Molly Donivan more beautiful than he remembered. Yet there was something new about her. An untouchable air. A hardness as clear as ice around the lovely woman. An invisible razor edge that warned anyone not to step too close.

Her sharp mind was another matter. It drew him to her. She made him believe he might have a full conversation with a lady for the first time in his life. She made him feel comfortable.

He thought he'd get to know the Molly who had drifted through his mind for eight years. He would gain her trust and maybe her respect, then explain who he really was. Maybe he'd ask if she remembered him and their shared kiss. Maybe he'd see if she was willing to start again. He could leave out enough details that she'd say yes. Or maybe he'd be better off lying. He told himself all day that he would think of something before the evening ended.

But that was all before this delivery now dancing in front of him. "What's your name?" he growled at the child.

"Callie Ann Digger," she answered as if singing a song. "But you can call me Princess."

The child was too young or too crazy to have sense enough to be afraid of him. After she'd kicked him a few times back in the drugstore, she'd decided he was harmless. Molly offered to keep her for the night, but Callie Ann cried and fought like a wild creature, insisting on going with Wolf.

He couldn't very well take her to Granny Gravy's, where he usually rented a room. Only men stayed in the boardinghouse and most tried not to eat more than one meal a day there even though Granny offered three for the price. She served sausage-flavored gravy for breakfast, chicken-flavored gravy for lunch, and whatever was left over for supper. She loved renting to rangers because they were never around and if they failed to return in three months, her house rules stated, she got to keep all gear left in the room.

"I don't like kids," he mumbled, wishing he'd had somewhere else to bring her besides the office. "And little girls are my least favorite creatures on this earth."

She stopped twirling and stared at him as if she'd suddenly forgotten how to understand English. But she still remembered how to speak it. "Can I have another cookie?"

Wolf grumbled and opened his jar of prize cookies Noma made for him. He'd been feeding them to the little princess for an hour. She looked no closer to settling down and going to bed than she had when she'd insisted he carry her from Molly's store.

"You promise to go to sleep?"

"If I eat one more cookie." She smiled a cherubic smile, as she had the other times, and he knew she lied, but he handed her the jar anyway.

She took two more cookies. "Did you really shoot my uncles?"

"Only one of them."

Wolf thought she might be upset by the news, but she just shrugged her tiny shoulders.

"I told the sheriff back home that Grandma always said they were worthless, but he sent me here anyway. He said kin is kin even if they're no-account and how bad could two men named Carrell and Francis be."

"Aren't you afraid of me?" Wolf decided maybe she wasn't a child at all but one of those pixies the gypsies say haunt the deep woods. She looked three, but she'd told Molly she was almost six.

"I might have been. You're the biggest man I remember ever seeing," she answered. "But Uncle Orson told me not to be."

He let out a long breath and smiled. "Finally, we're getting somewhere. You have another uncle?"

"Uh-huh." She crawled up in his lap and whispered, "But he's not like the others."

Wolf settled her in the bend of his arm. "He's not?

Why not?" Anything was bound to be better than the two Diggers he knew about.

She leaned her curls against his chest and yawned. "I can't say, but you can ask him."

Wolf relaxed; maybe his problems weren't near as deep as he thought. All he needed to do was contact her uncle Orson and send her in the right direction. Hopefully Orson wasn't an outlaw. Maybe he'd be a married man ready to take on another mouth to feed. "Where does Uncle Orson live, child?"

"With me," she answered, her eyes half closed. "Sometimes he sleeps in the barn when my grandma yells she doesn't want to hear his name one more time. But he doesn't like the barn. The cows keep him awake."

"Where is he now?" Wolf needed to get the information before she fell asleep. At daybreak he could send off a telegram.

"He's sitting over by the door. Has been since we came in. Said he wouldn't walk another step." She rubbed her eyes. "But he's too tired to talk anymore, so don't ask him any questions tonight."

Wolf caught himself looking at the empty chair by the door before he countered. "But . . ." It was no use, the child was asleep.

Carefully he carried her to the wide parson's bench beneath the windows and covered her with his wool coat. "I'll find out tomorrow," he said as he tucked her in. "Good night, Princess."

• • •

Just after dawn, Wolf shifted in his chair. His foot fell off the desk, rocking him forward. The thud of his boot against the hardwood brought him wide awake.

For a moment, he thought the child last night had been part of a dream. When the bundle by the window moved, he knew the dream was true.

The thought of trying to get the Diggers out of jail to take on their charge crossed his mind. But even if they weren't guilty of more murders than he could count, neither of them was fit to raise a child. When they weren't robbing stages, they drank. Carrell once bragged about killing a prostitute for overcharging him. Francis claimed they got Carrell's money back by selling the hooker's kid down in Mexico. Wolf wouldn't put it past the brothers to sell Callie Ann if they thought she'd bring a few dollars.

Wolf shook his head. He didn't even want to let the Digger brothers know they had a relative in town. Somehow they'd use the knowledge for their own purposes.

He glanced at the clock. In thirty minutes, they were due to hang.

A mass of blond curls poked out from beneath his coat. Round blue eyes blinked away sleep.

"Morning," he said, thinking she was cute as a shiny new button, but whoever taught the kid to talk pumped the churn a few too many times. "Are you hungry?"

She nodded and slid down from the bench. "But I have to go to the privy first, then wash up and comb my hair."

"Can you do that by yourself?"

She shook her head.

"Well, who usually helps?"

"Grandma." Callie Ann looked like she was about to cry. "But they put her in a box and planted it in the ground. The next morning the sheriff talked a couple into taking me on a train to a big city. I can't remember what their names were."

Wolf stood and motioned for her to lead the way out the door. "And . . . ?" he encouraged as they walked along the street.

Callie Ann thought for a minute. "And . . . when we got to a city, they walked with me to the stage place. They asked a woman named Mrs. Murphy to ride beside me to Austin since she was going the same way. She did, too. Even gave me apples and bread stuffed with butter and honey whenever I told her I was hungry."

She hurried ahead of him. "I didn't talk to her much, though. Uncle Orson told me not to. He said she was Sunday honest."

"Uncle Orson?" Wolf tried to piece together what she'd said about the man last night. "Where did you say he was?"

"I didn't." She peeked behind Wolf. "But he's following us. You can't see him because he's in the shadows now. He doesn't like to walk in the sun."

They reached the door to Molly's store. Wolf tried the knob then pounded. By the time Molly answered, Callie Ann was doing a one-legged dance beside him.

Molly's gaze met his for a moment, then lowered to the child.

"I . . . We . . ." He had no idea how to ask for her help in such a matter. He had no one else to turn to.

Molly took Callie Ann's hand and smiled down at her. "I understand. Come along, child."

Just before they disappeared upstairs, Molly glanced back at him and winked.

He grumbled as if finding the child a great bother, but grinned once Molly was out of sight. He couldn't help but wonder if the woman always woke up competing with the sun. She was so beautiful he didn't understand why there weren't suitors sleeping on her doorstep every night just to see her at dawn.

Following his nose to the coffeepot in the kitchen, Wolf stepped behind the curtain. The bony old man Molly referred to as Ephraim sat at a table for two. He was so slim his clothes hung on him like a scarecrow's. He held his head in his long spider-thin hands with blue veins as wide as his fingers.

"Mornin'." Wolf saw no sign he'd surprised the man and wondered if anything had in years.

"Welcome. Want a cup?" Ephraim stood one joint at a time.

"Thanks." Wolf glanced at the kitchen chair and doubted it would hold his weight. "Sorry to bust in on you this early."

"I've spent my life in the service of the Donivans. Callers have always been welcome at any hour. Or at least they have been until recently. We've been having a few late at night that I'd like to wallop with my cane."

The ranger waited. He knew the old man had something he needed to say. Ephraim seemed to chew on the words before he spoke.

A shaky hand poured coffee. When Ephraim returned to his chair, he looked up at Wolf with eyes as clear as fresh water.

"She won't tell you rangers, or anyone else, but Molly's in trouble. Bad trouble, and for the life of me I can't figure where it's coming from."

Wolf cradled the cup and listened. The old man didn't strike him as one given to idle gossip. He wouldn't be speaking out of turn if he didn't consider it necessary.

"I asked around about you, Captain." Ephraim lowered his voice. "You're respected in this town. Talked about like a legend for the good you've done since you've been in Texas."

Wolf took a sip. "What's the problem?"

Ephraim nodded as if understanding Wolf's modesty. Any man who was old enough to have fought in the war had memories and regrets enough to keep him from getting too proud. "She's a fighter, just like her father. Some folks can see a wrong and walk right past it. Others got to stop and try to fix it. She's like that, Molly, always wanting the world to be a better place and taking on the job of improving it like it was her calling.

"Her father was the same. I remember when the first battle of the war was over, he watched the wounded try to walk and crawl back to Washington because all the ambulance wagons the army hired took off at the first shots. He fired up like an avenging angel, donating his own buggy to use as transport and demanding at gunpoint others able to walk do the same." Ephraim laughed. "He made some gentlefolks mighty mad, but he saved many a life that day."

Wolf fought his impatience. He'd also been at that battle, only on the other side. The South claimed victory, but when the fighting was over and there was one doctor per thousand men, it was hard to see the win. He'd heard the North hadn't been any more prepared. Wounded wandered the streets of Washington waiting for room in the hospitals.

If Molly was in trouble today, though, he needed answers. "How's trouble finding her?"

Ephraim swallowed his coffee hard, as if it were only grounds. "We hadn't been here a week when she started fighting the opium trade on the back streets. I told her there was nothing we could do about it. Folks got a right to sleep in them beds if they want. There's no more law against it than against drinking. Half the men who came back from the war have been trying to drown their memories in alcohol."

"She needs to stay away from the back streets." Wolf hated to think of Molly walking in front of some of the shacks where opium was sold.

"I told her that. But—"

Footsteps sounded on the stairs, bringing the discussion to a halt. Wolf walked back into the store as Molly and Callie Ann reached ground level. The child let go of Molly's hand and ran to the door. Opened it. Then closed it back.

When she turned to Wolf, she was clean-faced, and

fighting mad. Tiny fists rested on her hips. "You left him outside!" She stormed at Wolf. "Don't do that again."

The ranger frowned and glanced at Molly. Molly shrugged.

"I left who outside, Princess?" He tried to sound calm before the child's anger.

"Uncle Orson! He doesn't like to be left outside."

Wolf raised one bushy eyebrow. He refused to look around the room for the invisible uncle.

Molly winked at him. "The captain is sorry," she said to Callie Ann. "May we meet your uncle?"

"Oh, no. He never meets anyone this early." Callie Ann looked bothered that Molly would even ask such a thing. "He would like a chair."

Molly stared at Wolf. "Well, Captain? Get Uncle Orson a chair."

Wolf opened his mouth to argue that he'd be damned if he'd get a chair for a transparent man, but Molly's eyes warned him to tread carefully.

"There's one in the kitchen," Wolf mumbled. "He can talk to Ephraim while he sits."

Callie Ann opened the curtain wide. After a moment, she passed through.

He looked at Molly. "I not only got stuck with a kid who wants me to call her Princess, she's got an invisible relative." He tried his best to whisper.

Molly slapped both hands across her mouth to keep her merriment inside. She motioned with her head toward the door.

Wolf held it open for her. He couldn't help but grin

as she ran outside, unable to keep quiet any longer. Her laughter filled the early morning air.

He couldn't take his gaze off her as she held her sides. She was even more beautiful than she'd been yesterday. Her hair pulled free of a single night braid that reached her waist. Honey-brown strands curled around her cheeks in warm wisps. The white of her nightgown peeked above her robe at her throat. And her eyes. Wolf couldn't stop staring. Her eyes danced with glee.

"I'm sorry," she said with no remorse. "I shouldn't be laughing at your predicament. But, don't you see, the child is all alone in this world. She needs Uncle Orson."

Wolf shook his head. "I don't see how encouraging her in make-believe can help her."

"But surely it can't hurt. Oh, Captain, play along with her, at least until you get her settled."

Wolf stared at Molly. He was not a man who figured he would ever be talked into anything in his life. Black was black, and white was white. The real world had no room for fantasy.

But when he looked at Molly Donivan, he knew he could deny her nothing. "If you think it best," he said with a raised eyebrow. "Then I guess Uncle Orson can tag along for a while." He winked. "As long as he keeps quiet."

That morning, while the princess helped Ephraim make lunch, Wolf built beds, one on top of the other, in Molly's spare room upstairs. The top bed was for Callie Ann, the bottom for Uncle Orson, of course.

Molly agreed to keep the child until Wolf could wire the sheriff in Savannah for another place to send her. At the most, Wolf assured Molly, it would be for a week, no more.

He picked up Callie Ann's trunk at the stage station, and they discovered that not only was her wardrobe of the best quality, but her name had been carefully embroidered into the folds of each piece.

"She's not an orphan abandoned," Molly whispered as she placed the child's clothes back in the trunk. "She's been loved and cared for by someone of means."

Wolf lifted one of the dolls that were nestled among the clothes. "Then why'd she arrive here without a cent or a note? The office said Mrs. Murphy only knew that a Francis Digger was to pick the child up when they reached Austin. She told the ranger in charge that she'd assumed Francis Digger was a woman."

"I'm sure there is just a misunderstanding. Surely it won't take more than a few days to straighten everything out." Molly folded back an outfit. "Until then I'll love having her around."

Wolf didn't believe problems were solved so easily, but he was in no hurry for this one to be resolved. The child had made it possible for him to be near Molly. He told himself he needed to be close in case Ephraim's warning was right about Molly being in trouble, but in truth he couldn't get enough of the woman who for so long had been his only dream of paradise.

"Thanks for your help," he said, wondering if he

should offer to pay for the child's keep. From the looks of her living quarters, it appeared Molly Donivan could use extra money. "Is there any way I can pay you back?"

Molly turned from where she'd been dusting Callie Ann's temporary room. Her hands shifted a cloth nervously from hand to hand. She moved toward him until her words only had to travel a few feet. "I could use a friend," she whispered. "A friend to cover my back if trouble rides in. I know that's asking a great deal since we've only just met and if you say no I'll understand and still keep the child."

Wolf felt his long-dormant heart roll over in his chest. He dented the bed frame with his grip, knowing if his hands were free, he'd have to hold her. "That's a tall order."

She met his stare. "More than you might want to take on at this time."

He could see the worry in her eyes, and maybe a bit of fear. He wanted to tell her his life was hers, but he couldn't frighten her so with the raw truth. "I'll be your friend, Molly Donivan, for as long as you need me."

"But you don't know the trouble . . ."

"It doesn't matter," he answered. "The offer stands."

FOUR

TWILIGHT ALWAYS FRIGHTENED MOLLY. NOT THE darkness of night, where she knew things moved unseen, or the brightness of day, where horror could be clearly identified. But the soft, blurry twilight, where all in the world seemed neither good nor bad.

She stood at the window of her store and watched the light fade, feeling as if she'd lived her entire life in the few moments between day and night. She wasn't a young maid who'd never loved, nor a woman who had known full love. Somewhere in between, she waited.

Closing her eyes, Molly hugged herself, wondering if she'd been a fool.

The memories of those first few days of the war drifted through her mind. She'd been so young, barely seventeen. Life whirled around her, and she never dreamed the merry-go-round would slow. Her father accepted an important position with the Union medical staff. She took a semester off from school to travel and work with him. All seemed a mad chaos of excitement and adventure.

Then, one day at a train station amid hundreds of departing soldiers and returning wounded, she found the anchor to her world. He said his name was Benjamin, and his lips tasted of forever.

Somehow, she'd built a world of waiting and dreaming of what would be. As the years passed, she'd written him a hundred letters in her journal, telling him everything. She'd lived a lifetime of daydreams with a man who'd kissed her once and whispered only his first name.

Molly forced thoughts of the past away. She'd believed in him for so long, she felt she'd go mad if she faced the truth. He'd said he'd find her. The words echoed through her mind. He would find her.

"Molly?" Ephraim pulled her from her daydream. "You ready for supper? I made a meat pie out of what that woman at the market called a chicken. Looked more seagull-size to me."

"I'll be there in a minute," she answered as she pulled the shade on the door. Though she thought of locking the door, she guessed it to be a waste of time; most of the people in the town seemed to think of it as locked anyway, judging from the few customers who ventured in. To date most of her work had come from the school for the Blind and the State Lunatic Asylum. They'd gladly let her fill orders for medicines and creams because other alchemists didn't want to make the trip twice a week and then hope for payment.

"Aren't we going to wait for Captain Hayward?"

Ephraim cleared his throat as if fighting down a cough. "He said he'd be back in a few hours. I figured that meant for dinner. A man his size probably doesn't miss many meals."

"No. I don't think we should wait. I'll leave the door unlocked in case he shows up, but he probably has far more on his mind than us." Molly raised her chin slightly. "You and Callie Ann go ahead and eat. I've a few things to finish, then I'll join you."

Crossing to her work counter, she began to clean and organize the bottles and powders. Ephraim and Callie Ann's voices drifted from behind the curtain. Molly couldn't help but smile. The old man had no trouble playing Callie Ann's game of Uncle Orson. He carried on a conversation with the invisible uncle as though they were old friends.

Molly slid her mortar and pestle closer and began grinding crystals of antimony and potassium tartrate together to make tartar emetic. She knew any doctor coming by would want a few doses to add to his bag.

So far, the doctors who dropped in were giving her the simplest of prescriptions. Wishing they'd trust her more, Molly accepted their work. She'd grown up around medicine and attended medical school for two years. As she twisted on the crystals, she told herself she knew more about medicine than some of these doctors ever would. Yet they treated her as little more than a clerk.

Since the war, medical schools had popped up like weeds. Some schools saw graduating doctors as a fast way to make money. They might offer only four months of instruction, with the second year offering the same lectures as the first, then the schools would hand out diplomas to students who'd never examined a patient.

"Evening."

Molly glanced up, startled to see Wolf standing only a few feet away. She hadn't heard the door open and close. He moved as silently as the warm Texas wind.

"I think you've won the battle. Those rocks look dead to me." Wolf's grin wrinkled his beard. He leaned against the counter so near her arm they were almost touching.

Turning loose of the pestle, she tried to make her hands relax atop the marble counter. "I was finishing up a formula." She didn't want to admit she'd been lost in thought or that his nearness affected her.

The large captain folded his arms. "Don't let me interrupt you. I can wait."

She brushed a loose strand of hair back behind her ear. "Oh, no. I'm finished for tonight." She liked the captain, but he made her nervous. She told herself it wasn't the number of weapons he carried, or his long hair and beard. Even his size was more comforting than frightening. But something about the way he looked at her made her uneasy. Almost as though she were the first and only woman he'd ever seen in his life. "I guess you're here to see Callie Ann?" she managed to keep her voice level.

"And you," he answered with an honesty that surprised them both.

Molly closed her eyes, dreading the words she knew

she'd have to say. How many times had she said them to other men? Men who hoped for a chance she'd marry them or men who dreamed of something more than friendship for a night. She had to stop them before they stepped too close. There could never be more. Not with them or with this strong ranger. She'd already given her heart away on a train station platform. There was nothing left to give.

"You did wait dinner on me?"

Wolf surprised her with his question. She'd thought he meant more than dinner when he came to see her.

She couldn't help but smile at her own foolishness. Of course, the ranger had come to see Callie Ann and to have dinner with her as he'd promised they would. Nothing more. She wasn't some fancy lady bothered by suitors flocking at her door. She was an old maid. An old maid who could share a meal with a man probably far more interested in the food than in her.

"I thought we'd take Callie Ann, and Ephraim if he wants to go, over to Noma's," Wolf offered.

At the sound of his name, Ephraim slipped from between the folds of the curtain concealing the back rooms. He was so thin his body barely made a ripple in the cloth. "I don't much feel like stepping out, Captain, but thanks for considering me. I think I'll turn in early tonight. As for Callie Ann, she fell asleep in her chair at the table. The princess has had a long day."

Wolf glanced at Molly. "I'll carry her up to that bed I made her and then be on my way. I'm sorry I was too late for supper. We had some problems come up this afternoon."

"Oh, you're not too late," Ephraim volunteered, ignoring Molly's frown. "Molly hasn't eaten yet and I'm afraid, what with Uncle Orson chowing down, there's hardly crumbs left of the meat pie I made."

"But I can't leave . . ." Molly began.

Ephraim stopped her. "Go ahead. It will do you good to get out of this store for an hour. I'll listen for the girl in case she wakes."

Before Molly realized quite how it happened, she was walking down the street on Wolf's arm. Dinner with the captain was nothing important, but the way Ephraim had turned on her was shocking. He'd done everything short of put a For Rent sign on her forehead. Captain Hayward must think her desperate if her oldest friend, with all the subtlety of a carnival barker, encouraged her to step out. Why hadn't Ephraim just stood in the middle of Congress Avenue and yelled, "One old maid free for dinner"?

"I'm sorry about Ephraim." She tried to find a place to start the apology. "If you'd rather dine alone?"

Wolf slowed. After several steps, he answered, "I'd rather dine with you, Molly. If it's agreeable?"

She was thankful for the shadows as a warm blush climbed her throat. "It's agreeable with me. But you must allow me to pay. It's only fair."

Wolf stopped so quickly she almost stumbled. He widened his stance in front of her as if preparing for a fight. "I asked you to join me for dinner, Molly Donivan. I'll be the one paying. You've done me a great favor this day by keeping up with the princess, but the meals we share are in no way payment." The huge man looked nervous as more than one person passed them, staring. He lowered his voice, realizing he addressed her far too harshly. "You do me an honor by allowing me to take you to dinner."

He cleared his throat. Molly wouldn't have been surprised to hear him say, "Dismissed."

His outburst might have frightened some women, but it made her feel right at home. Molly slipped her hand beneath his arm. "Thank you, Captain, for reminding me of my manners. You do me an honor by being my friend."

"Then it's settled, I'll pay."

The muscles along his arm were so hard she had trouble believing they were covered with flesh. Yet she knew he'd never hurt her. "You may regret your words, Captain, for I'm starving."

He laughed as they hurried into the cafe. His laughter, like the man, was full, warm, and welcoming. Fewer people stopped eating to stare than had last night. The waitress gave them a table at the side by the windows instead of in the middle. Molly relaxed, realizing she wasn't on stage. No one cared if she had dinner with the ranger two nights in a row. As a general's daughter, she'd always felt as though her every move was being watched and talked about. It felt good to be just one of the crowd.

Suddenly, they both had a hundred things to tell the other. Molly related stories about Callie Ann. Wolf talked of his problems at the office. The Digger brothers had missed their hangings, thanks to a newly arrived witness who swore they were with him at the time of the stage robbery. No one but the Diggers believed the man, but the judge said it was worth checking out the story.

There were also reports of trouble on the border. Several of the young rangers were antsy to go. Wolf knew if they went, he'd have to go along to watch over them. Now, four years after the war, men who hadn't seen battle were receiving the circle-star badge. They were fine young men who grew up with the stories of the War Between the States. As Texans, they'd been weaned on hardship and they handled weapons as though born with a gun in their hand. But they still had lessons to learn, if they planned to stay alive.

"To add one more problem to my list," Wolf said as he finished off his sixth piece of pie, "the judge told me that since the Diggers are still alive, they have to be told about their niece. He'll give me a few days to locate another relative. If there is none, and the Diggers are still breathing, it will be their decision as to what to do with Callie Ann."

Without caring who might be watching, Molly placed her hand on Wolf's. "We can't let that happen. There must be something we can do. The child has been sheltered and loved, even doted on, I suspect. She can't be given over to two outlaws."

He stared at her fingers warming his hand with a caring grip. He didn't move, didn't breathe.

"We'll think of something," she said. Her touch appeared to turn his hand to granite.

Molly straightened, embarrassed by her own boldness. She wasn't the kind of woman to make advances.

She told herself she wasn't even attracted to Captain Hayward. He'd certainly been nothing but a gentleman and of course offered only friendship. She shouldn't have put him in such a situation. Planting her hands in her lap, she stared down at them.

"Molly?" he questioned. "What is it?"

"Nothing." She couldn't meet his gaze. She was too old to be holding hands in public with a man she'd just met. Her father had always held her to a high standard. She'd let that standard slip.

Wolf sat waiting, as if he planned not to move until she answered. She could feel him staring at her, but her pride wouldn't allow her to say more. The waitress stopped by and asked if they'd like more pie. She raised an eyebrow when Wolf said no.

Molly folded her napkin. "I'd better be getting back." She stood.

He hurried to stand beside her and pay, then offered her his arm as they stepped outside. Molly accepted, but didn't allow herself to move close against him as she had last night.

"What's wrong?" he asked again when they were alone. "And don't say nothing. We were talking, really talking, as I've done very few times in my life with a woman, then all at once you won't even look at me."

She could hear the frustration in his voice, reminding her of a little boy beneath all the muscles and hair. The boy reached her where the man never could have.

"It wasn't you. It was me. I'm never so forward. I hope you don't misread my action."

Wolf was silent for several steps. She could hear the

click of her heels along the walk, but he moved silently in moccasin boots.

With a sudden sideways step, he pulled her into the total blackness between two buildings. She let out a little cry as her back brushed against the wood of the side wall of the mercantile. She could feel the warmth of his body only an inch in front of her.

Her heart pounded in her throat, but she didn't move. To her surprise, she still felt no peril from the man before her. The nearness of him seemed more protective than endangering. She could hear him struggling to find words and waited, guessing he needed the darkness as his crutch.

"I can read a week-old trail even after a rain."

She could feel his words brush her cheek.

"I can read a lie in a man's face and know the instant he'll draw a gun by watching his eyes."

Even straining, she couldn't see his outline, but the warmth of his body so near made her very much aware of him.

"I haven't been around many women in my life, Molly, but I swear to you, I'll never misread anything you say or do."

"But I didn't want you to think . . ."

"Think what? That you were being forward? You touched my hand, Molly, nothing more. I think that's allowed if we're to be friends."

She let out a long breath and relaxed. "Of course it is." There she went again, just like her father always said she did, making dragons out of clouds and wars from battles. "You must think me foolish."

Wolf laughed suddenly. "No, I don't think you're foolish. I just wish you would relax a little so I could. I know you must think I'm a man of the world, but when it comes to women, my education runs a bit short."

Molly couldn't stop her laughter. She'd never, for one moment, thought him a "man of the world." He was a man destined to remain alone just as she was a woman who'd always wear the tag "old maid" like her two aunts back in Philly. She felt like they were two people who'd never had a partner to dance with and, suddenly, they had the floor to themselves.

"Shall we dance, Captain?" Molly giggled as she reached out her hands and touched his shoulders.

If Wolf thought her mad, he gave no sign. His hands moved around her waist, and he lifted her off the ground, twirling her around amid the shadows. What he lacked in grace, he made up for in enthusiasm.

For the first time since her father died, Molly felt young. She chuckled into the blackness around her and felt his strong arms holding her high as he spun.

They were still laughing as they staggered like dizzy drunks to her store.

Wolf reached to open the door, but her hand stopped him before he touched the knob. He glanced at her in confusion.

Directing his attention with her stare, Molly watched a drop of crimson drip from the top half of the door.

She watched as he pulled his hand away and smelled the liquid.

"Paint," he whispered.

Molly continued to stare at the door as her eyes adjusted to the shadows. Printed in paint the color of blood were the words *Move or Die!*

FIVE

MOLLY WATCHED WOLF CAREFULLY OPEN THE PAINT-
splattered door and edge inside the drugstore with his
Colt drawn. She followed, holding her breath.

No one greeted them. The place was tomb quiet.
Light from the street flickered off the colored bottles
along the walls, creating tiny rainbows against the
shadowy backdrop. Familiar smells tiptoed in the semi-
darkness, welcoming Molly and reminding her of
home.

Wolf replaced his gun as soundlessly as he'd drawn
it. He pointed up. She understood he meant for her to
check on Callie Ann.

When Molly returned, he had his back to her as he
waited at the bottom of the steps. He didn't move as
she neared, but she had no doubt he was aware of her
presence.

"She's sound asleep," Molly whispered.

"So is Ephraim. Sawing logs with the best of them,"

Wolf answered in a low voice he must have thought was a whisper.

She'd figured the lawman would ask questions and try to get to the bottom of her problem. He'd have to be blind not to see she had trouble.

But he simply said, "How can I help?"

Molly sat on the second step and put her chin in her hands. "I don't know. Someone wants me out of here. Maybe it's because I'm a Yankee. Or maybe it's my being a woman, or that I'm taking business away from another. All I know for sure is they want me long gone and have since I arrived."

"Any idea who?" Wolf lowered himself to the step above her. His knee brushed her shoulder, but neither of them acted like they noticed.

"Half the people I've met in Austin. It started as veiled comments and hints the day we moved in. More a feeling that I didn't belong here than anything one person said. Someone even suggested Ephraim might be contagious with his cough, but I convinced them otherwise. Even after a month the Open sign might as well say 'Quarantined.'

"After I spoke out to try and clear the back streets of opium, the threats seemed more directed at me. I've had to replace windows and clean paint off the sidewalk and back door. But if they think they can pester me into leaving, they'd better think again."

Wolf rested his hand lightly on her shoulder. "I hoped tonight was the first threat. The kind of person who'd do this doesn't like to be ignored."

She shook her head. "Someone's trying to put me out of business, that's all I know. Or maybe it's more than that. The threats aren't aimed at Ephraim or really even at the store."

He leaned back against the steps and said in what sounded official, "You made any enemies, Miss Donivan?"

Molly laughed. "More than you'd think, Captain. Even my two old-maid aunts threatened me a few months ago when I said I was heading to Texas."

When he didn't laugh, she continued, "They threatened to come for a visit."

He relaxed.

"But seriously," Molly added, "my father was always fighting for one cause or another, even before the war. I was right by his side. After he died, a few gentlemen in Philadelphia wanted me to marry them so they could handle my affairs. When I refused, some predicted I'd never make it on my own." She shook her head. "But I don't think any of them would go so far as to follow me to Texas to destroy me."

"Your father left you well off?" Wolf inquired.

Molly closed her eyes, knowing how she answered the question might determine whether or not they remained friends. Men always said a woman having money made no difference, but she'd learned the hard way that it did. "My father never made much more than his military pay his entire life. His legacy to me was a few hundred dollars, which I used to get here," she answered, telling herself it was the truth. After all, he hadn't asked how much her mother left her.

"Any reason someone wants you out? Maybe it's not you at all but the property."

"Not unless you count Mr. Miller. He offered to buy the store so he can expand. Caskets seem to be a growing business in this town."

Wolf leaned forward, brushing his hand over her shoulder, gently spreading a warmth that passed through her clothes to her skin.

"Don't worry," he encouraged. "You can make a go of it. Maybe it's just a prank and we've seen the worst."

Molly rested against his leg as naturally as if she'd done so for years. "It's good to have someone to talk to. I've tried to make light of the threats in front of Ephraim. He's not well. I think the worry would be bad for him."

"I noticed how ill he is." Wolf's fingers rested at the back of her neck, moving slowly over the flesh between her collar and where her hair pulled upward into a bun. "This morning there was blood in his handkerchief after he coughed. He tried to hide it from you and the child."

Molly rested her chin atop his knee. "I didn't know about the blood. He said he was getting better. He said the bleeding had stopped," she whispered, more to herself than to Wolf. "He's all the real family I have left. My aunts told me never to speak to them again if I left without their permission. I feel like I'm out here all alone and Ephraim doesn't have the strength to fight beside me much longer."

A cry caught in her throat, drowned by sudden tears.

"Maybe I shouldn't have insisted on coming west." She mumbled the words between sobs. "I'd hoped to prolong his life, if only by weeks or even days. I didn't think I'd be heading for trouble."

An avalanche of feelings bombarded Wolf's heart. He fought to keep from reaching for her. She'd never left his thoughts, and now she was so close. She didn't have to tell him her only friend was dying. Wolf had already seen the signs.

She buried her face against his leg. Her silent sobs rocked them both. "I can't go back to my life in Philadelphia," she whispered. "And there's no place for me here."

The sorrow in her words brought the loneliness of his own life into focus. He lost the battle to keep his distance.

With one mighty sweep, he pulled her into his arms. He held her tightly against him, knowing he'd fight any dragon for this woman, but unsure how to help her now.

She pressed her face against his chest and cried softly, as she hadn't cried since the year her father died. All her dreams of coming to Texas and making Ephraim better and starting a new life were crumbling.

Wolf cradled her in his arms, realizing the feel of her would be forever burned into his flesh. He'd told himself he would never touch her. He was happy to be just her friend. It was better this way. She had no room for him in her life. If she knew who he was, she'd probably hate him.

But she needed him to hold her as no one in his life

had ever needed him. She needed him there, not as a lover, but as a friend.

Could he touch her like this and be that . . . only that?

Maybe the gods were punishing him for not going back to her after the war. He told himself it would have been impossible, but had he let his pride rule the day and not his heart? Maybe if he'd found her when the war ended, she would have understood. Maybe even accepted that he'd had his reasons for fighting for the South, for being a spy, for lying.

His hand cupped the side of her face. Warm tears trickled between his fingers. "I'm here, Molly, I'm here."

She wasn't listening.

He rocked her gently in his arms and smiled. In a few minutes, she'd be all stiff and proper again, probably apologizing for letting her emotions run wild. And then he'd try to convince her it didn't matter. He planned to be here for her.

But as her sobs became sniffles, she didn't pull away. Instead she relaxed in his embrace. He thought of saying something but couldn't think of anything. He figured saying nothing was better than voicing the wrong words. He didn't have to tell her people died. She knew all too well, as he did. Reminding her Ephraim was old didn't seem polite, and talking of Heaven was a little premature since the man snored only a room away.

He held her gently, ready to let her go whenever she wanted as she settled against his chest like a cat curling into a basket. The step above where he sat pushed into his back, but he hardly noticed.

Finally, Molly straightened slightly, smoothing his tear-stained shirt with her fingers. "It appears you're holding more than my hand, Captain."

Wolf raised her off his lap and returned her to the step beside him. "I hope you won't misread my action."

She smiled. "I can't read a trail the day it's made, and I've never been able to tell if a man's lying by his eyes. But I promise you, Captain, I'll try never to misread your actions."

Her hand covered his as it had in the cafe. "Thank you."

"You're welcome," he answered.

They were getting used to one another, he thought. Not just how they talked or what each thought about, but how it felt to be near. He'd watched couples who were balanced in one another's company. They were like a paired set of horses. They moved in harmony with one other. Even their steps matched as they walked.

He'd never known that with a woman . . . until now.

A lantern moved past the windows facing the street, then another, and another, until the lamp lights formed a chain like a bright centipede moving along the road.

Wolf braced himself to stand. "Looks like we're about to have company."

Molly's gentle touch stilled his progress. "Let me handle it," she whispered. "Please stay here unless I need you."

Words log-piled in his throat. She didn't know how

rough strangers could be in this part of the country. She was a woman going up against what looked to be a dozen men descending on her place. He wanted to protect her. But all he could do was nod, for he didn't trust himself to speak.

Wolf sank into the shadows of the stairs as Miller, the undertaker, opened the door. The little man ushered several others into the store with the formality of a sergeant-at-arms at a town meeting.

Wolf pressed deeper into the darkness where he could watch and wait in case Molly needed him. She would only have to breathe his name, and he'd be by her side.

Miller nodded continuously when he spotted Molly as if pointing her out with his head to the others.

"Good, good." He hurried forward. "You're here."

Wolf couldn't help but admire how calmly Molly faced the crowd. He could see a touch of her father in her.

"The store's closed," Molly began. "I'll have to ask you gentlemen to leave."

She lied, Wolf thought. There wasn't a gentleman among them.

The undertaker nervously took the lead. "We've not come to buy, Miss Molly. We've got other business."

"Get to the point," a stranger in black ordered. The outline of a rifle showed beneath his duster, and his boots chimed the jingle of spurs.

Miller's chin pushed forward as if he needed to stretch his neck in order to get words out. "Yes, well."

He took a step toward Molly. "We've come to ask you to leave."

"But I don't—" Molly began.

The little man interrupted. "We've got together enough money to pay you a fair price for the shop."

"Are you the cowards who painted my door?" Molly stared at the men.

Miller's denial came too fast. "Of course not! The painters make it plain, however, that we're not the only ones who want you gone."

"A woman shouldn't be trying to run a business alone." The black-clad man took a step forward. "You don't belong here interfering in our town and its laws. Anyone can see if you stay, there'll be nothing but trouble. Go back up north, where you came from."

"There's more to this than my being a woman or from the North." Molly could tell by the way Miller's eyes enlarged slightly that she was right, but no man spoke.

"Take our offer," Miller almost begged now. "There's no one to protect you against the mischief that's bound to come if you keep voicing your opinion. A woman who talks is about as useless as a crowing hen."

Several of the men laughed.

"I'll not take your offer or remain quiet about the poison being sold in the alleys," Molly answered coldly. "I'm staying, so I guess you'll just have to get used to me."

Wolf fought the urge to join her, but she'd made it plain this was her battle, not his.

She stood like a statue as the men left one by one. Miller mumbled that he'd try again tomorrow, but the others remained silent. The man with the spurs walked with heavy steps, leaving an echoing chink after he'd gone.

She stood watching the lanterns move away from her door. Wolf stepped up behind, almost touching her but not quite daring to.

"They'll be back," he said an inch from her ear. "You're right. They want you out, but it makes no sense. Other women run businesses here in Austin. Lord knows we got a bushelful of Northerners walking the streets."

"They won't speak of the real reason. But somehow I feel there is something that makes it very important that I go."

Wolf spread his large hand along the small of her back, touching her so lightly he wasn't sure she even knew of his caress.

She leaned back slightly into the warmth of his hand. "It's hard to fight when I'm unsure where the enemy stands."

Closing his eyes, Wolf breathed deeply of the fragrance of her hair. She smelled of lavender and rose water. The battle he fought with himself to keep from holding her seemed far greater than her conflict with the town.

This wasn't some woman he'd just met. This was his Molly, the girl he'd loved for years. The one he'd measured every woman against all his life, it seemed. The only woman whose lips he could remember the taste of after eight long years. He'd given his heart to her that day on the train station platform, and he couldn't withdraw it just because worlds forced them apart.

Wolf tried to forget about her nearness and think of how she'd react if he revealed his identity. Would she hate him for his lie? Or worse yet, had she forgotten the day that meant so much to him?

"Did you ever think of marrying?" The words were out of his mouth before he thought to stop them.

She stepped away. "Are you asking or offering, Captain?"

Wolf cleared his throat. "I was just thinking that if you had a husband, these men might back off. Coming over to frighten a woman is one thing, but these didn't look like the type to face a man equally."

"You're right. Miller even loses his bravery when Ephraim is in the room." She straightened her back. "But to answer your question, no. I never plan to marry."

Wolf faced the windows. He didn't think he knew her well enough to ask her why. "Nor do I," he responded. "I guess some people weren't meant to be married. I'm never in one place for more than a few days. It wouldn't be fair to give a woman my name and nothing else."

She didn't answer but seemed lost in her own thoughts. He mumbled his good-night and listened just outside the door until he was sure she'd locked up.

"Sleep well, my Molly," he whispered as he walked away. "I'll be near if you need me."

SIX

JUST AFTER DAWN, WOLF POURED HIS FIRST CUP OF
coffee. It had been a long night. With Austin's small
police force, rangers were often called in as backup and
last night had been one of those times. Voters across
the state had decided Austin would be the capital, not
Houston. Sam Houston had fought hard to move the
state offices to his namesake. From the early counts it
looked like Houston Town had lost. The folks in Austin
celebrated throughout the night. If Wolf were a betting
man, he'd guess half the population was drunk right
now.

The sound of gunfire suddenly echoed down the
street from the direction of Molly's place. The shots
came in rapid fire, the way only a gunslinger knew how
to fan a weapon. Wolf was out the door and running
toward the drugstore before the other rangers could lift
their Colts from the pegs by the door.

The men sounded like a herd of buffalo storming a

canyon as they thundered down the street with Wolf in the lead.

The drunken gunslinger outside Molly's store never saw the mountain of muscle coming. Wolf was airborne when he plowed into the man like a fully steamed train without brakes.

One round of gunfire, aimed skyward, resounded off the buildings as both men hit the dirt at full force.

Only one got up. Wolf.

Josh Weston was a few steps behind Wolf and almost tripped over the men before he could stop. He glanced at the gunfighter, then at his captain. "What happened?"

"Arrest him." Wolf shoved his toe against the man's side. "When he wakes up, charge him with disturbing the peace. I'll check on Molly and Callie Ann."

Josh nodded as he grabbed the criminal's arm and lifted him over one shoulder. It was too early in the morning to argue with the captain, but he tried. "This drunk will be out by noon on such a minor charge. If we made everyone in town serve time in jail for firing a weapon in the city limits we wouldn't have room for all the criminals."

Wolf showed no sign of listening as he dusted himself off.

Josh gave it another try. "And drinking is hardly unusual in Austin. The city fathers back in eighteen fifty had to pass an ordinance requiring their policemen to stay sober on the job."

Wolf never looked back as he stepped onto the walk in front of the drugstore. "Molly!" he shouted in a voice that would have awakened anyone who slept through the gunfire.

When she didn't answer, he jerked the door open. Callie Ann jumped into his arms and scrambled to his shoulder like an organ grinder's monkey. "The man was shooting at us," she cried. "He tried to kill us all."

Wolf held her tightly. In her cotton gown, she looked even smaller than she had yesterday. "It's going to be all right, Princess."

Molly stood at the bottom of the stairs. Her hair was in a long braid, and she wore only a nightgown. She held herself as calmly and regally as a queen.

"I think the man was shooting at the bottles," she said without emotion, slowly lowering the Navy Colt in her hand. "He wasn't trying to harm us."

Wolf glanced at the shattered glass scattered across the floor. He carried Callie Ann to the stairs and set her on the third step. "Run up there and get some shoes on," he ordered. "The trouble's over for now."

Callie Ann began hopping up each step like a rabbit. "I'll wash and comb my hair like I'm supposed to do before I come back down to breakfast."

She disappeared around the landing. Wolf turned to Molly. "You'll need shoes, too," he teased.

When Molly turned her gaze toward him, all laughter died in his throat. Terror seemed to drown her where she stood.

"What is it?" he demanded.

She bolted suddenly, running across the glass-cluttered floor. "I have to check on Ephraim! Something's wrong. He's always ready with the rifle when there's trouble."

She didn't have to say that Ephraim should have been there. Wolf had the feeling the old soldier had been present in every crisis of her life. His absence now seemed to suck the air from the room.

"Ephraim?" she called as she reached the curtain. "Ephraim, are you all right?"

Wolf pulled the curtain aside and glanced around. The tiny kitchen was deserted, the stove cold.

"He usually starts the coffee by first light," Molly whispered, running through the room to where her friend slept in the back. "He's always up and dressed by dawn."

Molly drew in a deep breath before she opened his door as if she feared it might be her last.

Wolf stood close behind her, ready to help with whatever met them.

For a moment, when she pushed the door wide, he saw nothing. Only lazy dust motes drifting in a beam of white sunshine shifting through the window. Then, slowly the room washed into focus like something rising to the surface from deep water.

Ephraim lay on his side, a pool of blood circling the sheet below his mouth. His thin hands were twisted into a blanket in a last desperate clutch at life.

Molly cried his name softly as she knelt beside him. She brushed thin gray strands of hair back from his face. "Ephraim," she whispered, "oh, Ephraim."

"I can't make formation this morning, General," he mumbled. "I'm under the weather."

"Ephraim." She blotted at his mouth with a clean corner of the sheet. "Why didn't you tell me? You need medicine. I can fix you something for the pain."

The old man rolled onto his back. His eyes cleared. He stared at her. His expression seemed to ask who she was, or maybe where he was.

A coughing fit racked his body. When he finally spoke, his voice was hoarse and weak. "I've been around hospitals and dying all my life. I know when it's time. The medicine will ease the pain, but it'll take my mind. I'd prefer to meet my Maker with as many of my faculties working as I can muster."

Molly shook her head violently as if she could rid herself of the sight of him dying.

"I'm sorry," he mumbled. "I promised your father I'd take care of you." He lifted his hand to her cheek. "Brave little Molly, always trying to be as strong as the general. Go back home. This wild land is not for you."

"Only if you'll go with me, Ephraim." Tears ran unchecked down Molly's face. "I'll go back. We can live at Allen Farm with the aunts. We'll fish for our breakfast like we used to do when I was a kid."

Ephraim shook his head. "I can't go this time," he whispered. "My tour of duty is over."

He coughed again. Blood dripped from the corner of his mouth. "Don't spend your life alone. Promise me, Molly."

She was crying so hard she couldn't speak, fighting back sobs with gulps.

Ephraim reached for her with wrinkled fingers. His

watery blue eyes closed. For a moment Molly and Wolf were quiet, waiting for the ragged breathing to start up once more. The plop of a drop of blood falling from his mouth to the sheet seemed as loud as the gunfire had been earlier.

Silence hung stagnant in the air as the old man's hand slid along her arm and came to rest on the bed.

Wolf watched Molly for a long while. He wanted to touch her, comfort her, but he wasn't sure she'd welcome him interfering in her private grief.

Slowly, she pulled her feelings close around her. Her back straightened and her chin lifted. She'd not share her grief any more than she shared her life.

She stood, tucking the covers around Ephraim as if he were only sleeping. "If you'll tell Miller he has work, Captain, I'll dress. I'll have to ask you to watch Callie Ann while I make arrangements. There is no need for Ephraim to lie in state. No one knew him in this town. As soon as I can find a preacher and have the grave dug, we'll have a service."

Most folks would have been shocked by her cool manner, but Wolf saw the general's daughter in her once again. How many times during the war had she watched her father do what had to be done without time to allow feelings to interfere? How many times had she pushed her own needs aside to do what she had to do? She'd grown up in the hospitals of war. She'd grown up around death.

As she turned to leave, she flinched with pain, but didn't make a sound.

Wolf lifted her off the ground and moved to the

kitchen. "Your foot's bleeding," he said as he sat her on the counter. "You should have said something."

She watched, disinterested, as blood trickled from her foot.

Wolf pumped enough water to dampen a towel and wrapped it around the cut. Then he stepped into the drugstore and collected all the supplies he needed. When he returned, she was still sitting on the counter.

As tenderly as he could, he checked the sole of her foot to make sure there was no glass left in the wound. With skill he cleaned the cut, then carefully wrapped a clean dry cloth around her foot.

Callie Ann followed him from the store and sat watching while he did his best to doctor Molly. "A man shouldn't see a lady's feet before they're married," she said matter-of-factly.

Wolf raised an eyebrow. "That so?"

"That's so. My grandma told me. I think it's a law."

"Sounds like a good one to me," Wolf answered. "After all, a woman who'll show a man her feet will show him practically anything. The next thing he knows, he'll be staring at her elbows or knees."

He finished tying the bandage and glanced at Callie Ann. "You stay here. I'll carry Molly to the stairs, then you can help me clean up the glass."

Callie nodded as Wolf lifted Molly. He walked carefully across the floor. When he sat her on the first step, he whispered, "Don't worry about the child or the store. I'll keep her busy and run off any customers who wander in."

Molly smiled at him. "Thanks," she whispered as she

moved away. "I'll be back as soon as I can. I have to wash Ephraim's body and give him a shave. He wouldn't want to meet his Maker without passing muster."

"I'll help if you like."

Molly shook her head.

It was afternoon when Callie Ann walked between Wolf and Molly to the cemetery at the end of Congress Avenue. A preacher read from his Bible while huge raindrops plopped atop the box, which had been constructed with little skill or patience. Molly had dressed the old soldier in his Union blues. She placed a folded Stars and Stripes beneath his arm just before Miller lowered the coffin lid.

Three mourners, a preacher, and the undertaker were all who attended the service. Ephraim's death wouldn't even be recorded in the paper, the *Statesman*. He died, as he had lived, a soldier on unfriendly ground.

When the prayers were over, Wolf lifted Callie Ann in one arm and the three of them walked back toward town. If Molly noticed the rain, she made no comment. She seemed lost in her own thoughts. Wolf wrapped his leather coat around the child and let Molly set the pace. The low clouds brought an early dusk and the drizzling rain kept folks inside, giving the town a deserted look.

Wolf wanted to ask her what her plans were now. He knew the main reason she'd come west was for Ephraim's health. Or at least that was what she said. He couldn't help but wonder if there weren't other factors. Would she be going home now? Or staying? And could he let her go without saying anything to her?

They stopped for an almost silent meal at the cafe. Callie Ann talked to Uncle Orson, telling him all about death and dying. Since she'd been to two funerals in as many weeks, she considered herself an expert.

It was obvious the waitress thought Callie's chatter a game they all played with the invisible relative. She set a place for the imaginary man and offered him dessert.

Wolf thought of putting a stop to the game but decided tonight was not the night. And if Molly didn't come out of her silent trance, he might start talking to Uncle Orson himself.

Twice during the meal she reached for his hand and held it between both hers as if needing to hold to the living. Wolf read her thoughts and touched her as often as he could without causing others to notice.

Wolf paid their bill and was about to walk out when Josh rushed into the cafe. "Captain," he almost shouted with relief. "We've been looking for you."

"What is it?" Wolf automatically lifted the child to his arm.

"You'd better come see for yourself." Josh whispered now that everyone in the place was staring at him.

Wolf followed Josh to Molly's, but when she saw the open door, Molly bolted past them and ran inside.

Powders and medicines, creams and crystals were scattered everywhere. All the shelves had been emptied to the floor in a multicolored pile, then Molly's book of handwritten formulas had been carefully cut into tiny pieces and ground into the mixture.

"They must have done this during the funeral," Josh guessed. "Miller said he thought he saw someone moving around in here when he returned, but by the time we got here, they'd gone out the back door. Who would do this kind of thing, Captain, and on this day of all days?"

If Wolf expected Molly to cry, he would have been disappointed. She picked up a piece of her formula book and gripped it in a fist.

"I've had enough." She said the words like an oath.

"You going back home?" He wouldn't blame her if she did.

Molly looked up at him with almost a smile on her face. "No, Captain, I've decided to fight."

If he'd ever thought he loved this woman, he'd been mistaken. Compared to the intensity of his love for her now, all else had been a slight infatuation.

She tossed the scrap of book down and said calmly, "Captain Hayward, may I have a few words with you in private?"

Wolf handed Callie Ann over to Josh, who held her away from his body as if she were poisonous.

Molly stepped onto the porch. The rain closed out the rest of the world, making Wolf feel they were alone even though they were in the middle of town.

"Did you mean it when you said you'd help?"

"I did." He wondered how many men she wanted killed.

"We are friends and must remain friends, no matter what I now ask, or how you answer."

"Agreed." He studied her closely. He could almost see her logical mind plotting what must be done.

"You said this morning you'd never marry because all you'd have to offer was a name. Well, Captain, I'm asking for that name. There is no one to protect me while I rebuild my business. Being a ranger's wife might offer me that protection long enough for me to become prepared. I'll ask nothing more of you except your name for a while."

Wolf was wrong. She wasn't like her father, the general. She was ten times tougher. Any other woman he knew would be crying and running, but Molly was only looking for a shelter until she had time to regroup. She wasn't deserting, she was merely retreating to prepare to fight another day.

He leaned his head out into the sheet of rain coming off the porch roof. When he finally pulled back, his hair was plastered to his head. Her offer still rolled around in his brain. "Are you sure you want to ask me to marry you, Molly Donivan?"

"I am," she said as if she'd just been sworn in during a trial. "I offer no great bargain in exchange for the use of your name. You can store your gear here when you're gone, and on the few days you make it into town, we'll have dinner together. I'll redo Ephraim's room and have a bed built that will fit your size, so you'll have somewhere comfortable to sleep."

Wolf watched her pace the porch, talking more to herself than him. "Oh, I'll never dishonor your name.

Should you die in the line of your duty, I'll see that you're buried properly."

Wolf wiped his face with the dry sleeve of his shirt. "And how long do you plan to be needing my name, Miss Donivan?"

"A few months—six at the most—but if you agree to the marriage you can set the date for it to end."

"All right. I agree to the marriage on those terms. I set the date for it to end."

She hesitated for the first time. "I'll change clothes while you get the preacher, if it's agreeable. I'll not be married in black, even if the marriage is in name only."

Wolf smiled. "I'd better hurry. After all, I've already seen your feet."

Molly didn't laugh as she turned and marched back into her store.

Wolf didn't even notice the rain as he stepped into the mud and headed for the church. After all, he was marrying his Molly for as long as he wanted. Out of the blue, she'd made the offer and he had no intention of giving her time to change her mind.

SEVEN

WOLF FELT HE WAS PLOWING UPSTREAM IN TEN FEET of water as he fought the rain, trying to get back to Molly's place. He'd had to wake up three preachers before he found one who'd brave the weather for a wedding. Reverend Ford was Baptist. He should be used to services under water, Wolf laughed to himself. Ford probably figured he could count this as both a wedding and a baptism at the same time.

"You all right?" Wolf yelled to the thin man at his side. The preacher's clothes flapped like sails in the wind.

"March on, Brother Hayward. March on." Ford looked like a man who'd never let a little storm slow him from doing the Lord's work. Or collecting the ten-dollar fee he charged for unplanned weddings after dark.

Wolf smiled. He enjoyed preachers. He considered himself kin to the McLain family his sister, Nichole, married into after the war. One of the McLains was a preacher. Daniel McLain, the kindest man he'd ever met. Who knows, if Molly agreed, he might take her to meet Daniel's little family. Daniel taught at a college not more than a hard day's ride from Austin. His wife, Karlee, had just given birth to the second set of McLain twins.

Wolf had always considered his sister, Nichole, his only kin. But that was before he met the McLain brothers. Adam, Wes, and Daniel had sworn him into their family, and he knew he'd always be thought of as blood related.

When he had time, Wolf would set Molly down and tell her about them. She'd understand Adam with his skilled, healing hands. And Wes would charm her as soon as she got past his scarred face. She'd like the McLain women, too. They were all strong like his Molly. Nichole had strapped on a gun belt more than once to stand beside her husband in a fight.

Wolf smiled, thinking of the children, some adopted, some born into the McLains. They made family get-togethers ring with laughter.

The thought of him and Molly not having any children made Wolf forget the rain. She might have done the asking, but she'd made it plain she didn't want anything but his name. She wasn't offering her bed. All she needed was a temporary solution to a serious problem.

She probably wouldn't be around long enough to even meet the friends he thought of as family. There'd be no children, no holidays in a marriage measured in weeks.

He told himself he didn't care. He'd take his Molly on whatever terms she offered. He told himself nothing mattered but keeping her safe. No one would dare bother her while she wore his ring.

His ring! Damn, he didn't have a ring.

"You want to slow down some?" Reverend Ford yelled. "I ain't never seen a man in such a hurry to get married."

Wolf stopped so suddenly, the preacher ran into him.

"I forgot the ring!" he yelled over the storm.

Before the preacher could stop him, Wolf waded across the street, now floating a foot deep in mud. "I'll be right back!" he yelled as he glanced back to see Ford huddle underneath a tin awning over a law office window. The rain wasn't cold, just wet. Which made it all the more bothersome, to Wolf's way of thinking. A man would have sense enough to come in out of a cold rain, but a rain like this didn't stop anyone.

Three businesses down the street, he found a mercantile advertising everything from feed to spectacles. He pounded on the door until the owner answered. Ten minutes later, with a ring in his pocket and mud caked halfway up his legs, Wolf rejoined the pastor.

They continued down the street without a word until they reached Molly's place.

When Wolf stomped into the drugstore, shedding water like a fully primed pump, she didn't say a word. She stood at the foot of the stairs in parade dress. Her tailored red jacket and matching gloves could have been a uniform, for there was no softness of lace or gathering. She wore a hat that reminded Wolf of a drawing he saw once of Napoleon. She looked a general's daughter from the top of her head to the shine on her black boots. He wasn't sure whether she planned to wed or go to war.

He glanced down at his clothes in comparison. The leather jacket he wore had turned dark brown with rain and smelled somewhat of the animal who first wore it. His hair and beard were thick with natural curl when dry and downright bushy when wet. Mud clung to him by the pound.

He glanced at Molly, who silently stared at him. She was probably wondering whether to marry him or plant him.

Wolf took out his handkerchief and wiped his face as he introduced his future wife to the preacher.

She shook hands nervously then turned to face Wolf. "Will you shave before we marry?"

Wolf watched her closely. He could see the anxiety in her eyes, blended with determination. She was going through with this wedding because she saw no other road to take. He shouldn't try to fool himself into believing it was for any different reason. "I will not," he answered. "Does that change your mind about the ceremony?"

"It does not." She lifted her chin. "Only there will be no kissing afterward. I'll never kiss a man who isn't clean-shaven."

"Fair enough," he decided. Right now all he wanted to do was marry her and know that she'd be safe. If he shaved before the service, she might refuse to marry him on other grounds. "I'll do without a kiss."

The preacher removed his Bible from a pouch beneath his coat and cleared his throat. "We'll need two witnesses before we start."

Josh stepped from the kitchen with Callie Ann in tow. "I'll witness," he offered as he finished off a biscuit.

Ford nodded. "And one more."

"I want to be a witness too," Callie Ann said, wiping her mouth with the back of her hand. "If Mr. Josh is one, I want to be one."

"I'm afraid you're too young," the preacher answered sternly.

"Then Uncle Orson will," she said. "He's older than dirt."

Wolf left the room with Molly trying to explain to Callie Ann why Uncle Orson couldn't witness and Callie Ann threatening to cry if she didn't get her way. The preacher muttered what sounded like Bible verses about children. No one, including the child, seemed to be listening.

Walking out the back door of the store onto a small screened-in porch, Wolf grinned as he looked through the rain. Just as he'd hoped, he saw Charlie Filmore huddled beneath the undertaker's woodshed. He could see the little man's holey boots propped at one end of a long line of lumber.

"Charlie! Charlie Filmore!" Wolf yelled. "Come here a minute."

A man less than five feet tall staggered from beneath the wood, dusting shavings from his unruly hair. "I ain't done nothing, Captain. I swear I ain't."

"I didn't say you had." Wolf waved him in. "I just need you to witness a wedding."

Charlie stared at the distance between his warm hiding place and the back porch of Molly's store. "Does it pay?"

"Two drinks," Wolf yelled.

"A bottle."

"Three drinks." Wolf swore beneath his breath. He was one of the few people in town who didn't buy Charlie drinks, but the man considered nothing else worth bargaining for. Most men in the saloons would buy him a shot just to have the little man move on down the bar and not linger too long at their side.

"A bottle." Charlie must have been able to tell even through the rain that he had the upper hand.

"All right. Get over here."

The drunk wrapped his only blanket over him and limped toward the drugstore's back entrance.

When he entered, he hung the blanket on a hook meant for coats.

Wolf tried not to react to the shock of seeing Charlie close up. But the damage three bullets had done to his face always startled Wolf at first glance.

Charlie told folks he considered himself the luckiest man alive. He'd fought in four battles of the war and been shot and left among the dead three times. Death certificates had already been signed before he managed to convince them he still lived. The fourth time he went into battle he'd made it through the day without a scratch and drank himself to sleep to celebrate. An hour later, a supply wagon loaded down with wounded drove over his legs, breaking the bones in so many places they never healed completely. After that, Charlie quit the war and went on to his chosen career of town drunk.

"Where's the bottle?" When Charlie smiled, his face looked even more distorted. He was a walking reminder to every man who fought off the nightmares of war.

"You'll get it after you witness. You can write your name on the marriage certificate, can't you?"

Charlie looked insulted. "I went to fourth grade. Not all my brains splattered out. I can write my name forward and backward." He lifted his chin. "Besides, I know all about certificates. I got three death certificates with my name on them. I reckon I was the dyingest man in the war."

"Forward will do. Come on." Wolf had to wonder about a man whose only source of pride lay in dying.

Wolf hoped he looked apologetic as he brought Charlie in. He probably should have taken the time to find someone respectable, or at least a person who bathed yearly, but he was afraid Molly might change her mind if there were many more delays. He hoped she'd seen the man before or she might scream. Charlie had caused more than one woman around town to faint when he'd appeared during daylight hours.

To Molly's credit, she only blinked as Charlie stepped from behind Wolf.

Wolf thought the preacher might break into a full round of fire-and-brimstone preaching when he took one look at Charlie. He shook like he might be the one to turn and run, but Callie Ann broke Pastor Ford's trance by hurrying over to Charlie and shaking his hand.

"Evening, Mr. Charlie. I'm glad you came inside. Uncle Orson worried about you being out there in the rain."

Charlie patted the child's head. "I'm dry enough. Tell Orson thanks for the worry, though."

"Did you come in to be a witness?"

Charlie stood a little taller. "I reckon I did."

"They wouldn't let me. Uncle Orson and I are the watchers. Which is a very important thing to have at a wedding. But not as important as being a witness."

Charlie's grin sent one side of his face into a thousand wrinkles. "Maybe you'll grow up to be a witness if you do a good job as a watcher."

"Maybe." Callie Ann moved to the counter and climbed atop Molly's work stool. "I'm ready," she said as if they'd all been waiting for her to start watching.

The preacher cleared his throat and positioned himself so he didn't have to look at Charlie during the service. "Shall we begin? Captain Hayward, Miss Donivan, are you both ready?"

Charlie snorted. "Captain, you the one getting married?"

Wolf glared at the little man in what he hoped was a threat-of-death stare. "I am, and I'll remind you, Charlie Filmore, you are a witness, not a participant."

Charlie nodded and tried his best to stand straight and sober.

"We're ready," Molly answered the preacher as she placed her gloved hand on Wolf's arm.

Wolf didn't hear most of the words. He kept saying over and over in his mind that he was marrying Molly. His Molly. It didn't matter about his clothes or how he looked; she was standing up with him.

The preacher stopped to ask their given names, but Wolf just said Wolf would do and Ford didn't argue, saying only that as long as he used proper names on the paper that was enough.

When it came time to put the ring on, Wolf's hand shook for the first time in his life. The plain gold band looked perfect on Molly's long slender finger and she smiled that he'd thought of such a detail.

"It's lovely," she whispered. "I'll give it back whenever you ask."

"Promise you'll wear it until then," Wolf answered, ignoring the preacher's shocked expression at her comment.

"I promise."

Brother Ford collected the signatures of Charlie and Josh while Wolf and Molly faced one another. He wasn't sure what to do. She'd said there would be no kissing, and he had a feeling Molly usually meant every word she said. But he thought they should do something, and shaking hands seemed a little odd for two people who'd just said they would "love, honor and obey."

"Mrs. Hayward," he said close to her ear, "would you have any objection to a hug?"

She lifted her gaze to his. "I would not." Her hands rose to rest on his shoulders.

Wolf closed the distance between them, lifting her off the ground and into his embrace. She laughed as he hugged her, twirling her around as though she were weightless.

His Molly felt as she had all those years ago. A perfect fit in his arms.

EIGHT

MOLLY DRESSED CALLIE ANN FOR BED AND SAT BE-
side her long after the child drifted off to sleep. The
little princess had been in Molly's life only a few days,
yet somehow she and her strange ways had become a
part of Molly's routine. She'd be sad when Wolf put
the child, and her invisible uncle, on the stage to another stop. Another relative.

Moonlight filtered in through the designs in the lace
curtains of the windows, making the walls a gallery of
pale shapes and forms. All that had happened during
the day circled around Molly amid the shadowy pat-
terns.

"What have I done?" she whispered to the empty
bunk below the girl's bed.

Uncle Orson didn't seem any more inclined to answer than he did to appear.

Leaning against the wall, Molly closed her eyes. She
was a rational woman, never given to unpredictability
or foolishness. She liked everything organized and

planned. Even during the war, when traveling with her father, they'd always functioned with rules and routine. Molly knew what to do. What was expected of her.

But these past few days something had happened in her world . . . something far more than the threats against her and the store and even greater than finding herself truly alone for the first time.

A man named Wolf had walked, or rather crashed, into her life. He was no gentleman. Not like the fine ones who flirted with her back home. But there was a gentleness about him that touched her as none of them ever could. He would never be her love. He'd always be her friend, though, and for her, that would be enough. He wasn't much to look at, but she felt no shame with him at her side.

Molly closed her eyes. Maybe she married him for protection. Maybe because she didn't want to be an old maid like her two aunts, who wrote of their pets as if they were children. Or maybe, for once, something just felt right without explanation. Marrying Wolf felt right.

This could be the best of both worlds. She could still have her dreams of Benjamin and his perfect love in her imagination, and she'd have Wolf as a friend in her reality. She could trust him. Any man who settled for a hug on his wedding day was not interested in her as a woman. He had his life. She had hers. With the marriage, their worlds crossed nicely, without friction or complication. His name would give her protection, and she, in turn, offered him a base to return to.

Molly jerked suddenly and realized she'd fallen asleep in the chair. She wasn't sure how much time had passed, but her back ached and her shoulder tingled with numbness from leaning into the wall.

She stretched and moved silently out of Callie Ann's room and down the stairs. Wolf waited for her in the kitchen. His empty coffee cup and papers covered the table.

"I thought you'd turned in," he said as he rubbed his eyes.

"I just came to say good night and make sure you got settled." She glanced at the few bags in one corner, wanting to ask if that was all he had, but knowing it must be. "Was your landlord surprised when you picked up your things?"

"Granny Gravy?" Wolf laughed. "She hugged me then scolded me for never bringing you by for supper. Seems she thinks the least I should have done was introduce you to her before I married you."

"The two of you were close?"

Wolf winked. "Jealous wife already?"

"Oh no." Molly felt her face redden before she realized he was kidding. "I just wondered."

"I've stored my gear there for two years, but I doubt I've spent more than two weeks beneath her roof. I think she'll miss the steady money more than me. She's a nosy old bag, but there's a good heart in there somewhere. I imagine she'd come through if you needed a friend."

He refilled his cup and changed the subject. "I thought I'd sleep on the floor in the front tonight. Just in case anyone plans to make a midnight call." He pointed to where he'd spread a bedroll that looked to be made of hides. "Tomorrow, I'll help you clean out Ephraim's room, but I don't know how long I'll be in town. Several of the young rangers have already headed for the border to fight off trouble brewing there."

Molly poured herself less than half a cup of coffee, then added milk. Without a word, she sat in the other chair. The small room seemed tiny with Wolf's bulk beside her. She pulled her journal from between the flour tin and the salt shaker. Every night, without fail, she wrote in her journal, as she had since she was a child.

Before she could start writing, Wolf pushed a paper across the table. "I made a list of those I think of as family. It's not very long. I'd appreciate you notifying them if something happens to me since, I guess, legally, you're now my next of kin."

Wolf studied the other papers. "These are statements from a handful of banks. Over the past few years, I've opened small accounts here and there so I could have money on the road if I needed it. I've already written notes informing them you're to be given whatever is in the accounts if you ask."

Molly stared in disbelief. "Captain, you don't have to do this." All she'd expected was his name in the bargain they'd made, nothing more. "I don't expect you to support me. I can take care of myself."

"I guessed you'd say that, but the money is there if you need it. I want this completed tonight. In my line of work, a man never knows how long he'll live. I'll not leave a wife owing for my funeral . . . even a wife in name only."

"But surely you have someone else?"

Wolf shook his head. "No one. My sister in Fort Worth has her hands full with two little ones. My friends, the McLains, would have taken care of things. Even after I'm gone, they'll stand beside you if you have any trouble. But should something happen to me, I'd appreciate you making any arrangements."

He said the words directly, without emotion. Molly felt the loneliness in his statement. Some folks might have thought him cold to be organizing his affairs on what was his wedding night, but Molly understood. He was trying. He knew she was a woman of order. He wanted to leave his books the same. But judging from the stains and wrinkles on most of the papers, order was not one of his strong traits.

"Can I help?" she asked, realizing he was doing all this for her, just in case something happened to him.

Within a few minutes, they had their heads together, adding up numbers and trying to figure out where some of the small towns were that he'd left money. Compared to many she'd known back East, Wolf Hayward had very little, but he was solid. He had enough to handle anything life might toss his way.

His willingness to give her all he had worked for over the past four years overwhelmed her. She could write him a draft for ten times that much from her bank in Philadelphia and it would not be nearly as great a gift.

As she figured the last list of accounts, he leaned

close, sliding his arm along the back of her chair. The action was natural. Something most couples wouldn't even notice. But Molly felt the warmth of his arm. She had to start over twice, for her mind kept wishing he would pull her an inch closer into his embrace and just hold her.

She'd always been so proper, so distant no man had ever just grabbed her and hugged her. Even her father held her gently as if she might break if he embraced her. His almost hugs and her aunts' air kisses near her cheek were all she'd ever known growing up. She'd already learned this man she married knew how to hug.

But of course he didn't hug her now. She'd been clear. She wanted only his name.

His nearness made her relax, and the worry she felt earlier slipped away. When he finally stacked the papers neatly into a tin box, dropped their marriage license on top, and locked it, they both felt that all was in order.

He handed her the key. "Put this in a safe place, Molly. I'll store the box under my bed once we get it built."

While she put the key in a tiny drawer on the kitchen shelf, he stood, almost knocking the chair over. "I'll be saying good night now." He straightened the chair but didn't look at her.

She turned to face him. With his coat and vest off, she could see that the man she married was as solid as his accounts. He certainly wasn't a man who dressed to impress anyone. Somehow his clothes fit him and the life he lived. She couldn't help but wonder what he'd look like in a suit, all shaved and trimmed.

"Thank you," she whispered. "For helping me out. I think no matter what, married or not, we'll always be friends."

"But never lovers." His foot had caught the corner of the table, and he mumbled the words as he stumbled forward.

His face was unreadable. His eyes didn't meet hers. Yet his statement surprised her, caught her off guard, for she hadn't thought of it and was shocked he had.

"No." She tried to keep her voice just as level, just as unreadable. "Never lovers. I gave my heart once. Once was enough."

"Did he hurt you so badly?" Wolf kept his head low as if he knew he were prying, yet couldn't help asking.

"No," she answered as she moved toward the stairs. Now it was her turn to look away and not meet his eyes. "He just never returned as he promised he would. But a part of me still loves him, and there is no room for another. A part of me will always belong to Benjamin."

She hurried up the steps before he could see her tears. Molly hadn't said Benjamin's name out loud in years. She thought the pain would have grown dull, but it still stabbed her heart. To try to explain would only make matters worse. Wolf would think her a fool for loving a man she'd only met once, for staking her life on a promise and a kiss, for believing a stranger.

Undressing quickly, Molly slipped into bed and snuggled under the covers, not for warmth, but to feel somehow surrounded and not so alone. As she twisted, the quilts held her, hid her, buffered her from the world. A world that had shattered around her feet in one day. A world where her only friend for thousands of miles was probably downstairs thinking he'd just married the craziest woman west of the Mississippi.

Wolf stood rooted to the floor as he heard her moving above him. His huge fists formed tight white-knuckled balls, but he didn't take a step. Every part of him wanted to climb the stairs and tell Molly who he really was. But he stood, listening to his own heart pound and calling himself every kind of fool.

His new wife had just told him she was still in love with another man—him.

NINE

Wolf didn't bother to close his eyes most of the night. Molly, his Molly, was one floor up. She might as well still be back East. He'd married her, but she had made it plain he would never hold her. He would never sleep beside her. Never make love to her.

He watched the sun lighten the street outside on Congress Avenue and wondered how he could make it through another day without touching her. Another night without holding her. He'd never longed for any woman but Molly. She was the one in all his dreams and the few hopes he'd allowed himself to have over the years. Even during the war, when he was young and hot-blooded, he'd preferred a dream of her to the reality of an unknown woman beside him.

Now she was close, so close, but she might as well still be the dream, for she would not be filling his arms.

By the time he heard her moving about in the drugstore, he'd rolled up his bed and wandered into the kitchen looking for coffee.

She stepped into the tiny room. He nodded a greeting and tried not to react to her nearness. She was all proper and dressed in black. Her cheeks were rosy, as though she'd just returned from a morning ride in the dawn mist. He, on the other hand, figured he looked more like a Pony Express horse who had just pulled a double shift.

She said something about making breakfast. He circled past her to go wash up. She offered her room, but he said he'd feel more comfortable out back at the washstand Ephraim had set up on the porch.

In truth, Wolf didn't know if he could be in Molly's room with all her things surrounding him. The smell of the rose soap she used must linger in the air. He'd have to touch her clothes that always felt freshly starched and sunshine bleached. He wouldn't be able to stop himself from running his fingers over the pillow where she slept. He'd go mad.

"The washstand out back," he mumbled again as if he hadn't heard himself before.

The alley was deserted and already hot. Half of the porch was crowded with boxes, but the washstand was tidy and fully stocked.

Wolf stripped down to his trousers and washed in a bucket of cold water. He combed his hair, knowing that, within minutes, the natural curl would remove any order to it. With the scissors he found cradled in leather he cut another inch off his beard. It now hugged his jawline in a thick bush.

As he cleaned his teeth, Charlie Filmore slid from beneath Miller's disorderly pile of wood twenty feet away and staggered to the edge of the porch. Thanks to Wolf he'd finished a whole bottle last night. "Morning," he mumbled, staring up at Wolf.

"Morning." Wolf watched him in the shaving mirror. He could smell the man from three feet away. Charlie had that aged ripeness of a dirty saloon floor.

Charlie stuck his tongue out and wiped his face with the back of his hand, reminding Wolf of a stray cat grooming. "How's married life treating you, Captain?"

"Fine," Wolf grumbled. Charlie Filmore was even uglier in daylight than at night. The wrinkles in his bullet-marked face were caked with dirt. His attempt at grooming only smeared the dirt around.

Wolf glanced back at the small mirror reflecting his own face. Compared to Charlie, Wolf didn't think he looked so bad. He scratched his beard and tried to remember what he looked like clean-shaven. "Want to earn four bits?" he asked Charlie as he put the mirror down.

"I might if the work's not hard." Charlie raised an eyebrow, sending his face into a new collection of creases. "If you need something, anything, I can get it if you got the money. I know what's in every storage shed in this town."

Wolf tossed him a half dollar. "All you have to do is what comes natural to you. Let everyone you see today know that I married the lady last night."

Charlie grinned. "I'll do that. But you could have saved your money. Preacher Ford has probably told half the town by now." He winked. "That bride of yours cooking breakfast?"

Wolf nodded, hoping Charlie didn't plan on inviting himself. He wanted to spend what little time he had left in town with Molly, not trying to avoid looking at Charlie Filmore head on.

"Well then, I'll be moving along. Her friend Ephraim cooked like an old army sergeant I once had. He could burn water and sour sugar. We never had a meal that we didn't lose at least one man to stomach pains for the night. We'd line up for grub, starting at the back. Last man to check in had to eat first. If he started showing signs of turning green, the boys at the end of the line usually lost their appetites."

"Ephraim's not around anymore, Charlie. He died, so there's no need to worry about his cooking."

Charlie shook his head. "I know. Helped Miller with the coffin. He couldn't have got it finished without me." He straightened at his bragging. "What I'm trying to say is, near as I can tell, Ephraim was the *good* cook between the two of them."

When Wolf didn't comment, Charlie leaned closer and whispered, "Yanks can't cook, you know. They ain't never been taught right. I heard they toss okra and even black-eyed peas to the hogs up north. Imagine that. Not one of them can beat a steak thin enough to chicken-fry it." He shook his head. "It's a wonder they won the war."

Laughing, Wolf asked, "Are you trying to tell me my bride is missing talent in the kitchen?"

"Worse than that. It's only a matter of time before she'll be arrested for poisonin' you. Your coffin'll take more wood than most and Miller'll be beggin' for my help, as always."

Wolf tried to look concerned. "Thanks for the warning. My family, men who are like brothers to me, are the McLain boys. Between the three of them, they didn't marry a cook. Karlee tries, but she just doesn't have the gift. Allie burns everything, and my sister, Nichole, has a cook who lives in. But they love their men. I guess that's why I've never heard a McLain complain."

Charlie shook his rat's nest of hair again. "But, Captain, you don't understand. It ain't that she can't cook. It's more like the stove is a weapon to her, and she's out for blood. I've seen roaches hightailing it out of the alley when she throws out leftovers. Since she moved in, I ain't seen one stray cat or dog stop by this place to even sniff for food."

Wolf frowned, wondering if he'd have the guts to eat whatever she put in front of him for breakfast. "Thanks for the warning, Charlie, but I think I'll be fine."

Charlie wiggled around as though fighting himself to get out more words. "There's something else I better tell you, Captain, since you married the lady."

Wolf wasn't sure he wanted to hear anything else Charlie had to say. If it was something bad about Molly, he wouldn't believe it, and he'd hate to hit a man as down on his luck as Charlie.

"She's in trouble," Charlie mumbled. "Someone wants her out of here worse than I've ever seen. Word is, they'll pay plenty to have her removed or if she just happened to disappear that would suit someone fine."

Wolf's interest piqued. "Who?"

"I don't know." Charlie scratched his head. "I just heard things. Maybe they ain't true. Even if they were, there ain't a man in his right mind who'd mess with her now they know she belongs to you."

"Maybe. Let me know if you hear anything else. And get the word spread that any man who messes with Molly will answer to me."

"All right, Captain." Charlie straightened. "I guess that makes me now working for the Rangers."

Wolf nodded. "Right. You're the secret ranger. No one, not even the pay clerk, knows. But don't worry, if you come up with something, I'll see you get paid."

Charlie saluted. "Yes, sir. You can count on me, Captain. I'll keep my ears and my good eye open."

Wolf returned the salute and walked inside, buttoning a clean shirt. As soon as he could, he'd go to the office and let them know he wouldn't be leaving for the border or anywhere else for a few days. He planned to stay close to Molly and nothing short of an earthquake would move him. Charlie was probably only repeating rumors, but he'd do some checking.

If there were folks out to bother Molly, they'd have to deal with him from now on.

When he reached the kitchen, Molly poured coffee. Breakfast sat on the little table, looking pretty as a dessert display in a fancy Harvey House.

"Just in time." She smiled. "I was afraid it would get cold."

Wolf stared down at lean ham and fat scrambled

eggs on each plate. A stack of biscuits rested between two place settings, with butter and jam beside them.

"This looks great," he said honestly and waited for her to sit down.

When she took her place, he hurried to the other chair. The smell of the bread made him smile. Charlie was a liar.

They ate in silence. Wolf couldn't believe how good everything tasted. When she pulled out two cinnamon rolls the size of his fist from a cold oven, he was amazed. Even Noma's cafe didn't make better. In fact, these tasted almost exactly like the ones he'd had at Noma's yesterday.

"That was a fine meal, Molly," he said, giving her an opportunity should she feel the need to confess anything.

"Thank you." She calmly cleared the table without meeting his eyes. "I set Callie Ann's meal aside. She should be up soon."

Wolf didn't know what to do. He wasn't about to confront her. What if his suspicions were wrong? Maybe there was some way to cook breakfast without heating the oven. Maybe she cooked it last night without waking him. Maybe she was a witch and conjured it up. He didn't care. Molly had fixed him breakfast, and that was all he needed to know.

The jingle of the front door saved him from worry. A young ranger called out and Wolf directed him to the kitchen area.

He gave a quick nod to Molly as he handed Wolf a message. He looked like he wanted to leave but stood waiting for orders as if he'd been told to do so.

"What is it?" Molly asked as she slipped into the chair across from him.

"Trouble," Wolf answered before even opening the paper. No one would have bothered him if it wasn't something important. "Good news can be told. It doesn't need to be written."

He almost tore the paper in half and tossed it in the stove, but without a fire, it wouldn't stand much chance of burning. He was staying here. Whatever the note said, he was staying by Molly.

Slowly he flipped the note open, his body already tense, preparing to stand his ground. But the words called to him, drawing him from his resolve. With grim lines across his forehead, he set his mind to what must be done.

Molly touched his arm. "What is it?"

Wolf could hear fear in her voice.

"I have to go," he said, forcing his gaze to leave the words on the paper. Forcing the words he didn't want to say.

For a moment, he stared at Molly, knowing he was leaving again. Leaving before she knew who he really was. There was no time to explain all that was in his heart. If a part of the love she'd said she had for Benjamin was still alive, then there was a chance she could love him. He'd claim that part of yesterday and build their tomorrows on it.

"Will you take care of Callie Ann . . ."

"Of course."

". . . and take care of yourself?"

Molly nodded slowly, like a soldier accepting an order.

She'd been trained well, he thought. So well, she'd given up having dreams or plans of any future with anyone. People leaving her was a pattern in her life.

"Philip, saddle my horse and pack the standard bag of supplies," Wolf ordered the young ranger. "I'll be ready in ten minutes."

Philip, who had waited impatiently, hurried away now that he'd received his orders.

Wolf stood slowly, watching Molly's fingers slide away from his arm. He wondered if he'd ever have the time to grow so used to her touch that he didn't notice it.

With determination, he moved to his saddlebags and checked them as he spoke. "You know I wouldn't go if I had a choice. The note is from my sister, Nichole McLain. She says John Catlin is in trouble. John is part of my family, or as much of a family as I've ever had until I married you last night. He's a wild kid, no stranger to trouble."

As he rolled the chamber in his Colt, he tried to think of how to tell her quickly all that had happened before. Why John had to live, not just because he was still a boy, but because he was all the family Allie McLain, Wes's wife, had left, thanks to an Indian raid years ago. Allie was the one they had all thought was little more than a savage when Wes saved her and brought her home. She'd been kidnapped and tortured for years, thinking all her family dead. Then they'd found John, her brother. He'd lost his early memories of the settle-

ment and of Allie. John believed himself to be Comanche. But somewhere inside him beat the heart of a
little boy who'd been happy and known love before the
day he'd had to watch his parents killed. If there was
a goodness deep inside, John deserved a chance.

Wolf had to try to make Molly understand. "My sister, in Fort Worth, received a telegram yesterday from
a friend who is a U.S. marshal near Waco. He saw John
arrested, but said nothing, only sent the message. She,
in turn, sent messages to Daniel in College Station,
Wes near Denton, and me. She said her husband,
Adam, would take the next train. One of us has to get
to Waco before John is hanged. He may be a fighter,
but he's not a killer."

Molly nodded, but her eyes told him she didn't fully
understand. "What can I do to help?" she asked as she
helped him collect things.

Wolf tied the leather on his saddlebags, then stared
up at her. Unsaid words were like the Rockies between
them. He didn't know where to start. "Don't take any
chances while I'm gone. Lock your doors at night.
Sleep with a Colt under your pillow."

He knelt and finished packing, unsure if he could
face her and still leave.

"I know what to do," she answered calmly as though
she'd said the words a hundred times.

He glanced up and saw her frowning at him. She
was a woman fully grown, a general's daughter. She
knew how to take care of herself. She'd lived much of
her life in dangerous territory.

"I'll be back as soon as I can," he said, fighting the

urge to swear. All he wanted to do was stay with her, convince her that a part of him was still the young Benjamin who'd kissed her. But duty called, and honor demanded he go.

He strapped on his gun belt and lifted his gear. "Follow me out to say good-bye, would you, Molly?" he said as he moved through the door.

"Of course," she answered almost formally as she wrapped a bit of food in a lace napkin.

Several people waited in the street. Word must have spread, Wolf thought. Three of the rangers walked down from the office to see him off. They offered help if he needed it.

Wherever more than one ranger stood, folks gathered to see what was about to happen. Even though Austin was the base they all returned to from time to time, it was rare to see a group of them. They wore no uniform other than a circle-star badge, and most kept that pinned beneath a coat. Yet, people in Texas knew a ranger on sight. Maybe it was his walk, tall and straight. Or maybe the way twin Colts were usually strapped to his legs so snug they appeared to have naturally grown there. Wolf wasn't sure, but he'd seen it again and again. Folks stopped and watched when a ranger walked the street. It was no different this morning.

He laced his saddlebags in place and swung onto the blood-red horse. Wolf couldn't help but groan. He'd thought he'd have more days in town this time. He didn't even feel like his legs had straightened this stay. They were still bowed and ready to ride.

No thoughts of staying were considered. He had to help John Catlin if it were in his power. Not only for the young man's sake, but for Allie's. Wolf didn't want to have to tell Allie McLain her brother was dead. She'd had enough sorrow to last one lifetime.

The street came alive with folks moving to work and merchants sweeping their storefronts. But he hardly noticed them. All he saw was a tall woman dressed in black, back held straight, chin lifted, hands at her sides. He didn't understand why everyone wasn't staring at her beauty. Couldn't they see the softness of her honey-brown hair or the way her green eyes sparkled with a tear she'd never let fall. She seemed to move invisibly through the crowd, yet she took his breath away.

"Molly," Wolf called, as though she weren't standing five feet away.

She hesitated and, for a moment, he thought she'd remain a statue in the crowd.

When she finally neared, he leaned over so that he could whisper in her ear.

She stood on her tiptoes.

"Put your arms around my neck," he ordered.

"What?"

"You want the town to know you're my wife, don't you? Then put your arms around me, darlin'."

She raised her arms awkwardly about his neck, brushing his hair with her hands as she followed his command.

With one mighty swing, he circled her waist and pulled her up onto his lap.

A cry escaped her before she realized what he was

doing. Frantically, she held to him as his huge horse pranced at Wolf's sudden movement. The few people on the street who weren't already watching them turned to stare. The lady and the ranger made an odd pair.

"This should let the town know we're married," Wolf whispered as he lowered his mouth to hers.

He'd expected her to protest, maybe even fight his advance. But she didn't. He had no idea if it was because she realized what he was trying to do or she was too shocked to react. He'd meant the kiss to be for show, nothing more. But when his lips pressed against hers, he felt a longing so deep in his soul he couldn't pull away.

One hand held the reins while his other drew her to him. He could feel her breasts rising and falling against his chest . . . the pounding of her heartbeat against his own.

When her lips moved against his in protest, he pulled back slightly so that only words could pass between them. He'd expected her to scream or slap him or push away, but she only whispered, "Be careful. Please come back."

As she spoke, her mouth brushed against his, driving him mad with their softness.

This time, when he closed the space between them, his mouth was tender, hesitant, hopeful. Her lips made him ache with need. Her bottom lip trembled as he tasted, and her body yielded so completely in his arms, he could feel her melting into him.

When the kiss ended, he lowered her to the ground, so rattled by her reaction that he feared he might drop her. "I'll be back as soon as I can." He pulled the reins and stared down at her.

She was as shaken by what had happened as he. He could see it in her dancing green eyes. In the way she touched her lips as if to hold on to his kiss for one more moment. In the blush that rose to her cheeks, making her look like a young girl.

Suddenly, he was aware of the people standing around them. Shop clerks, rangers, bankers. They all stood silently watching, their mouths open. For a man to kiss his wife in public was one thing, but to kiss her as he'd just kissed Molly was outrageous.

Wolf tipped his hat to Molly and smiled. There was no one on the street who would doubt that the captain and his lady were in love.

He'd deal with her anger at his breaking their agreement later. He kicked his horse into action, in a hurry to do what he must and return. For when he returned, not only would he deal with her anger, he'd deal with the passion he tasted in her kiss.

TEN

Molly lifted her head and walked slowly back into her store. She'd show no shame for kissing her own husband good-bye. Not in front of the town. Not in front of anyone.

As soon as she was alone, she touched her face with trembling fingers. His beard had made her skin tingle. Now her cheek felt raw and newborn. Her lips felt slightly swollen and very much kissed.

She could tell herself the kiss had been just to make a point, nothing more, but she knew the truth. When his lips had touched hers, it was as though they both discovered at the same time that they wanted the kiss. Or maybe *needed* it would be more accurate. She'd been no victim, but a willing partner. Never in her life had she so boldly pressed herself against a man. In the few days she'd known Wolf Hayward, she'd gone from a respectable lady to a wanton hussy, kissing a man brazenly in the street.

She sat down at the table still littered with the dishes

from Noma's cafe and lifted her journal from the shelf. If she wrote down every emotion, every thought, maybe she could save all the feelings running through her right now. Then someday, when there was nothing but memories in her life, she could turn back the pages and recall how she'd felt the day she'd been kissed boldly in the street.

As she finished writing, Callie Ann came down and it was time to begin the day.

If the people of the town thought she'd acted improper when Wolf left, they showed no sign. For the first time since she'd opened her doors, folks actually came into her store. They were polite, respectful, calling her Mrs. Hayward and introducing her to others as the captain's wife. Many expressed their sorrow at Ephraim's passing, though most had only seen the man, never spoken to him. The young doctor who'd treated Ephraim, Frank Washburn, came by with a pie and fresh bread his wife had made. He spoke highly of Ephraim even though Molly doubted he'd had time to know the old man well.

Two gentlemen from the State Lunatic Asylum dropped in to ask if she'd be interested in providing drug needs to the hospital. It lay three miles north of the capital, which meant Molly would have to rent a buggy once a week. But with luck she could make all her calls in one evening.

Rangers wandered in to check on her as regularly as tiny soldiers on a Swiss clock. Women came by to chat and ask advice about creams and soaps. One aging doctor wanted to introduce himself and ask if she'd start filling the prescriptions he didn't keep in his office. Even Miller stopped in, offering to hang her sign back up. He no longer looked at her strangely, but kept his eyes respectfully focused on her face.

By afternoon, the rangers had pestered her so often with wanting to help that she assigned them the task of cleaning out Ephraim's room and building a large bed. They smiled at one another and winked, never guessing the bed would be for Wolf alone.

Ephraim's room was military in orderliness—a few books, two drawers of clothes, and an empty trunk. In all the years of his life he'd never owned more than could fit in a trunk. The rangers packed his things with care.

Molly lost track of the number of times she ran to the storage room for supplies. If the days to come were like this one, she'd have to order more of everything by the end of the week. Between the drunken gunslinger and the vandals most of her beautiful bottles were gone, but by carefully stocking her supplies on the mirrored shelves the store still looked reasonably full.

Callie Ann played on the stairs with her dolls, setting up little rooms on each step. She seemed a child accustomed to being alone and liked playing where she could watch people but still be out from underfoot. In many ways, she reminded Molly of herself at that age, always looking for ways to play in an adult world.

By the end of the day, Molly had experienced more business than in the entire month she'd been open. A new shingle hung outside her door with Hayward as her last name.

Exhausted, she faced the tiny kitchen where Ephraim had always waited with tea. His decline had been slow. She hadn't realized the end was so near. Since the war and her father's death he'd been a staple in her life, always ready to help. The only time she'd heard him raise his voice was the day she'd told her aunts she was leaving. They'd protested as if she were a child planning to run away from home. Finally, after hours of arguing, Molly was about to give in and forget the idea. Ephraim helped her stand her ground.

Ephraim wasn't a relative or a paid employee; he was more. He'd been her second father. She never knew her mother, but she'd been lucky enough to have two fathers.

The general used to say her old-maid aunts had moved in like the plague when his wife died giving birth to Molly. They'd told her for years that they were her mothers now, but Molly never believed such a lie. Criticism was their only teaching tool.

She brushed the back of the chair where Ephraim always sat with a cup of coffee before him. A year ago he read every free moment; then, just breathing took all his energy.

Suddenly, the room . . . the store was too small. Molly hurried Callie Ann out the door, promising dinner at one of the fancy hotel restaurants where state congressmen and their ladies dined. Austin might be a western town, but it was also the capital. With politics came society and fashion.

The child seemed at home in the hotel dining room, not even commenting on how grand it was. She sat up straight, folded her napkin, and knew which fork to use. Molly wondered anew how such a child could possibly arrive homeless and penniless.

After dinner, they walked home holding hands as though they had done so every day of the child's life. Molly smiled, thinking how much she enjoyed the company, when she realized Callie Ann hadn't mentioned her invisible relative once all day.

"Is Uncle Orson following us?" she had to ask. "I can't see him in the dark."

Callie skipped along without missing a step. "Oh, no. He decided to sleep in today. He's taken to his bed just like Grandma used to do."

"Oh, I hope he's not ill." Molly tried to sound serious. "Should I mix him up something to help?"

"Nope." Callie Ann walked along one board as if balancing above the earth on the single plank. "He just took to his bed. He's old as the hills, which was the same age of Grandma, but she died."

The sadness in the child's eyes reminded Molly how they both had lost everyone close to them. Molly changed the subject. "I hoped you would help me watch the people again tomorrow. You can still play on the steps, but every now and then glance down and see how many people are in the store."

"I'm a good watcher," Callie said proudly. "I even watched Mr. Miller take a key from a nail under the counter." She skipped along, only half interested in the conversation.

"Mr. Miller took my extra key?" Molly found that hard to believe.

"I watched him," Callie Ann answered. "He looked up at me and gave me cricket eyes."

"Cricket eyes?"

The child stopped and frowned, drawing her eyebrows as close together as she could. "You know, cricket eyes, like he could rub his eyebrows together. Grandma and me used to have a gardener who would do that every time I walked off the path. She told me some of his kin were probably still eating the crops every spring."

Molly tried to frown enough to pull her eyebrows together. "Do I have them?"

Callie Ann laughed. "You can't have them. You can't look that way 'cause you're pretty."

"Thanks." Molly took the compliment. "But I've never been pretty." In her life, she could never remember anyone accusing her of being pretty. Practical, useful, efficient, but never pretty.

"Yes, you are," Callie Ann objected. "Wolf told me you was the prettiest woman alive. I said, 'In all the world?' and he said, 'Yes, in all the world.' "

"And when were you talking to Wolf about me?"

Callie looked bored with the conversation. "All the time. He talks about you like there's nothing else to talk about."

Shocked by the statement, Molly tried to think back to one compliment Wolf had given her. If the man considered her a beauty, he was more nearsighted than she'd thought. Her old aunts used to remind her daily that there were more important things in life than being attractive.

When they reached the drugstore door, Molly turned the knob carefully. It was locked, just as she'd left it. She pulled out her key and opened it, then touched her finger to her lips and motioned for Callie Ann to follow.

They tiptoed into the store as soundlessly as mice.

All was silent. All was in order. If Miller planned to infiltrate her business, he'd waited too long. Now, she was prepared.

While Callie played, Molly moved all her weapons into place. Her father had taught her not all defenses were guns. She strung a bell between both doors, then slid a wedge against the back door just to be sure. Anyone coming in through the back would have to knock the door down. If the front was opened even a few inches the bell should ring. If the door swung enough to allow a man through, the bell would hit the floor.

She placed all the large knives she owned on shelves where she could reach them, but Callie Ann couldn't. Then Molly dug through Ephraim's trunk for the Navy Colt he'd owned since the war. She'd leave it downstairs and her father's matching gun upstairs. That way no matter where she was, she'd be near a weapon.

By the time she got Callie Ann to bed, Molly could feel her nerves tightening like a warrior ready to fight. If Miller and his friends had any plans to break in, they'd find a surprise waiting for them.

She dressed for bed and lay awake, waiting for the

bell to sound downstairs. By the time anyone could step three feet into her store, Molly would have her gun in hand and be halfway down. The street lamp pushed most of the shadows away in the store, but, to her advantage, the stairs remained dark until full dawn.

As the hours passed and no one came, Molly's mind sought the comfort of invisible arms. She curled against a vision who never slept beside her in the real world but had lived vividly in her dreams. "Benjamin," she whispered softly from her sleep. "Benjamin."

Over the years and through the pages of her journal Benjamin had drifted. She'd written him letters, described her dreams of holding him, and built in her mind a life that might have been.

But when her hand rose to touch his face, her dream shattered, bringing her full awake.

Molly rolled from the bed. Standing in the darkness, she took huge gulps of air, fighting away the memory of the dream. Her body was covered in sweat. She shivered as the night air circled around her.

She tried to force the real world to return, but the vision had been too strong.

Opening and closing her hand, she realized she could still feel the whiskers that had brushed her palm. In her dream it had been Wolf's face she touched and not Benjamin's.

Wolf rode hard out of Austin. The day grew warm, and the land flattened slightly. He changed horses at stagecoach stations along the way, promising he'd return in a few days to switch the stock. Most of the stage managers knew him and wouldn't charge him for the feed for the horses he left behind.

Finally, after dark, he stopped to rest. The grass was tall and soft along the San Gabriel River where he staked his horse. He'd seen the river rage and spread far over its banks after a storm, but tonight it flowed lazy and quiet.

Wolf didn't even bother with his bedroll. He stripped off his clothes and waded into the stream to wash off layers of sweat.

The soap Molly had insisted on putting in his bag smelled funny but it lathered well. How could he feel clean without the smell of lye surrounding him? If a soap didn't take off a few layers of hide when he washed, Wolf figured it wasn't worth much. But he couldn't have said he didn't want it, when she'd been running around making such an effort to help him pack.

At least the water was cool. Unfortunately, it wasn't more than a foot deep. As he knelt to wash, he thought of how accustomed to being alone he'd become. In the war it had been necessary. When he'd entered enemy territory his only safety lay in trusting no one. He'd walked into dozens of Union camps. He'd even spent a month once in Washington.

More often than not, he'd been alone when he'd traveled north. And, always, he found himself walking by the hospital tents, hoping for another glimpse of Molly, thinking that maybe she and her father might be touring at the same time he passed.

He told himself that, even if he saw her, he wouldn't approach her. Yet he looked, sometimes even asked if

anyone knew where General Donivan was stationed.
The boys in blue spoke highly of him. They talked of
how Donivan's standards never bent, never slackened.
The comments only served to remind Wolf of how un-
welcome he would be if he ever got brave enough to
knock on Molly Donivan's door. The general would
probably have him shot for even thinking of courting
her.

When the war ended, Wolf had been running too
long to settle down. His home had been burned, his
land claimed for taxes. There was nowhere for him to
go. He'd fought hard for what he thought was his right
for his state to be free, but his side lost. For him, there
would be no parade, no pension. For Wolf, only a warrant awaited him if he returned home.

Without putting on any clothes, he stepped from the
stream and stretched out in the grass. Eight years ago,
when he met Molly, he was almost the gentleman she
thought him to be. But now, too much had happened.
He lived off the land like an animal, sometimes for
months. He forgot all the rules of etiquette his mother
had drilled into him. He'd become Wolf. Benjamin no
longer existed.

The warm night air dried his skin as he remembered
Molly's kiss from only hours before. Slowly he realized how wrong he'd been to kiss her as he had. They
no longer fit together. He couldn't see himself settling
down and working a regular job. It would be better to
play the charade of the marriage until she was safe,
then walk away. He'd never belonged in her world. He
never would.

Wolf closed his eyes. He could tell himself that a hundred times, but he doubted he'd ever believe it in his heart.

He was so absorbed, Wolf didn't hear a horse walking in the stream until it was too close for him even to make an effort to bolt for his guns.

He lay perfectly still, hoping whoever it was would pass by without seeing a two-hundred-pound man lying nude in the grass.

A deep chuckle gave him away. What were the chances of that?

"Well, it was bound to happen." Wes McLain's familiar voice came from not ten feet away. "I always knew you'd go mad one day and start living like the animal you're named after."

Wolf opened his eyes and stared at the shadow. Even in the blackness, he could see the military bearing that still hung about Wes like a cloak.

Standing, Wolf pulled on his trousers and growled. "Either you're getting better, or I'm losing my hearing. Hell, time was I could smell a Yank for a good mile. Now you walk through the water a few feet away."

"Speaking of smell." Wes swung down from his horse with the ease of a cavalryman. "Is that lavender soap you're wearing this evening?"

"Shut up," Wolf growled again. "Don't say another word unless you wanta be counting your teeth in your hand."

Wes laughed. He might not be as big as Wolf, but his smile showed he'd known the ranger long enough to have no fear of the man. "Good to see you. I was hoping we'd meet up before Waco. I was down in the Hill Country buying cattle when I got the word. I guessed you'd be traveling the stage trails."

Wolf stacked a few logs for a fire. He knew he and Wes would talk a while before they slept, if they slept at all. "You heard how John is?"

Wes shook his head.

The men made camp in the rhythm of old friends. Wes boiled coffee. Wolf unrolled the biscuits Molly had packed, noticing she'd cut each and spread jam in the centers. Wes's brother was married to Wolf's sister, which made them close to being relatives. A mutual respect for one another made them friends.

"How's your bride, Allie?" Wolf finally asked, knowing he didn't want to hear the answer.

Wes was a hard man, scarred by war, yet when he thought of his wife, something softened about him. "I promised I'd bring the kid back alive. I've never broken my word to her."

Wolf remembered the tiny woman who was now Wes's wife. Wes pulled her from a cage where she'd been treated like a wild animal. With kindness he'd brought her back to the world from the hell of being passed around as a slave captive by first the Comanches, then the man who used her as little more than a side show attraction.

Wolf didn't want to think of sweet Allie sad now. "What's the kid done this time?" he asked about Allie's brother. For the past few years, Wolf felt like he and the McLain boys had been guardian angels to a wild kid who wished them all dead. He didn't take to being civilized any more than an alligator would.

"Allie thought we should send him to a real school. She's had no luck teaching him to read or speak English, for that matter." Wes ran a hand along his scarred cheek. "I swear, the kid looks civilized, but he lived with the Comanche so long, a part of him just won't listen. At night, when he's with us, I see him watching the path of the moon like he's a prisoner in chains and that's the only touch of freedom he has."

Wes poured Wolf a cup of coffee. "He went along with the idea of going away to school. And to tell the truth, I was kind of glad to see him leave. Except for his sister, he looks at everyone on my spread as if he'd just as soon see them floating facedown in the creek.

"I took him to Dallas to a good school. He stayed a few days before he disappeared. A month later, he turned up in a Waco bar fight. Seems a man died, and John was the last one standing, so he took the blame."

"You think he killed the fellow?" Wolf asked.

Wes shook his head. "No. A few months ago I might have, but wishing everyone around him dead and killing them are two different things. The kid's unhappy. His world has been turned upside down. First, seeing his parents killed, then being kidnapped and growing up on the move with one tribe after another. Finally, when he'd almost forgotten his family and grown accustomed to the Indian ways, he had that life ripped away and was told he could never go back. He doesn't know who he is. He thinks he belongs nowhere."

Wolf stood. "So how we going to get him out, friend?"

Wes stared up at him. "How far are you willing to go?"

"As far as it takes," Wolf answered honestly.

Wes smiled. "Good, then I have a plan."

ELEVEN

It was almost dawn when Molly finally fell asleep. In what seemed like minutes, Callie Ann stood by her bed, shaking her shoulder.

"Wake up," the little girl whispered. "Wake up, I think it's time we ate breakfast."

Molly forced her eyes open. "It can't be morning. Not yet."

Callie Ann laughed. "Yes, it is."

Molly pulled the pillow over her head. "Go away, Morning. I need sleep."

Giggling, Callie Ann lifted a corner of the pillow and yelled, "Morning won't go away."

"All right." Molly shoved her hair from her eyes. "I'm up."

They laughed as they dressed for the day then went down to a breakfast of cold rolls, apples, and tea. By the time Molly removed the alarm bells and unlocked the front door, people were waiting.

The day was busy and full for them both. The rangers finished Wolf's bed and asked if there was anything else they could do. Everyone from Mr. Miller to the old woman people called Granny Gravy dropped in to say hello. A few needed something, but most just came to pass the time.

By evening, when Molly finally sat down next to Callie Ann on the steps, she was surprised to realize how exhausted she felt. "Passing the time" was not an easy job.

The child rested her head in Molly's lap. "I don't want to go anywhere to eat tonight. I'm tired from watching all day. Can we stay here?"

Molly brushed the girl's curls. "I'd like that. When I used to travel with my dad in the army camps I watched men make peanut porridge. I put some on a while ago. Would you like some of that for supper?"

Callie Ann smiled. "Peanut porridge and rolls with apple slices in the middle."

"That sounds like as fine a meal as I've ever ordered in a restaurant."

By the time they cooked and ate, they were both ready for bed. Molly carefully rigged the alarms on the doors, then went up to tuck in Callie Ann. She marveled at how quickly the child had become a part of her life. When Wolf returned there would probably be word of other relatives she could live with. Molly knew Callie Ann was only company, but she felt like family.

"I forgot to tell you," Callie Ann said as she curled into her bed. "Uncle Orson watched Mr. Miller bring the key back this afternoon."

Raising an eyebrow, Molly asked, "Are you sure?"

"Uncle Orson said he put it back on the hook under the counter."

Molly didn't comment as she moved to her room across the hallway. Maybe Miller felt guilty about taking the key. Maybe he was afraid to carry through with whatever he'd planned. Maybe he thought she might miss the original and made a copy.

Until Molly was sure, she'd keep the doors locked and rigged with alarms. The Navy Colt would be by her bed until Wolf returned to sleep downstairs. If trouble came knocking, she'd be ready.

After sleeping very little the night before, she welcomed her bed. By the time she settled in, she was already dreaming of Benjamin and the make-believe life they had together in her fantasies. Her dreams of him changed over the years. At first she'd imagine him coming home in his uniform and dancing with her. As the years passed they had long walks and talks in her mind. Sometimes he'd save her, defending her against the world. Sometimes they'd just enjoy a quiet dinner and talk of the day. It didn't matter. Benjamin lived in her dreams.

Hours later, Molly thought she heard the bell clang twice before she fought through the deep sleep she'd entered. Grabbing her gun, she was at the stairs before she blinked sleep fully from her eyes. The bell chimed again, sounding muffled as if gloved hands had caught it in midair.

Molly searched the darkness. The store was still . . . empty.

Molly took the final few steps, trying to see into the

dark corners of the room for any movement. As her hand gripped the gun tighter, she told herself she had to be ready to fire. Her father always warned her never to draw a gun unless she was willing to use it. If she hesitated, it could mean not only her life, but Callie Ann's. No man stood by to protect her. She had only herself to depend on.

She reached the ground level. Nothing. As always, smells drifted through the air in greeting. The few colored bottles remaining on the shelves reflected light from the street. But all was silent.

Circling the counters, Molly checked the door. It had been unlocked and opened enough to sound the alarm, but the ropes were still intact. No one could have entered.

Pushing the door closed, she twisted the lock. The bell clanked again, falling back into place at guard. She took a deep breath. Whoever had tried to get in had failed. The alarm must have frightened them away. Lowering the gun, she walked back to the stairs.

As she headed up, the corner of her gaze caught a slight movement in the curtain separating her work area from the kitchen. A silent scream caught in Molly's throat. She wasn't alone. Someone *had* entered, maybe even replaced her bell system so she wouldn't know. Someone waited just beyond the curtain.

It took every ounce of her strength not to run. Slowly, she moved up the stairs and into the blackness. Halfway up, she turned and sat down, holding her gun steady atop her knees.

Afraid even to breathe, she waited. As she focused

on the curtain, she tried to keep from blinking. Her finger stayed poised on the trigger, ready for action.

The curtain shifted again, but there was no sound.

Molly raised the barrel to heart level. If the intruder were armed, she might get one shot before he answered with fire of his own. The stairway shadows protected her, yet the walls imprisoned her.

Seconds dragged by like hours. Her hands grew sweaty on the weapon. Her knees shook. She reminded herself she was a general's daughter. She could do what had to be done.

The curtain parted. For a moment, she thought something was horribly wrong. There was only a void where a man's chest and shoulders should have been.

Then she saw the blond curls and knew.

"Callie!" Molly dropped the gun and ran down the steps.

The startled child hiccuped a cry. The cup of milk she carried slipped from her fingers and shattered. In fright, Callie Ann backed up, entangling herself into the curtain.

"Callie," Molly lowered her voice. "You frightened me so."

Callie Ann frowned, then began to cry. "You scared me, too. I didn't do anything wrong, did I?"

"No," Molly whispered, trying to let her voice calm the child. "I guess we just scared each other half to death. Maybe we'll both think it was a dream when we wake up."

They laughed, suddenly embarrassed by their own fear.

"I came down for some of those cookies Ephraim called crackers. He always let me have one when I asked." She looked down at the crumbs in her hand. "My grandma used to leave a snack by my bed in case I got hungry. She said she didn't want me wandering about the house with a candle. I didn't tell her, but I used to eat the snack, then wander around."

"It's all right." Molly brushed the crumbs from Callie Ann's tiny fingers. "You can have a snack anytime, but I'd rather you not walk about down here alone at night."

" 'Cause you got the place triggered like a trap?"

Molly looked closely at Callie Ann. "Triggered . . . trap?"

The child nodded. "I saw the bells tied to the door but I didn't bother them none. My grandma used to show me how a trigger worked on a trap. But I don't understand yours. What are you hoping to catch?"

"Nothing." Molly cleaned up the milk and crumbs. "I only wanted to know if someone was in the store."

"Well, it worked. You found me." Callie Ann shoved a tear off her cheek. "You scared me, yelling my name."

"I'm sorry." Molly guessed the child was not half as frightened as she had been. What if in her fear she'd fired the gun? "How about we start over? I'll carry two milks, and you get the crackers. We'll go upstairs together so you won't be scared anymore." As she spoke, she guided the child into the kitchen area.

Callie Ann climbed on the chair and collected the

tin of crackers. "After we eat these, can I sleep with you tonight?"

"Of course." Molly reached for the pitcher of milk kept in a cold box near the floor. In Austin, no place was cool in the summer, but the cooler air beneath the house kept milk for a day. "Whenever you want to sleep with me, you're welcome to."

As she poured the milk, Molly thought she heard the splash echo through the night like someone pouring another liquid at the same time. A moment later, the smell of kerosene drifted past the thin curtains and filled the kitchen.

Molly set the pitcher down and reached for Callie Ann's hand. She'd been right, she thought. Someone was in the store. Somehow they'd gotten in and re-placed the bells before she could get down the stairs.

Panic climbed her spine. She'd left the Colt on the steps and the other one was in the store.

The sloshing sound came again. The liquid splashed lightly against the glass counters just beyond the kitchen. She could hear it spilling over, dripping down the edges.

Kerosene fumes burned her eyes. Slowly, she pulled Callie Ann backward. Their only hope was the alley door. Whoever was pouring had been too impatient to wait until they returned upstairs.

"Hurry," Molly whispered.

The child might not understand, but the fear echoing in Molly's voice kept her silent.

They moved quickly to the back of the kitchen and into Wolf's room. Molly's mind raced through their chances. If whoever was in the front room struck a match, the store would burn fast. She had no hope of retrieving anything from upstairs. There was nothing of value in the kitchen except her journal and she'd be backtracking to get that. It wasn't worth the risk.

As they moved through Wolf's room her eyes fell on Wolf's extra gear and the box that held his papers. Protectively, she grabbed the box with her free hand and headed for the back door.

A light flicked, as harmless as a falling star, for a fraction of a second. Molly blinked and the front room flashed bright.

Within seconds fire raged behind them, exploding containers. A sudden blast knocked them against the wall beside the door as though the very air fought to escape. Molly shoved open the bolt, then pulled the wedge, but the door wouldn't budge. She pulled the rope from the handle, listening to the clang of the bells calling too late a warning.

Flames lit the front room brighter than day. It was a matter of seconds before they engulfed the kitchen and spread across Wolf's room.

Molly shoved harder on the door, pounding against it, demanding escape. Callie Ann held tightly to her waist as if she believed Molly could protect her.

Shoving again, harder, Molly screamed in frustration.

The door didn't move. Callie Ann began to cry and burrow against her gown. Molly coughed and covered the child's face with her skirt.

Kneeling suddenly, Molly placed the box in the

child's hands, unclenching tiny fingers to force them to take hold. "Carry this!" she yelled then grabbed the army blanket off Wolf's bed and covered Callie Ann. "Stay under this tent. You'll be safe."

Molly backed up a step and rammed the door with her shoulder again. The wood groaned in answer. Her lungs felt like she was breathing fire. The air pressed against her, burning before the blaze even reached them.

She glanced back. Flames had crawled into the kitchen, running like vines along the old rug and racing up the curtain. The thin-legged table and chairs popped and crackled as they died.

Pounding with all the force she could muster, Molly screamed for help.

As she stepped back to hit the door one last time before the heat overpowered her, the portal suddenly opened, swinging wide as if in welcome.

For a moment, Molly couldn't see anything. Smoke raced her for the opening, then she felt the cool air.

"Come on, ma'am!" someone yelled from beyond the porch. "I can't carry you. You got to run."

Lifting Callie Ann, blanket, box, and all, she ran for their one chance to survive.

Tumbling more than walking down the back steps, Molly reached clear air and took a deep gulp. She pulled the blanket from Callie Ann and tightly hugged the crying child.

"It's all right," she whispered again and again, more to herself than to the child.

The fire lit up the alley. Men ran everywhere, forming bucket lines, beating out secondary fires born from wind-carried embers.

Molly held Callie Ann and moved backward until she hit the woodpile behind Miller's furniture store and coffin factory.

"You all right, ma'am?" a little man beside her asked. "I moved the boxes blocking your back door as fast as I could once I heard you screaming."

She blinked away tears to see Charlie Filmore. The little beggar's face was twisted in worry. "Thank you," she whispered. "You saved our lives."

Charlie looked embarrassed. "Weren't nothing, ma'am. Just part of the job."

TWELVE

WOLF HAD BEEN PREPARED TO FIGHT FOR JOHN CAT-
lin's freedom, but to his surprise, Wes asked only that
he tell the truth. Well, most of the truth. The plan was
to walk into the Waco sheriff's office and tell them
who he was and that he thought the boy was wanted
in Austin for another murder downstate.

All Wolf had to do was talk them into it. Nichole
told Wes the sheriff wasn't sure of the boy's name, so
Wolf stood a good chance. The man who'd wired Nichole hadn't bothered to step forward and identify the
boy as a Catlin. The law in Waco planned to hang him
as a John Doe, which always looked bad on the records
and in the cemetery.

They'd probably be happy to turn the boy over to
Wolf, who would, of course, convince the sheriff he
recognized him. As soon as they got out of town John
would slip through the ranger's fingers into Wes's.

Wes reasoned that since Wolf had never lost a prisoner, a few might think it strange that a boy got away,

but then, one loss wouldn't ruin his reputation. Some might think the mighty Captain Hayward was getting old, but Wolf could disprove that theory with the next good fight that came along.

Wolf agreed reluctantly. He wasn't a man who took to tarnishing easy.

The plan was simple. No one would get hurt. No one would get killed. Most important, no one would get hanged.

As they rode into what old-timers still called Waco Village, Wes McLain stretched in the saddle and asked, "You want to tell me what's going on with you?"

"What do you mean?" Wolf had always been amazed how Wes could read him like a book. Most men who'd known Wolf since he'd been in Texas couldn't tell you three facts about him without being wrong on at least two. But Wes, he'd somehow pieced the puzzle together.

"Lavender soap. Clean clothes. Biscuits with jam. A bath. It's not even Saturday night." Wes laughed. "Shall I go on?"

"No," Wolf grumbled. Hell! He might as well be wearing a sign. "You remember me telling you about the woman I met once at a crowded train station in Philadelphia?"

Wes tipped his hat as they passed a couple taking an evening walk. "Only every time you've had a few drinks."

Wolf growled, but Wes continued, "Her name was Molly, and she was a vision in Union blue. She helped take care of the wounded. You fell for her the minute you saw her. And, if I remember the story, you kissed her and swore you'd find her when the war was over."

The ranger didn't comment. The romantic peak of his life sounded almost comical coming from Wes.

"Don't tell me you ran into her again? Another crowded station? Another kiss?"

Wolf chewed on the words a minute before he answered. "Something like that. I married her."

"What?"

"I married her!" If they had more time, Wolf would've been angry at Wes for acting like the three words couldn't possibly be connected to him.

Wes shook his head. "Well, I'll be damned. When we get John out and away, I don't care if I have to sit on him for an hour, I'm hearing the rest of this story."

"There ain't no more 'rest.' I married her. That's all there is, except she doesn't know I'm the same fool who kissed her all those years ago." They pulled up to the sheriff's office.

A passer-by would never have guessed what the two tough men were talking about, Wolf thought.

"She's gone mad since the war, right?" Wes asked as he stepped down from the saddle. "Lost all her teeth, and you felt sorry for her. A widow with a litter of kids to feed, and you were her only meal ticket." He tied his horse. "Blind as a bat and just stumbled into you one night."

Wolf fought the urge to slug his good friend. "No, she's sane, got all her teeth, never been married, and more beautiful than I remember. As for her eyesight, I'm not sure about that."

"Congratulations." Wes slapped Wolf on the back. "Seriously. If she hasn't figured it out yet, she will. Beneath all that hair and muscle is a fine man."

"Thanks," Wolf said as they walked toward the office. "Only one problem. When she finds out who I am, she'll probably never speak to me again."

"You've got to tell her," Wes advised.

"I will." Wolf promised. "I hoped to give her time to fall in love with me as I am first."

Wes shook his head. "Time can go against you just as easily. Your best shot is to remind her of the good times."

"That won't take long. We only had about three minutes of good times."

They entered the sheriff's office laughing.

The deputy on duty nervously checked them out. Strangers dropping by after dark were usually not welcome. He almost shrank in the chair.

Wolf opened his coat to show his badge and the deputy relaxed a few degrees south of panic. "Evening," he mumbled as he leaned back in his chair, obviously trying to show his authority and hide his fear. "What can I do for you fellas?"

Wolf sobered his tone to sound official. "I'd like to have a word with the prisoner named John Doe. I'm Captain Hayward from Austin. We're after a killer who fits his description and is wanted for half a dozen murders near Austin."

The deputy rose. "You can talk to him, but he won't talk back. I don't think he understands a word we say. We couldn't even get a name out of him. But I've no doubt he's bad. One look at those eyes and you can see that." The deputy unlocked the door to the cells. "He's just a kid, but it's easy to see he was born to kill. A baby rattlesnake is just as deadly as a grown one."

The ranger waited without commenting. The deputy might be surprised to learn that the boy was John Catlin, heir to one of the biggest ranges in Texas. It was run by an aging couple waiting for their only grandson to stop believing himself to be Comanche and take on his birthright. From what Wes and Allie had told him, Wolf knew John saw the ranch as another prison and not his home.

"He's in there." The deputy opened the first door and pointed to a line of cells, all with doors open except one. "I'll be out here if you need me."

Wolf moved down the hall with Wes a few feet behind. "Kid," he said in a calm voice.

The boy didn't look up.

Wolf knew the kid recognized him. Hell, he'd tried to fight his way past the lot of them on more than one occasion. "You might as well face me. I've come to get you. There's folks waiting to see you, son." Wolf fought the urge to add "as usual." If the boy hadn't been Allie's only brother and Victoria Catlin's only grandson he would have given up long before now.

Wes gave it a try. "John?"

No response.

"John!"

The boy raised his head, and Wolf locked his jaw at what he saw. John's face looked purple and blue with marks the size of a fist beaten into several places. One eye was swollen completely closed, the other blood-red where white should have been. A wound at his hairline slowly dripped blood over dried scab.

Wolf moved against the bars for a better look. John's clothes were filthy and ripped to rags. He had no boots or socks. Blood had soaked through in several spots, telling Wolf there were injuries he couldn't see.

"Hasn't this man seen a doctor?" Wolf yelled.

"Couldn't find one to go in the cell with him," the deputy hollered back. "We got two men out on sick call because of this one. Word was he took down eight men in the bar that night. He ain't all that old, or big, but he's plenty mean. Only doc we got worth anything is out of town. The army doc said he values his own life too much to get within striking distance of the kid. He ain't fit to treat anything except horses anyway."

As Wes moved closer to John, Wolf took a few steps backward until he could see the deputy in the other room. "What time does the train get in from Fort Worth? I heard there's a doctor coming in."

The deputy shifted as if bothered by all the effort he was wasting answering questions. "How would I know? Sometime tonight."

"Fifteen minutes ago," a voice said from the front door.

Wolf glanced past the deputy to a tall, well-dressed man framed in the doorway. His greatcoat blew in the wind almost like angel wings.

"I got here as fast as I could, Captain," the man said as he lifted his doctor's bag. He addressed the deputy.

"I'm Dr. McLain from Fort Worth. I'd like to have a look at the boy."

Wolf nodded at his old friend and brother-in-law. If the deputy had been brighter, he might have wondered how a Texas Ranger from Austin knew a doctor from Fort Worth was coming in. But the deputy probably never wasted effort on too much thinking.

And, Adam McLain looked to be exactly what he claimed. In truth, he was much like his brother Wes in height and coloring, only there was a kindness in his eyes that marked him as a healer. While Wes spent the war as a soldier, Adam had been a doctor. To Wolf's way of thinking the most important person he'd treated was Nichole, Wolf's sister and only blood kin. He'd saved her life one night near the end of the war and in turn she'd saved his.

Wolf fought down what he wanted to say to Adam. The deputy listened. "I'm glad you're here, Doc. Looks like the boy could use your services."

Adam smiled in greeting first to Wolf, then to Wes as he moved toward the cell. "Open the door," he ordered after one glance. "I'll need clean water, bandages if you have them, and a stack of clean towels."

The deputy's features melted from bothered to worried. "I don't know. I ain't supposed to open the cell. I'm just here as a guard. We don't wet-nurse the prisoners. Clean towels would be across the street at the hotel, but I can't leave." He showed no interest in moving from the office.

"And if the prisoner dies on your watch?" Wolf

grumbled as he passed the man and lifted the keys off a nail.

The deputy was outnumbered. The three powerful men shooed him around like he was no more than a gnat. He said something about needing help with all the paperwork if John Doe died, but no one answered him. Wes went after the towels and Wolf got the water while Adam laid out the tools of his trade.

The deputy stood in the corner as far from the cell as he could and still be able to see. He stared as they congregated once more. He made no effort to assist while Wes, Adam, and Wolf entered the cell together.

"Now, son," Adam's calm voice began, "there's no use fighting us. We're here to help you."

Wolf didn't miss the fire in John's eyes as the wild kid looked from them to the knife Adam had placed on a table just outside the cell.

If John's sister, Allie, had been there, she might have been able to talk him into cooperating, but Wolf knew they didn't have a chance.

Sure enough, as soon as they were within striking distance, the boy swung. His blows weren't aimed at any one of them, but at the world in general. Wolf could see it in his eyes, he'd fight to the death. Only, not this time, Wolf thought. Not this time.

Wes and Wolf grabbed the boy and held him down as Adam covered his mouth with a cloth. John fought the chloroform for several breaths, then relaxed.

Standing by, Wes wiped sweat from his brow and whispered low enough the deputy wouldn't hear. "You know, the kid's getting stronger, and we're getting older. How long do you figure we'll be able to keep holding him down?"

"As long as it takes." Wolf hauled in the bucket of water and noticed the frightened deputy had slipped from the room and locked the door leading to the office as if he believed the boy might overpower them all. "John will come around one day and thank us."

Wes looked doubtful.

Adam wasted no time talking. He pulled off the kid's clothes and began working on the worst wounds first. Wes said something about getting him fresh clothes from his saddlebags.

As he yelled for the deputy to let him out, Adam and Wolf grinned at one another. They both knew, in truth, Wes couldn't hang around for the doctoring. He might be a hard man with a thin scar along his cheek to prove his battles, but something about the sight of blood, or Adam pulling a needle through flesh, made Wes McLain weak in the knees.

"Lucky you became the doctor and not your brother," Wolf mumbled as he helped Adam.

Adam laughed. "Allie's expecting their first this fall. I'm going to need help. Not with Allie, but with Wes."

Wolf nodded. "I'll be there. How long does this chloroform work?"

Adam shook his head. "Keep the cloth handy. If John starts to move, put it over his nose and add a few more drops to the cotton. I'm going to be awhile. After I get these cuts sewn up, I need to wrap the ribs. The kid may not tell us anything, but judging from these wounds, he's been in a world of hurt for a few days."

Wolf glanced down at the man who was little more than a boy. He looked so young as he slept, so helpless. He'd been living in hell since the army had found him and brought him in. His skin was tanned dark; he almost looked Comanche. But one soldier had seen his blue eyes when the army raided a camp and knew he was one of the missing children they'd searched years for.

John fought them all the way, but the army got him to Fort Griffin, where Wolf had claimed him. Sometimes Wolf wasn't sure he'd done the kid a favor.

By the time they had him bandaged and dressed, John was beginning to move. A few of the bandages were already spotted with blood and the floor was covered with crimson-stained towels.

Adam placed the cloth over the prisoner's nose. "I've an idea, but we'll be taking a chance with his life," he whispered to Wolf.

"If we don't get him out of here, the boy won't have a life."

Adam nodded and let another drop of chloroform fall onto the cloth. "It doesn't look good," he said in a loud voice. "The kid's lost a lot of blood."

The deputy opened the door and ventured in a few feet. "I thought you could help him. I thought you were a real doctor." He backed a step away in disgust. "Hell, look at the mess. Blood everywhere. You could have slaughtered a calf and left less."

Adam frowned, but to the criticism he answered, "Even a *real* doctor can only do so much. There's a head wound that must have been slowly spilling blood into his brain since the fight. His breathing is so shallow I can barely detect it."

Wolf joined in the charade. "I don't think he's breathing at all, Doc. Do something. I've got folks waiting to hang him in Austin."

The deputy backed away. His eyes rounded with a fear of getting too close to death. "Maybe I should get the sheriff."

He backed into Wes, who stood like a stone in the doorway.

Wolf tried to catch Wes's attention, to let him know it was a game. But Wes's attention was focused on the body of his wife's little brother.

Adam leaned close to John. After a moment, he shook his head. "It's too late, he's dead."

Wolf faced the deputy as Adam placed a towel over John's face. "He should have seen a doctor earlier. What kind of jail are you running here?"

The deputy panicked. "It weren't my fault. I'm only the night watch. I don't have no say."

Adam seemed to take pity on the deputy. "Get the papers. I'll write what happened in medical terms." He turned back to Wolf. "Leave the body. It won't stink much by morning. When a man dies in jail, they pay for the funeral." He looked straight at Wes. "There's no kin around."

Finally, Wes understood. Blood returned to his face. His gaze left the body. He glanced from Adam to Wolf. Adam's slight nod let him know a game was being played.

The deputy scrubbed his face. "I don't want to be

here guarding a body. The sheriff's going to be mad."

"He'll probably make you cover the cost of the funeral. If it wasn't for you, I'd have a live killer and not a dead John Doe." Wolf shook his head.

"But you said you knew who he was. You said you were going to take him back with you."

"I'm not identifying any corpse. Then I'd have to pay for the burying. He's all yours."

Panic spread like a fever across the deputy's face.

Wes mumbled from the doorway in a tone that hinted that he was only mildly interested in the situation. "Too bad the death didn't happen a few minutes later, when he had already checked him out of Waco and was on the road to Austin. Then it would be his problem and not yours."

The deputy gulped hard. "It might've happened that way. I could say this ranger came in asking to take the boy and I didn't know no better than to hand him over. It ain't right to hang him here if he's wanted for more murders."

Wolf shook his head. "I don't want my name connected to killing a man in transport."

Adam closed his bag. "Well, do I put a name on the death certificate or not? I'm just a doctor who treated a prisoner."

The deputy pointed at Wolf. "You know his name. You gotta tell us. You can take the body back to Austin and prove it."

Wolf shook his head. "I ain't taking him. It'll tarnish my reputation."

Wes seemed to come to the deputy's aid. He said to

Wolf, "How about if our friend here writes the dead man's name down, but forgets what your name was? As long as everyone knows you were a ranger, no one will question anything and the doc will be happy because he can complete the certificate."

The deputy nodded as fast as he could. "Right. You take the body and leave me the name."

Wolf rubbed his beard and caught the signal to hurry from Adam. "Oh, all right. I guess the law in Austin will want to see the body."

The deputy ran to get a pencil as Wes and Adam carefully lifted John. They carried him through the office while Wolf blocked the deputy's view.

"Tie him behind my saddle. I'll ride out tonight." Wolf yelled at them.

"His name?" The deputy was in as much hurry to be rid of the body as Wolf was to take it.

Wolf moved toward the door. "Charlie," he said. "Charlie Filmore is the killer's name."

Adam raised an eyebrow when he returned to sign the certificate, but didn't comment.

Before the deputy finished filling out the whole report, Wolf, the McLains, and John Catlin were deep into the shadows of the night.

THIRTEEN

WOLF STAYED WITH THE MCLAIN BROTHERS UNTIL John Catlin was safely loaded into a berth on a train headed north. The kid had come to, but didn't look grateful to his guardian angels.

Wes shook Wolf's hand as they moved off the train. "I'll keep him tied until we're home. With no record of his name in Waco I don't expect anyone will come looking for him."

"And when he runs away next time?" Wolf glanced back at Adam changing one of the kid's bandages.

Wes shook his head. "Allie will have to talk to him in Comanche, since I'm not sure how much English he understands. Once we get back he stays without ropes. I can't keep him tied up and I can't keep chasing him."

Feeling sorry for his friend, Wolf nodded in understanding. "I'll come if you need me."

Wes slapped him on the back. "Thanks, and as we McLains always say, keep an angel on your shoulder, friend."

Wolf laughed and added the old refrain usually used by the brothers. "And your fists drawn."

"Until your brother is there to cover your back," Wes finished as the train whistle blew. He winked. "I'll keep your wedding a secret, but not for long. We'll all want to meet her."

"Soon," Wolf promised as he climbed on his horse and watched the train begin to move. "Soon."

He rode southwest, following the stage trails home. His thoughts were full of Molly. The kiss they'd shared lingered in his mind, thick and rich like fine Kentucky bourbon. He decided that as soon as he saw her he'd tell her who he was. Maybe she'd laugh about it. Maybe she'd be madder than hell. But, by the end of the evening, she'd be in his arms. Wes was right, he needed to be honest with her as soon as possible. Time might not be on his side.

He never considered himself much of a talker. He'd fought his way out of most of his problems all his life. But when he got back to Molly, he had to say the right words to make her know the truth.

Wolf practiced their conversation so many times, the words began to mix. Finally, he gave up. She'd taken pity on a poor fool twice now. Maybe his best bet was that she'd take pity on him again.

The sun burned across the horizon in farewell as he galloped onto Congress Avenue and into town. At the far end of the street, the capitol glistened like a castle in the evening light. Folks moved in a "going home" hurry. Dust from rolling wagons rose from the street like a grayish-brown fog. A breeze would have swept it away, but the air was stagnant and hot.

Wolf pulled the reins and slowed his mount. He'd ridden hard to get home. Now that the time was near, he wished for a few minutes more to think. He was a fool for not going back for her after the war. Maybe she would've tossed him out, but she deserved the opportunity to do so. He owed her that much, when he'd kissed her and promised to find her. After all these years, his reasons had melted into excuses.

How could he explain what those first few months after the war had been like? As a spy, he was treated as an outlaw. He lived on the run, sending his sister to Texas for safekeeping. Finally, he split his men up, scattering them in every direction with new identities. He traveled to Texas to find his sister. This state was a different world, full of possibilities and chances. His life during the war and before seemed another lifetime and Molly had been only a fantasy.

Wolf swore beneath his breath. Maybe he hadn't wanted to trade the dream of Molly for the slim chance she might be glad to see him. By never going back, he kept her suspended in time. He took one perfect moment in his life and encased it in glass. As long as he did nothing, the moment stayed clear and flawless in his thoughts.

If he only could convince her how important that one moment had been to him. Maybe she would understand. She might accept that he had fallen in love with her at first sight and never stopped loving her. Somehow, doing nothing had been a way of never losing her love.

But he could no longer do nothing. He had seen her again. Molly was back in his life and more beautiful than he remembered. Only now, she was flesh and blood and warm in his arms. And by chance, she was his wife, if only for a short time.

The smell of burned wood drifted around him, far too strong to be an oven fire. Wolf swept the street with a tired gaze that missed little. The town appeared calm. He saw no flames, only a few tiny whiffs of smoke from chimneys. But the odor was there, strong, baked into the area like a spice.

He rode past the Ranger office and headed straight for Molly's place. He noticed the air dulling as though a gray cloud lay to ground. Halfway down the block, something was missing in the haze of a dying fire. He scanned the street and saw the huge gap, a cavity smoldering between two buildings.

Wolf urged his horse forward. Before anyone could flag him down to warn him of the sight, he was in front of the hull of the pharmacy. For a moment, he stared in disbelief. It couldn't be her place. He'd only been gone a few days. But the shingle with her first name and his last lay in the ashes.

A few studs from the walls remained standing, like blackened skeletons rising above the coals. The buildings on either side were scorched and burned in spots.

Wolf slid from his horse and moved up to what was left of the steps to the boardwalk in front of Molly's store. He felt the heat now, embers smoldered beneath the rubble where the second floor had crushed the first. He fought the urge to plow into the hot wood and scatter it until he had answers. Molly! Callie Ann!

"A total loss," a voice said from behind Wolf, startling him.

Wolf whirled. "My wife! The child!"

Miller backed up a few steps as if he feared Wolf might strike. "They're safe, Captain, now don't you worry. They got out the back right before the second floor crashed in." Miller flicked sawdust from his apron. "I can build this place back. I'll start as soon as everything cools off. I can use a heavier wood that'll make—"

Wolf grabbed the undertaker before he could jump away. "Did you or your friends have anything to do with this?"

Miller shook so badly Wolf lessened his grip. "No, sir. I swear. We wanted her gone before she married, thinking she was trouble, but none of us would do something like this. We're businessmen. We couldn't burn a person out. Whoever did this wanted her dead, not just out of business."

He looked so pitiful Wolf believed him.

"I'm gonna build it back. I swear."

Wolf shoved past Miller and grabbed the reins of his horse. He cared nothing for the store. "Where's Molly?"

Miller rubbed his throat and hiccuped his words. "She's over at Granny Gravy's place, I think. She didn't have nowhere to go. I suggested one of the hotels, but that little weasel of a man, Charlie Filmore, insisted you'd want her at Granny's. The young ranger who's always with you agreed."

Wolf was too far up the street to hear more. If Charlie and Josh put Molly at Granny's, there could be only
one reason. Molly still wasn't safe.

He rode at full speed to the boardinghouse, a rambling three-story in what once had been the best part
of town. As always, Noah, a former slave of Granny's,
sat on the porch waiting for arrivals. When Noah was
freed, he'd been too old to start out on his own. Granny
offered him a room and meals in exchange for him
keeping the barn. He made extra money by watching
after the lodgers' horses.

When he saw Wolf riding in, he stood to meet the
ranger. Wolf was one of the few who liked to take care
of his own animal, but tonight both men knew that
wouldn't be the case.

"Your lady's upstairs, Captain." Noah took the reins.
"I'll see to the horse."

"Thanks," Wolf answered as he hurried up the steps
three at a time.

In the parlor, two rangers sat where they could see
the stairway. Wolf nodded at them, wondering if they
were guests or guards.

They both stood. "We're glad you're back, Captain,"
one said as Wolf hurried up the stairs.

He met Granny on the third-floor landing. "How is
she?" He tried to pass the wide-girthed woman.

Granny would have none of his passing. "Slow
down," she ordered. "I'll not have you storming in
there, when it's taken us most of the day to make her
comfortable."

Wolf faced the woman. If she'd been a man, he

might have run the blockade, but Granny wasn't a person to be ignored.

A hundred questions shot through his mind like bullets from a Gatling gun. All he could think of was seeing Molly and making sure she was all right, but he simply said, "What happened?"

"I don't know about the fire. It must've started sometime before dawn two days ago." Granny shook her head. "Heard rumors, but you've time for that later. The important thing now is your family. The child is fine. Molly carried her out wrapped in a blanket. The wee one is asleep on the couch in my room."

"And my wife?" Wolf knew he'd heard the good news first. He braced himself for the rest.

"She's got some burns on her arms. The doctor from the School for the Blind came over to help. He said he knew Molly. He had me keep cool rags on her arms most of the day. He just finished wrapping them for the night. Her shoulder is black and blue, and her left wrist is badly sprained. She must've rammed the door as hard as she could trying to get out. Thank the Lord she made it."

Granny took a step backward up the stairs, and Wolf followed. "The doctor's with her now. He had to give her something to help her rest, so don't worry if she seems groggy." She moved up one more step.

"If you go in, you go in quiet. That poor child doesn't need any more shock today. Your voice will wake the dead, Wolf Hayward, so none of that ordering around."

Wolf thought of arguing that he never raised his

voice, but now wasn't the time. He simply nodded. She let him pass.

As he entered, the doctor moved from the foot of the bed. Wolf glanced around. This room was different from the others in the boardinghouse. It was large and spacious with a separate dressing area to the side. He guessed it had been built to serve as the master bedroom, but Granny could no longer climb two flights of stairs several times a day. She'd moved her quarters to the main floor and left the room intact.

One lamp burned low on a table near the windows. Molly lay in the center of the bed with only light covers, her hair spread across both pillows. She wore a high-necked nightgown several sizes too large. The bruise on her temple and the bandage on her hand were all that indicated she'd been injured. Other than that, she looked more like a fine painting than a real woman.

"I'm Doctor Washburn. Frank Washburn." The doctor offered his hand. "I've heard a great deal about you, Captain. May I say it's an honor to meet you."

Wolf shook the man's hand and returned his gaze to Molly's face.

"She's fine," Washburn added in a quiet voice developed for sickrooms. "I've given her something to help her sleep."

Feeling powerless, Wolf watched her. He'd gladly fight to the death for her, but how could he help her now? She looked so frail.

"The burns are minor, and the bruising along her shoulder will heal. She's been through a great deal. She coughed smoke for hours. From the looks of it, everything she owned burned up in that fire except that tin box over there."

Wolf glanced at his box on the table. The only thing she'd saved belonged to him.

"How . . . ?" Wolf didn't know where to start. His main fear was eased simply by watching her sleep.

"How'd the fire start?" Washburn rubbed his neck. For a young man, he seemed to be aging fast in this town. "I don't know. Talk is that it was set. Partly because the back exit was blocked from the outside with boxes. If it hadn't been for Charlie Filmore hearing your wife scream . . ."

"If she's sleeping and all right"—Wolf's voice didn't mold to a whisper so easily—"I'll go see what I can find out."

The doctor touched Wolf's arm. "You do what you think you have to do, but she needs you here as soon as you can get back." He hesitated. "Granny told me you two just married, and you only knew her a few days before that."

He stalled as though he must talk to a stranger about a very private matter and wasn't sure how to advance. "It's more than the burns and the shock that worries me. She feels like she's lost everything, not just the building, but everything in her life. I've seen a sadness like this before in folks. Soldiers coming home wounded to find nothing waiting for them. Farmers starved or burned out with nowhere to start over. When we asked her if there were relatives she needed to telegraph, she shook her head."

"What are you trying to tell me?" Wolf didn't see

Molly as a quitter. Something like a fire wouldn't stop her. Besides, she wasn't alone. Didn't she realize she had him?

The doctor looked frustrated. "I don't know. The mind is a fragile thing. Folks reach a point some-times—even strong folks full of spirit—when they don't want to fight anymore. They just want to rest. Their minds would rather drift in dreams than face loss and failure. I got the feeling that maybe the pharmacy was her one chance to make it, to prove herself, and now it's gone."

"Are you saying she's crazy?" Wolf couldn't help but wonder if the doctor hadn't missed his calling as a preacher.

"No, of course not," the doctor answered quickly. "I'm just saying she's had a hard time, what with mov-ing and losing her friend and the fire. She needs some-thing . . . somebody to hang on to. She keeps calling for Benjamin in her sleep. I know you're not him. He's probably another death in her life. But if you could just be here, it might help. She's feeling mighty lost and alone about now."

Wolf nodded, finally understanding. "What do I do?"

"When she wakes in a few hours, try to let her know you're here for her. If you can't keep her calm, give her this packet of powder in water. It'll help her sleep, but be careful. The less we have to give her, the better."

Washburn moved to the door. "Too bad I can't bring back the ghost of her father, or Ephraim, or even Ben-jamin, whoever he is. Tonight, she needs someone she feels safe with." His raised eyebrow left no doubt that a husband of a few days wouldn't fill the bill.

Wolf followed, biting his tongue to keep from yelling at the doctor that he *could* do whatever needed doing. Washburn knew nothing of how he felt.

As they shook hands, Wolf asked, "Do you know the beggar called Charlie Filmore?"

"I know him," the doctor answered. "He's been sitting on the stairs most of the day, worrying about your wife. Seems he saved her life."

"I'd like to see him," Wolf said in a tone that was half asking, half ordering.

"I'll find him for you. If he's not in Granny's kitchen eating leftovers, he'll be at the nearest saloon."

"Thanks." Wolf closed the door and moved to Molly's bedside. He carefully lifted her unbandaged hand off the sheet and lightly kissed her fingers. More bandages showed beneath her cuff.

"Molly," he whispered.

She moved her head slightly.

"Molly, my love."

"Benjamin," she mumbled without opening her eyes. "Benjamin."

Wolf kissed her hand once more and replaced it at her side. As he stood, he knew what he had to do. One more time he'd play a role, this time not for the South, but for his Molly's peace of mind.

FOURTEEN

IN THE DRESSING AREA AT THE SIDE OF MOLLY'S ROOM, Wolf faced the mirror with the determination of a hired killer. After he'd shortened his mane to collar length, he pinched his beard with two fingers while he continued to cut. Hair slowly filled the bowl below.

As he shaved the last of the stubble away, he hardly recognized the face staring back at him. There were a few more lines, but he felt as if he were stepping back in time. He was becoming someone else. Someone from his past. Someone fabricated.

He dropped the towel from around his waist and dressed in the clothes Charlie had brought him. The little man had been right, he did know what was in every warehouse in town. It had only taken him an hour to find a uniform that would fit. A uniform of Union blue.

To Wolf's amazement, Charlie asked no questions. He brought the clothes, including boots and socks, as though the request had been easy to fill.

Wolf disliked putting on the outfit. The uniform was a reminder of all he wanted to forget. Except for Molly, he thought. He never forgot how she'd looked that first day he saw her. How she held him, a total stranger, in her arms as though she also knew they were made to be together.

As he buttoned the jacket, he glanced at the mirror once more. An officer looked back at him. The officer who'd slipped so easily behind the lines, watching troop movements, mapping railroad routes, and counting heavy artillery. The officer who'd met Molly.

Wolf cleared his throat as he set his mind on losing his accent. If she were to believe he was Benjamin, he had to remember everything. He had to move like an officer, talk like a Yankee, think of nothing but this moment in time. Tonight might be his best performance to date, for this time, he'd be trying to convince someone who knew him as Wolf. Somehow, in this shadowy room, Molly had to see Benjamin and not him. She couldn't see the actor, the spy. She had to believe she saw only Benjamin.

Molly twisted in sleep, tossing the covers. The medicine was wearing off. It had been almost two hours since the doctor left. Wolf had talked to the rangers downstairs while he'd waited for Charlie. They couldn't give him any answers about the fire, but they all agreed that Molly might still be in danger.

Once Charlie showed up, Wolf listened to every detail about what had happened from the beggar's point of view. Wolf couldn't find the words to thank him, but both knew that the captain would consider himself forever in Charlie's debt.

The knowledge made Charlie walk a little taller. He was now Wolf's friend. When Wolf asked about a uniform, he didn't ask why; after all, it was a favor between friends. While Charlie went to find it, Wolf hauled water to the third floor for a bath and retrieved his saddlebags. Then he told everyone he would stay with Molly and they could relax for the night.

The others nodded, seeming relieved to turn over the watch. Granny disappeared into her room. The rangers left, and Wolf closed the door to the world as he stepped into Molly's room.

As she muttered something in her sleep, Wolf buttoned the final button of the uniform and walked toward the bed. He stood at attention and waited. Mentally, he practiced saying her name without drawing out the syllables, as his Southern tones always did.

Finally, Molly's eyelids fluttered open. She smiled a sleepy, drug-filled grin. "Benjamin," she said, "I knew you'd come."

Wolf knelt on one knee. "I'm here, darling. I'm here. I'll sit beside you all night. You're not alone any longer."

"No," she whispered, more asleep than awake. "Lie beside me. I have so much to tell you. I lost my journals in the fire. I lost all my memories of feeling. You have to lie beside me."

Wolf wasn't prepared for her request. He'd thought she'd rest easy just seeing him. "But you've been hurt. You'll sleep better without me so close."

"Hold me, Benjamin. Hold me all night."

Wolf froze. This had been a crazy idea. If he hadn't been the one who thought of it, he'd have beaten up the man who did for even suggesting such a cruel plan. He'd thought to be a vision beside her for the night, not to climb into her bed.

Her hand lifted, and she brushed the smooth surface of his clean-shaven jaw. Slowly, her fingers found his hair and moved gently through the damp strands.

"Do you want more medicine?" he asked, stumbling over his Northern accent.

"No," she answered, slurring her words a little, almost like a drunk. "I need you to hold me."

Wolf stood and pulled off his boots and jacket. It was too late to turn back now; he'd already infiltrated too deeply into her dreams. If he refused her request, she might grow upset. The last thing the doctor said to him was to keep her calm.

For a long while, he stood in his white cotton undershirt and trousers, as if climbing into bed with his wife was too difficult a job to tackle without some thought.

Her fingers reached out again, taking his hand, pulling him to her.

Wolf slowly stretched out beside her, careful not to touch her. Awkwardly, he lifted her head and slid his arm beneath. She curled against him without opening her eyes. He moved her bandaged hand atop her gown so that it wouldn't get crushed between them.

"I'm so sleepy." Her words brushed against his throat. "I feel like I could sleep for days and days."

Wolf rolled slightly toward her. "It's only the powder the doctor gave you. You'll be fine tomorrow." He held his free arm in midair, trying to figure out where to put his hand. Finally, he lowered it to her waist.

"I love you, you know," she whispered. "I think I always have."

Wolf could hear his heart cracking. Somehow he'd stepped into her dreams. He was seeing her private thoughts. Her dream was of him . . . had always been of him. And he'd tumbled into the middle of it.

Tenderly, Wolf lowered his mouth to hers. The kiss was so light it could have been a prayer. "I love you, Molly," he mumbled against her lips. He'd thought the words a hundred times in his mind, but he never dared say them aloud. Suddenly, he longed to drop the charade and say them with the accent of his birth. The way his father had said them to his mother. The way his sister whispered them to her husband when she thought no one listened. A low, Southern way that warms the blood, stirs the heart, and echoes of forever.

He felt her body relax beside him and knew she slipped into a deep sleep. He'd accomplished his goal, he'd given her peace.

For a long while, he held her, listening to her breathe, feeling her warm beside him. Then, finally, the hours caught up with him and he slept also. A deep, dreamless sleep for the first time in his life. For all he'd ever dreamed of was in his arms.

Molly drifted between reality and fantasy. All the fears of the night before were held at bay as she felt Benjamin at her side. He was more real than she'd ever dreamed before. She could smell the shaving cream he used and feel the warmth of his chest slowly rising and falling beneath her cheek.

"Benjamin," she whispered as she spread her hand across his chest. The soft cotton welcomed her touch.

He jerked slightly and caught her fingers in his grasp. "Are you all right?" he asked, sounding sleepy and almost boyish.

"I'm fine." Pulling her hand from his, she fanned her fingers once more over his broad chest. "I just wanted to feel you."

She felt the chuckle more than heard it.

"Of course, feel away," he whispered against her ear.

As her hand moved over him, he remained still. She liked the strong line of his jaw and the surprising softness of his bottom lip. She might have been very proper in her life, but in her dreams she grew bold. Her fingers slid over his clothes, loving the contrast of the cotton of his shirt and the wool of his trousers. When she brushed below the belt, she heard his sudden intake of air.

"Molly." He sounded out of breath and guarded. "Do you really think . . . ?"

"Would you stop me?" she challenged, opening her eyes to stare at him for the first time. He was in the shadows of early morning, but there was no mistaking her Benjamin. She loved the way his hair curled as it had in the wind of the train station all those years ago. And the power in his jaw that promised stubbornness and strength. "Would you stop me?" she repeated.

"No," he finally replied, as formally as though at attention even as he lay beside her.

Settling against him, she breathed deeply of the smell of him. In all her dreams, she never remembered the aroma. Soap, shaving cream, starch, all lay above a deep-baked smell that could only be his. A hint of horses, and wind, and sun, and adventure.

Her hand slipped boldly along his trousers to the inside of his thigh. The powerful muscles in his leg tightened.

"Do you mind?" she asked.

He swallowed. "No."

"I can do whatever I want. After all, it's my dream." Molly felt terribly wicked. He seemed so real tonight, she wanted to sink into the senses and not think, but only feel.

Her hand moved up to the buttons of his shirt. Slowly, she began unfastening each as she listened to the rhythm of his pounding heart in her ear and felt his warm breath against her face.

As she slipped her fingers beneath the cotton of his shirt, his hand tightened at her waist, pulling her gown into his fist. She'd seen men take stitches with less reaction.

"Do you wish me to stop, Benjamin?"

"No." He seemed barely able to get the word out.

"Then relax." She raised her face and kissed him lightly on the mouth. "Relax, I said." She kissed him again. His lips had never felt so soft, or tasted so sweet.

In fact, until tonight, they'd never tasted at all. Even

the memory of how they'd felt faded over time. But not tonight.

Tonight they were as real as Wolf's lips had been when he'd kissed her farewell a few days ago. Only Wolf's kiss had been to show the town that they were married. Nothing more, she told herself, nothing more. She would never allow it to be, for Benjamin was in her heart. There was no room for another.

Molly let her lips brush his as her hand moved over the hair and muscle above his heart. His chest hair was soft in contrast to the muscles. She pulled away and began unbuttoning the rest of his shirt, suddenly in a hurry to drink her fill of the pleasure she'd discovered.

He didn't move to stop her, but she wasn't sure if he was breathing.

About the time his hand relaxed once more at her waist, she pulled the shirt fully open.

Molly raised her head and stared at him. His eyes were closed. She wasn't sure if he'd fallen asleep or was simply trying to endure extreme torture.

Smiling, she lowered her mouth to his chest. He was so delicious tonight. She had to taste him.

She felt his fist tighten once more at her side, but he didn't say a word as her tongue brushed his skin.

While she let her hand drift along the soft sprinkling of hair to his waist, she felt his sudden intake of breath and laughed. In all her dreams, he'd never reacted so to her touch, and now the feel of him so aware of her every move thrilled and excited her.

Returning to his mouth, she kissed him deeply. At first, he let her kiss him, exploring at her leisure.

Slowly, the kiss shifted, and he took control. The kiss came in waves, first tender, then demanding and more fully than she'd ever known a kiss could be. He filled her very soul with a passion she'd never before experienced.

His hand spread out at her waist and moved in gentle strokes until his fingers brushed against the underside of her breasts and circled low across her abdomen.

She breathed with his kiss as if she had no breath of her own. She relaxed to his touch, welcoming all he wanted to give her. Never in all the years had she dreamed like this. The taste of him was deep in her mouth, the feel of his hand forever branded across her body.

She wanted to touch him more, but all she could do was drift on the sea of pleasure. Finally, when her senses overflowed with sensations, his hand stilled across her abdomen and his kisses softened. She settled against his shoulder, feeling a warmth she'd never known burning deep inside her. Her fingers lazily fanned his chest for one last touch. She listened to the beat of his heart and fell deeper into sleep, knowing she'd return to the dream and he'd be waiting as always.

The last thought that drifted through her mind, too airy to take root, was that he'd whispered, "I love you" against her ear in a low Southern tone.

FIFTEEN

Voices buzzed around Molly like flies. Bothering. Awakening her from a dream where she longed to stay.

"Can you hear me?" someone kept asking.

"Doctor," another voice whined. "Can't we wait? Do we have to tell her now? Doesn't she need to be stronger?"

Molly pulled herself through the fog of her brain and smiled. The night's sleep and dreams left her refreshed, reborn.

She noticed Granny Gravy and the young doctor named Frank Washburn standing by the window. He picked up medicines for the School for the Blind at her store and also treated Ephraim.

"Good morning." Molly sat up in bed, feeling the ache in her shoulder with every movement. The pain couldn't erase the grin that lingered on her lips.

Washburn was at her side. "How are you this morning, Mrs. Hayward?"

"I'm sore but much better." Her father used to say that she took trouble hard, like her mother, but bounced back ready to fight like him.

"Careful." The doctor gave her his undivided attention. "Don't move too fast." He acted as if she were about to take her first steps.

Molly slipped from the bed and stood slowly. "I'm fine. All I needed was a good night's sleep. How's Callie Ann? Is she up yet?"

Granny snorted. "That child's been up for hours asking about you." She seemed in a hurry as she fretted with the curtains, yet didn't leave.

Washburn lifted the packet of powders he'd left by the bed. "How much of this did you take last night?"

"None. Except what you gave me," Molly answered. "I slept the clock around." She wanted to add "in the arms of Benjamin" but knew they would think her mad.

Smiling, Granny added, "My husband used to say there ain't nothing better than a woman who wakes up grinning. He said she's worth her weight in gold."

Molly didn't want to explain how her dreams had helped more than any medicine. She could still feel the heat of the drugstore fire along her arms. Her shoulder and wrist throbbed with a dull pain, but through the night, Benjamin had held her. Somehow that made everything all right.

She almost laughed aloud. Wouldn't the world be surprised to know that she had a lover as invisible as Callie Ann's uncle? Only last night, he'd been so real to her that she could almost hear the echo of his heartbeat in her ear and taste his kiss lingering on her lips.

The doctor tilted his head as he watched her. "Are you sure you're better, Mrs. Hayward? You had quite a shock."

The smile faded from Molly's mouth as she heard him say her name. He'd called her that earlier. Hayward! How could she have forgotten she was married? Had she betrayed Benjamin by marrying, even in name only? Or had she shamed Wolf Hayward with her secret life and love, who came to her only in her dreams?

She wasn't sure from what direction guilt flew in, but it perched heavy atop her heart. She felt its weight, hollow and bitter. Somehow, she'd dishonored one man, but which?

Molly rubbed her forehead. The terror of the fire hadn't destroyed her sanity. She was doing that simply by dreaming. "Perhaps I'd better sit down."

Granny moved out of the way. Molly melted into the only chair in the room. The table wobbled when she rested her arm on a lace cover that had been washed and bleached so many times the material appeared feathered.

Looking around the room, Molly saw beneath the first layer of warm comfort. The place she'd seen as finely decorated aged before her eyes. The drapes were heavy with dust. The design in the rug had almost disappeared with wear. Wood, from headboard to dresser, was weathered and cracked in age.

"That's it, ma'am." Granny patted her hand. "You rest easy for a spell. The soul takes time, just like the body, to recover from losses like you had. I'll have old Noah bring you up a cup of tea. You missed breakfast, but lunch will be ready in a few shakes."

The old woman reached to touch Molly's shoulder in comfort but pulled back. "Don't you worry none, child." She glanced at the doctor. "A body can face anything once the stomach is full." She looked back at Molly. "I'd be willing to bet three meals a day of my grits and gravy will put some meat on those bones. You'll be filling out my nightgown in no time."

As Granny hurried off, the doctor checked Molly's arms and removed the bandages.

Red puffy flesh, no worse than a sunburn, Molly thought. The doctor pampered her, but she wasn't sure why.

"I need to ask you this, Mrs. Hayward. Is there any chance that you could be with child?"

Molly wanted to laugh. Surely dream lovers couldn't accomplish that feat. "No," she answered, wanting to be honest with him. "Wolf and I have never . . . will never . . . well, not yet, anyway." She felt she had to be honest about her condition, but she didn't want to give away the agreement of their marriage. "Wolf left within hours after our wedding."

"I think I understand." The doctor was a poor liar. "You rushed into a marriage, don't rush into . . ." He couldn't find the words. ". . . Into what you're not ready for. I know a great many marriages that are strong with the husband and wife in separate bedrooms."

She'd heard of them, also. Marriages where no love was involved. Marriages where children were not wanted. Marriages where one of the partners had a lover.

Blinking, she realized, that would be her. *I'm the one with a lover.*

Washburn reddened when she didn't comment. "If you like, we can talk about how it could be between the two of you. Understanding can sometimes take the fear away from a new bride."

She almost giggled. She'd bet all she had, which at the moment was one slightly burned gown, that the doctor had never given this talk before. "No. I understand about that. I went to the backroom classes at medical school."

Now it was the doctor's turn to be embarrassed. The backroom classes were those group meetings held at the bars after the lectures. Diseases and ailments never discussed in lecture halls were described over a mug of beer. Theories on how to prevent pregnancy that ran from old bayou methods to new scientific research from Germany were discussed. Diseases that ran rampant across the country, but were never mentioned in parlors, were talked about. A classmate of Molly's had laughingly called what they debated over beer as the "ailments of the heart." But as far as Molly could figure, not one round of talking had anything to do with the heart.

Washburn changed the subject. "Did you finish medical school, Mrs. Hayward?"

"Yes, but most of my intern work was in pharmacy."

"Have you ever considered practicing medicine?"

Molly shook her head. She'd seen enough of the

"practice" during the war. "I enjoy helping people with my mixtures." She leaned back in the chair. "I'd just ordered a wagonload of supplies the morning before the fire. Now I'll have no place to put them."

Washburn closed his bag. "If you'd consider it, I think the school could loan you a room to work in, in exchange for a reduced fee on what we need."

Molly grinned. Everything was going to work out. "I'll consider it and thanks for the offer."

The doctor cleared his throat. "Well, I guess if you have no questions, I'll be leaving. I'll check on you again this afternoon."

"Thank you. But it won't be necessary for you to return." Molly saw no point in his making another call. Yesterday she'd had a shock. She'd been hurt and frightened. Her lungs were full of smoke, her spirit near broken. But today she felt her strength returning. She knew how to treat the burns and bruises. She could take care of herself. "I know you're busy. I'll be fine."

Nodding his agreement, Washburn added, "I'll speak to your husband."

"That won't be necessary either, I assure you." Molly wanted to fire more angry words back at Washburn, but knew he was only saying what most doctors said. Once a woman married, her medical care, or sometimes the lack of it, was dependent on her husband's decisions. In most states, a doctor couldn't even treat a woman without her husband's consent.

A moment ago Washburn had treated her like a colleague and now she was back to being a woman.

A tapping on the door saved the doctor from having

to reply. Callie Ann rushed in. She ran to Molly but halted just out of reach.

"I was going to hug you," she said and pouted, "but I don't want to hurt you."

Molly laughed. "A hug could never hurt." She opened her arms to the child. Over Callie Ann's head, Molly watched the doctor slip from the room.

After hugging her, Callie Ann pushed back Molly's hair and kissed her on both cheeks. "I missed you. Granny Gravy said you had to sleep. I didn't have anyone to play with but Uncle Orson."

"I'm sorry." Molly took the child's face in her hands and kissed her cheeks in return. "Promise to stay with me a while today."

Callie Ann giggled. "We can't go anywhere. We don't have any clothes. But we got boxes and boxes downstairs that Mr. Wolf had delivered."

"You're right." Molly looked down at her gown, as if she'd just noticed it. "We'll have to stay here." She hoped she could find something to wear before Wolf returned. She didn't want to face him in only a nightgown.

Foolish, she thought. Why shouldn't her husband see her in a nightgown? Most of the town had last night. They'd surrounded her in a mob once the fire was under control, asking questions all at once. Charlie Filmore had shielded her as best he could until the rangers showed up.

Callie Ann suddenly danced around the room while Noah brought in a tray of tea with cookies on it that could only have come from Wolf's favorite cafe. As they ate, more boxes arrived—dresses for them both to try on, shoes, underthings, even a doll for Callie Ann and a new leather-bound journal for her. All from Wolf. His thoughtfulness overwhelmed her.

Molly was amazed at how closely Wolf guessed her size, but decided it had been blind luck. He obviously hadn't really looked at her, or he'd have known she only wore black. She'd started when her father died and never stopped when the year of mourning ended. The white blouses were fine, but the skirts of wine red and hunter green were colors she'd never choose.

But she had to wear something. She couldn't very well go shopping in the nightgown she now wore. So she picked three of the simplest outfits along with underthings.

Callie Ann, on the other hand, liked everything she tried on, as if she were playing dress-up. She even tried Molly's rejected clothes and asked if she could have a shawl with golden fringe. Molly knew Wolf was probably spending most of his savings on the clothes. She should keep only what were necessities, yet she couldn't tell the child no.

As soon as she could, she'd get to the bank and wire Philadelphia for money to repay Wolf. She knew what he had in savings and guessed he'd spent very little on himself over the years. She couldn't allow him to drain his account for her.

Molly lifted Wolf's tin box, planning to check his original balance and replace it. But the box was locked and the key had been left in her kitchen. She thought of trying to break the lock, but decided she could guess the amount close enough.

With her hand bandaged, it was impossible to do more than comb through her hair. Molly worked to make herself look presentable. By noon she and Callie Ann were ready to go downstairs. Carefully, Molly took each step.

When she reached the long dining room that could easily seat a dozen, the table was set for only three. Fresh flowers fanned from a bowl in the middle, amid blue and white china.

Granny set a pot of dumplings on the table and looked up. "My, my, don't you look fine. As grand a lady as I've ever served."

Callie Ann twirled. "I have new clothes, too."

Granny made a fuss over the child, then tied a huge napkin around her so she wouldn't spill anything on her new dress.

Molly took her seat. "I thought you had other guests staying here."

Granny filled the plates without bothering to ask what or how much anyone wanted. "I do, but I ran them all off. I thought we needed to spend some time talking. I've had this place for years, and you are the first lady I've ever had stay here."

Accepting her plate, Molly watched the old woman closely. She could feel something wrong. No one had been up to her room to check on her. The house was quiet. Something *was* wrong.

"I talked with Wolf this morning when he came

down a little after dawn," Granny mumbled as she took a bite of a biscuit-size dumpling.

"Wolf was here last night?"

Granny nodded. "He came in just before dark and didn't leave until after sunrise. Said he sat by your bed most of the night. Didn't you even wake up enough to see him?"

"No." Molly felt her cheeks redden. She couldn't believe he'd watched her while she'd dreamed. "Where is he now?"

"When he brought the last of them boxes in this morning, there were men waiting to talk to him. He took off like lightning. Ranger problem, I imagine."

Molly tasted the bland food as Granny continued.

"I haven't had a chance to tell you my Luther was a ranger back in the early forties when Texas was a country all to itself. He weren't more than a kid when he rode with Sam Houston at San Jacinto."

Granny looked insulted when Molly didn't comment. "It was the great battle of Texas's rebellion against Mexico. Houston and his men caught old Santa Anna napping. A few hundred men took an army of thousands. Luther said they rode in firing like wild men and yelling, 'Remember the Alamo!' and 'Remember Goliad!' Santa Anna's men didn't have time to form a line, much less hold it. They ran like chickens at the sound of thunder."

Molly nodded as if she remembered.

Managing to filter in bites, Granny kept talking. "My Luther was a big fella, just like Wolf, and took to rangering. All full of gruff and spit, he was. If he ran out of bullets, he'd just frighten most troublemakers to death by yelling."

Granny snorted. "Lord, how I miss that man! When you're hugged by a bear of a man like that, you know you've been held," Granny mumbled around another bite. "But I guess you understand that, don't you, hon?"

In truth, she did know that. The few times Wolf had pulled her into his arms, she knew she'd been hugged. There was something warm and safe about the way he put his arms around her and lifted her off the ground. He might not be polished and handsome like Benjamin, but Wolf Hayward had a way about him that made her feel good about herself. He treated her like she was fine china, something to treasure.

"My Luther was killed down on the border one winter," Granny continued. "He was chasing outlaws who raided ranches then ran back across the Rio Grande to hide. Luther was alone when he met up with them. There was a horrible gunfight. The men who found him said the ground was thick with spent shells. Luther took four bullets before he quit firing. They said he killed twelve of them." She lifted the first of her chins in pride. "Imagine that! It took more'n twelve men to bring my man down."

Suddenly, Molly didn't want to hear Granny's story. She didn't want to think about Wolf fighting to the death in a gun battle. She couldn't imagine ever bragging about such a thing in her widow days.

Finishing her meal, Callie Ann asked if she could go out to the barn with Noah. He'd promised to let her feed a carrot to the goat he kept for milk.

When the child disappeared around the corner, Granny straightened, as if getting down to business. "Some men came in this morning and told me something you need to know."

Molly waited for what she knew was coming. Maybe they'd found who set the fire.

"That night"—Granny swallowed a dumpling without bothering to chew—"amid all the excitement over the fire at your place, two men escaped from jail."

Without speaking, Molly watched Granny finish off another bite.

"The Digger boys. Meanest men you'd ever want to meet. They had help by someone on the outside."

Panic made Molly's blood rush. "Do they know about Callie Ann? Will they come after her because she's kin?"

"I don't think so. Far as I know, the rangers saw no reason to tell them about her. Besides, they wouldn't care nothing about a kid."

Molly hadn't realized she'd been holding her breath.

"Wolf rode out to try and catch them." Granny wiped her chin. "He said to tell you he'd be back as soon as he could. He's got to try and get to the Diggers before they kill. With them two it's not a question of if, but *when.*"

Reaching across the table, Granny took Molly's hand. "I told him you can stay with me. With most of the rangers rooming here when they're in town, this is as safe a place as you'll find." She patted her apron pocket. "And I got my derringer, just in case."

Molly tried not to look frightened. She wasn't positive the fire had been set. It seemed reasonable that some folks didn't like her, or might want her to leave, but they wouldn't go so far as to kill her, not even in this wild place. Maybe a bottle spilled over and started the fire? Children, looking for money, may have destroyed her book and stayed to spill things for fun. The cowboy who shot up her place was drunk, nothing more. Wolf had to do his job. He couldn't stay here worrying about her. She could take care of herself.

Granny stood and cleared the table. "Wolf said you had the names of those he counted as family. You could go to them if you like. They'd welcome you." She looked over her shoulder and made a face. "Wolf also paid for Charlie Filmore to stay here. He'll be sleeping and eating on the porch unless he gets in a bathing mood. Charlie's about as useful as a yard dog in town, but he did save your life. I guess now he figures he's got to keep watch over you."

Shaking her head, she added, "Lady, you got the ugliest guardian angel I ever seen. He'd scare paint off a fence post."

"I'll stay here until I sort things out," Molly whispered, almost lost in her own thoughts.

Granny smiled. "I figured you would. A wife wants to be where her man will come back to first."

Molly didn't have the nerve to tell Granny that wasn't it at all. She simply refused to retreat. Somehow she had to stay and rebuild. And straighten out the mess she'd made of her personal life.

• • •

Wolf pushed himself to exhaustion. He rode after the Digger brothers at twice the speed he normally tracked. He told himself it was the need to catch the killers, but deep inside, he knew he had to put distance between himself and Molly's dreams.

After the night by her side, he had no doubt she was in love with Benjamin. He should be elated that their chance meeting years ago had made such an impact, but all he could think of was she'd never love him as Wolf. He'd believed their friendship would have a chance to grow, but after he'd shaved and held her, he doubted it. She had her lover. Dressed as Wolf, he'd never be more than a friend.

At sunset he stopped, knowing only a fool would try to track by moonlight. He made camp and tried to relax, but the memory of Molly so close against him kept him awake long after midnight. All he had to do was close his eyes and he was back on the third floor of Granny's with Molly by his side.

But he didn't want a dream lover, as she obviously did. He needed a real flesh-and-blood woman staring at him, good or bad, in broad daylight.

Yet each night the ache for her pounded through his body. He told himself it would lessen, but a week later he could tell no difference.

Two weeks passed and, still, the need to feel her by his side throbbed like an open wound across his heart. A hundred times, he fought to keep from turning back. He told himself he'd shave again and lie beside her. He'd walk into her dreams as he had before. If he could have nothing else of Molly, he'd have that.

But duty drove him on. Blind, frustrating loyalty to a course he knew was right. No matter how much he ached inside for her, Wolf knew he'd never be able to make love to her unless he first did his job. He'd never forgive himself if others died because he hadn't tried his best to find the Digger brothers.

By the end of the third week, it was obvious the brothers were well aware he followed. They were basically a lazy pair who wouldn't have traveled so far or fast if they felt safe. They tried to cover tracks, but their bungling made the trail even easier to follow.

Wolf concentrated on finding them. They were covering familiar ground, for the pair seemed to know this part of Texas better than he did. First, they rode west past the fort lines where roads crisscrossed the countryside. Then the outlaws doubled back and skirted the Hill Country, where hunting was good and hideouts plentiful among the rocks and uneven terrain.

If the Diggers made one mistake—backtracked because of a swollen river, or took a wrong turn into a box canyon—he would catch them. But their luck held into the fourth week.

Early fall chilled the air. Wolf pulled his saddle off, hobbled his horse, and rubbed the red down with dried grass. He stopped before dark, for once, to take time to hunt. His supplies were so low, he knew even if he caught game tonight, it would be only a matter of days before he'd have to stop in a town. The delay would cost him dearly, but he had no other choice.

After dropping a line in the spring and setting a trap in the brush for rabbits, Wolf boiled the last of his coffee and waited. He was covered in dirt from head to foot, but bathing took valuable time. Scratching his thick, inch-long beard, he laughed. Molly wouldn't recognize him as Benjamin tonight. He knew he looked more like a wild animal than a human.

But that was a part of him, too. For every month he'd worn an officer's uniform, he'd spent twice that time combing the woods, moving like a shadow, living off the land. Once, when he'd been caught behind enemy lines without supplies, he survived in the woods a month. He had sat, gnawing on hard roots and listening to the Yanks camped all around him. He could smell their fires, hear their jokes, almost taste their coffee.

While he waited for them to move on, he had nothing, not even a blanket. When it snowed, he'd burrowed beneath dried leaves like an animal.

Half-starved and freezing, he never allowed himself to consider giving up. He knew he could walk into their midst with his hands up. They would probably take him to a prisoner camp. Probably even give him a blanket and maybe coffee. Lord, how he had missed the feel of hot coffee sliding down his throat.

But he wasn't a quitter—not then, not now.

Wolf took a deep breath as his coffee boiled. He would go into town for supplies. He would keep tracking. He would see the Diggers back in jail.

The rabbit trap he'd set snapped, and Wolf knew supper had arrived. With luck, there would be fish for breakfast as well.

He stood, framed against the dying sun. From the

corner of his gaze, he caught a glimmer of reflected light, like a star sparkling before sundown.

It took his mind a fraction of a second to react. He jumped for his rifle.

In an instant, he saw the flicker spark and smoke. The sound of gunfire reached his ears a moment before a bullet struck, knocking him to the ground.

His fingers closed around his rifle as the world faded. No stars. No moon. Nothing.

SIXTEEN

MOLLY WALKED THROUGH THE FRAMED BEGINNINGS of her new emporium with Callie Ann at her side. True to his word, Miller had worked hard to rebuild her business this past month. Dry days and few funerals to distract him kept the construction moving along.

Since Charlie Filmore saved her life, he'd taken on a new status in the community. He'd sobered and worked regularly with Miller when he wasn't watching over Molly. To everyone's surprise Charlie had the hands of a craftsman.

The walls of the store would stand as before, but Molly planned to change the inside. She wanted the store part larger, with a storage room in back half the size of Ephraim's old quarters. Then she planned one huge room upstairs to serve as an office and play area for Callie Ann.

There would be no kitchen or sleeping quarters. She'd been looking for a house nearby to rent. After what she'd been through, she wasn't sure she ever wanted to live above a store again.

Molly had thought to talk it over with Wolf. She'd tell him it was her decision to rebuild differently, and therefore, she'd bear the cost of a house that would, of course, include quarters for him. Surely he'd understand the logic. Living above the store was fine when she was single, but she was a married lady with a child to worry about now.

She watched as Callie Ann circled through the columns of wooden studs. A child, she thought. I have a child. After all these weeks, Callie was hers. Molly would fight before giving her up. At first, she'd hoped they'd find her a nice relative to live with, but as the days passed the possibility grew slimmer, and her hope broadened that the child would stay.

She had an almost-husband, who'd been gone for weeks now, and a hand-me-down daughter no one else wanted. But sometimes, in the bustle of the day, they seemed real to her, more solid than dreams on which to build.

Even in his absence, Wolf was a part of her life. Folks asked about him, told stories they'd heard of him, worried with her about when he might return. She found herself forgetting his gruffness and remembering only his kindness.

"I'd rather check with your husband about this," Miller said as he approached, breaking into her thoughts. In his hand he had the plans she'd drawn up for the interior. "Captain Hayward might have something to say about all these changes you're making."

"It's my store. There is no need to talk it over with him," she answered. What gave the little man the idea that Wolf would know more about the workings of her store than she would? Miller reminded her of her old-maid aunts, who always had to check everything with the general, as if they had no minds of their own.

Miller insisted she pay half the money for the building up front. He wanted it all, but Molly doubted he'd finish without incentive.

"When my husband returns, he'll expect the store rebuilt, not awaiting his approval of the plans."

Miller seemed to chew on what she said. It was obvious he didn't like taking orders from a woman, but he needed the work.

"Mrs. Hayward?" Josh was almost at her side before she noticed him. The young ranger walked softly, as though in a funeral procession. With a slight tip of his hat in greeting, he delivered a white envelope.

When he handed her the note, she didn't bother to open it. Wolf had told her only bad news came written.

"What is it?" she asked.

Shifting from boot to boot, Josh said, "It's for you, Mrs. Hayward. From the sheriff's office."

She checked to make sure Callie Ann wasn't listening, then turned her stare to Josh. "What does it say?" She wanted to hear the message, let it hit her full, not read the news.

He answered as though responding to an order. "Wolf's been shot. I don't know how bad. A cowhand found him miles south of here. Said he'd been left for dead."

Josh waited for her to react. When she didn't comment, he continued, "The man got Wolf as far as a little settlement called San Marcos. It lies between here and San Antonio where the Blanco River crosses the road." Josh hesitated. "He's been there a few days, by the way the priest's note to the sheriff reads."

Molly had watched her father tell women of their husband's wounds or death many times. Until this moment, she had no idea how it must have felt.

The air rushed from her lungs. Her throat blocked with tears. "Anything else?" She would not cry, she told herself, or show any emotion.

"No, ma'am." Josh's lips formed a hard line as he fought his own feelings. "Except it's a pretty sure bet that it was them Digger brothers. Word came in, even before we heard from the priest at San Marcos, that the Diggers were in a saloon in San Antonio, bragging about killing a ranger. We're rounding up every spare man to go after them now. Don't worry, ma'am, we'll bring them back."

Molly didn't care about the Diggers. All that mattered was Wolf. He might be her husband in name only, but he was a friend. A good friend. He'd been there for her when she'd needed to marry, when she'd buried Ephraim, after the fire. He'd shared his little wealth with her willingly.

"Where will I find my husband?" she asked, holding herself at full attention.

"He's at a temporary mission set up near the springs at San Marcos until the Indian trouble's over. But you shouldn't go. He's being looked after. The place is hardly big enough to be called a town."

"I'll be leaving as soon as possible."

"But . . ." He stopped. Josh was wise enough not to comment.

She thanked the young ranger and watched him walk away. He acted like he wanted to say more, to help her in some way. But Molly showed no emotion and asked for no favor.

"I'll need a wagon," Molly said to Miller, who obviously had heard every word the ranger said.

The undertaker shook his head. "A wagon would take two days. You could book a place on the stage. There's one leaving every morning for San Antonio. It stops at San Marcos to change horses. You should have no problem renting a rig to get you out to the mission and back home."

Miller's sound advice surprised Molly. A fast-moving stage on a good road could cover in an hour what it would take a day to travel by wagon. "Thank you, sir. I'll do that."

"Me, too," Callie Ann echoed. "I'm going with you."

Surprised that Callie Ann was listening, she tried to think of how to explain.

The child stood up straight. "I'm going," she said with the determination of a lawyer.

"All right," Molly answered. She couldn't help but wonder if the little girl was worried about Wolf or couldn't stand the thought of another night at Granny's. Each day they'd been there, she'd looked more diligently for a house to rent or even buy. Each day

Granny's advice spread and her meat serving shrank.

Molly held Callie Ann's hand tightly as they hurried down the street, stopping first at the bank then at the stage line.

The Wells Fargo office bragged in their advertisements that the Concord Stage could carry nine passengers inside and nine more on top, but Molly didn't see how. Most passages were booked for six, sometimes seven or eight if at least two were children. However, the children had to sit in seats against the doors, taking up other passengers' leg room.

Molly bought the sixth and seventh spot for tomorrow's stage. She knew she'd be greeted with frowns from the male passengers who'd lose their stretching room, but Callie Ann was going.

That night Granny hardly spoke at supper except to mumble comments like, "Hope he's alive when you get there." "Wonder where he took the shot?" "If it's gut, he can count his remaining days on his fingers." "Some men are never the same after a head wound, but still, that's better than in the privates."

Molly hurried through the meal and went up to pack. She had no idea how long she'd be gone, but having so few clothes since the fire, packing wasn't a problem. She planned to get to San Marcos and bring Wolf back as quickly as possible.

Callie Ann crawled into bed with her, as she had since the second night they'd been at Granny's. She was asleep before Molly turned down the light.

Closing her eyes, Molly tried to think of Benjamin. Except for the night after the fire, her dreams of him had been foggy, unreal. Tonight, he wouldn't come to her at all. Worry over Wolf occupied her thoughts.

She thought of the way he'd held her in the shadows, dancing in the darkness, the way he'd hugged her at their wedding, the way he'd kissed her good-bye. She'd never feel passion with him, but there was something warm and safe about the man. She knew without doubt that he was a true friend. A forever friend.

"Be alive when I get there," she whispered. "Please, be alive."

She never remembered falling asleep. By dawn, she was dressed. As they stepped from Granny's house, Charlie Filmore arrived. He'd managed to locate two boxes of medical supplies with the ten dollars Molly had given him. She wasn't sure what she would find when she reached Wolf. Molly believed in being prepared for anything. She pretended she didn't notice the boxes were marked with government codes.

"I think I found you a place," Charlie whispered so Granny wouldn't hear from the porch. "Not more than a half mile from your store. A real nice house if you got the money."

"Really?" Molly found his statement hard to believe. She'd circled the area too carefully. At first she'd been picky, having a list of things a residence must have. But after the weeks at Granny's, any place would be fine.

"It won't be available until the owner sobers up, but it's a nice size. Plenty of room for kids."

"The owner sobers up?"

"Don't ask."

She wanted to know how much, but it didn't matter at this point. She would pay dearly to have a house to bring Wolf home to.

"I'll take it." She jumped in with both feet. "How much?"

"Owner said he'd talk it over with your husband." Charlie had been around her long enough to duck, figuring she'd hit him for what he just said.

Granny moved down the stairs. They'd been talking long enough to pique her curiosity.

But when she drew close enough to hear, Molly was asking Charlie to let Dr. Washburn know she wouldn't be in for a few days. She then offered him more money for the supplies.

To Molly's surprise and Granny's shock, he took only half the money she offered him, refusing any more than what it cost him for the goods. He loaded the boxes in Noah's wagon and waved good-bye as Molly helped Callie Ann up.

Noah left them at the station. The time posted for departure was eight o'clock, but the clerk told her the stage would leave as soon as it was full. So someone arriving late might find his seat sold to another and himself on the next stage. Or, if it was a slow day, passengers might have to wait until nine or even ten until everyone wandered in.

Molly read the rules posted on the door half a dozen times. The only one she found interesting was number three, which stated there would be no smoking on the stage if a lady were present. Chewing tobacco was allowed with the warning, all in capitals, SPIT WITH THE WIND, NOT AGAINST IT.

Finally, the driver yelled for everyone to board. While Molly helped Callie Ann fold the shawl Wolf had bought her, three men who looked to be salesmen tossed their cases up. They stepped inside without seeming to notice the women standing about.

A woman two seats wide almost had to make a running effort to shove herself in. The girl with her looked to be almost Molly's age but had the manner of someone following behind a mother. She looked plain and bone thin with sad eyes.

Molly lifted her skirt and stepped in. As she had feared, the only seat left was in the center space between two men. No wonder the men were less than chivalrous. A window seat would be prime property on this long, hot drive.

She lowered the small folding seat that rested against the door for Callie Ann. The colorful shawl made a perfect cushion. The seat had straps on either side to keep the passenger in place should the stage stop suddenly. It seemed to cradle her comfortably.

"I'd like to ride up top the second half of the trip, Momma," the sad-eyed girl mumbled as she tried to squeeze between her mother and one of the salesmen. She appeared to be layered in clothes too big for her.

"You will only if I say so, missy," the mother snapped. "I'll have to check the weather. I'll not be dragging a sickly child along who rode in the rain." She flipped the covering from the window. "I swear to goodness, on a cloudy day like this, you'd think it would be cooler." She shoved her daughter in an effort to gain more space.

"Wish it would rain," the man next to the girl said, as he turned sideways trying to allow her room. He had black curly hair and a mustache that almost reached his ears. "Cool everything off for a few hours at least."

Molly watched him closely. Of the three salesmen, he appeared to be the drummer. She guessed the name came from men who "drummed" up business as they traveled. He was flashy, with a gift for talking and an easy smile.

"I've always enjoyed a little rain. How about you, miss?" He smiled at the girl.

The mother gave her daughter a sharp look, daring her to speak to the stranger.

The girl melted down in her place, her eyes staring straight ahead. She was taller than both her mother and the drummer, making her look all the more strange as she tried to shrink between them.

"Where will Uncle Orson sit?" Callie Ann asked. Two of the men groaned and glanced toward the door, expecting another person to try to crowd in. "He has to have a place. I don't want him catching cold from sitting up top in the almost rain."

No one but Molly appeared to notice how Callie Ann mocked the mother.

Molly pulled the door closed and lowered the second extra seat. "Here." She grinned. "He'll be comfortable in this seat. That way he'll be straight across from you."

Callie Ann smiled. "He said, 'Thank you kindly.' I

think he'll enjoy sitting in a chair just like mine."

The oldest salesman, who reeked of whiskey, laughed and winked at Molly as if he understood the game. The other two men didn't seem to care as long as no one took the seat and therefore the leg room. But the huge woman puffed up in disgust. She folded her arms as best she could over her chest.

The stage rocked into action. For a few minutes, Molly thought the large woman wasn't going to say a word and the ride would be made in blessed silence. But peace didn't last.

As soon as they were away from Austin, the woman began talking to no one and everyone. "I'd never let a daughter of mine weaken her mind with imagining. There is enough of real life to deal with."

Molly didn't respond. Callie Ann pulled two tiny handkerchief dolls from her pockets and didn't seem to be listening.

"I said," the woman grew louder, "I said, I wouldn't allow a daughter of mine to weaken her mind with such foolishness."

The older salesman who'd winked leaned forward. "Why, ma'am, I would be surprised to learn you had a daughter old enough to talk. You being so young."

The woman thumbed toward the silent girl. "I got her and two more younger at home. So don't go trying to sweet-talk me."

"I'd never tell anything but the truth to a woman so obviously intelligent." His eyes might be bloodshot from drink, but his tone was smooth as fine whiskey.

"Better not," she answered with less conviction.

"And may I say," the man continued, "that it is rare I see a woman with such delicate skin in this hot climate. Peaches and cream, ma'am, peaches and cream."

The woman patted her round cheek. "I do always wear my bonnet in the sun. Just like I've told my daughters a thousand times, the Lord gives us fine skin. It's our responsibility to take care of it."

Molly caught the older man's gaze as it cut briefly to the drummer with the black hair and mustache. The drummer smiled and nodded slightly toward the senior salesman.

The older man paid yet another compliment to the huge woman. In an instant, Molly understood his game. She leaned back and closed her eyes. The thought of warning the woman never reached her lips.

She listened to flattery that stretched further into fantasy than Uncle Orson. The third salesman fell asleep against the frame and snored in rhythm to the stage's rocking. The shy daughter pulled a handkerchief from her pocket and made Callie Ann another doll. The drummer remained silent, but the hint of a smile never left his face.

By the time the driver yelled, "San Marcos," three hours later, the bossy mother had bought half the creams and lotions in the older salesman's sample case. As they stepped from the stage, Molly saw the drummer slip the salesman money. This was obviously a game they played to pass the time from place to place.

"I'll be getting off here," Molly told the driver as he offered his hand to help her down.

He grunted without interest. It obviously made no

difference to him what she did. He was paid to drive, nothing more.

The huge woman leaned out of the window and then nodded her permission for her daughter to ride up top. The mother glared at Molly. "Why would anyone in their right mind want to stay in a godforsaken place like this?"

"It's Uncle Orson's home," Molly answered politely as she took Callie Ann's hand and moved away. "He owns a ranch just west of town. Runs a hundred head all by himself." Molly linked her arm to the air as though she were walking with a man.

She could hear the woman spouting her wisdom about the weak-minded to all who would listen. Molly couldn't help but grin. The drummer who sold her next would have his work cut out for him.

Crossing to the livery, Molly thought how good it felt to be free here in Texas. Trouble had certainly been raining on her, but at least she no longer had to bear the constant criticism of her aunts. The woman on the stage reminded her of how good that felt.

It took only a few minutes to rent a wagon. While waiting for the stable hand to hook up the team, Molly got directions to the mission.

By the time the stage pulled out across the street, Molly was climbing into her wagon. She'd put Callie Ann in the back with their bags and supplies boxing her in. The child was already curling into a ball atop her shawl, like a kitten at nap time.

Molly took the reins in her hands. Ephraim had taught her to drive a team years ago, but since the war, she hadn't had much practice. The feel of the reins came back to her though.

Just as she slapped the horses into action, a person from seemingly nowhere stepped in front of the wagon.

Jerking the lines, Molly stood to make sure a horse hadn't knocked the bystander down.

The girl who'd ridden all morning across from her hurried to the side of the wagon. "I'm sorry," she wailed. "I didn't mean to step out like that. I guess I wasn't watching where I was going. I was trying to stay out of my momma's sight."

Molly glanced at the dust of the Concord a half mile away. "Aren't you supposed to be on that stage?"

The girl looked like she might cry. "I asked Momma if I could ride up top. For once, she let me. Then she was too busy shouting at you to notice I didn't climb up. She won't know I'm gone until San Antonio, and there's not another stage back this direction until morning."

Molly was in a hurry to get to Wolf, but she couldn't help asking, "You're running away from home, aren't you?"

The girl shook her head. "I'll be twenty this fall, I think. My momma never celebrates a birthday for me so I ain't sure. I'm not running, though, I'm just leaving home. I've got enough money to catch the next stage to Austin, where I hope to find a job. Momma won't come after me. She always said she'd never look for a dog or child who didn't have sense enough to come home."

"Have you ever been on your own?"

Tears bubbled in the girl's eyes. "No," she answered. "But I had to leave. Momma always said none of us could make it without her. I figure I'd rather die of hunger on the street than live at home one more day. She won't even let me go to the privy until my chores are done ever' morning. She says we're all too dumb to get married, so we have to live with her 'til we die."

Molly moved over on the wagon bench. "Can you drive a team?"

The girl looked up in surprise and nodded.

"Then you can go with us, if you like. I have to pick up my injured husband and get him back to Austin. If you'll do half the driving, you can keep your money and still get to Austin." Molly had a feeling she'd be having a talk with herself later about being so impulsive, but right now another pair of hands sounded like a good idea, and she couldn't leave the girl. "What's your name?"

"Early. Momma tried to convince the man she married that I was just gonna come early. But he knew enough not to let me be called by his last name when I weren't, and he left Momma for trying to fool him. The name Early just stuck. Momma married a man, not long after I was born, named Ed Willis, but he didn't want me using his name either."

The girl smiled as if she'd just completed the longest speech of her life. She climbed up and took the reins with callused hands. "You won't be sorry, ma'am. I won't be no more trouble than Uncle Orson."

Molly pointed the way, suddenly glad that she wouldn't have to face whatever lay ahead alone.

SEVENTEEN

Twenty years old, the settlement of San Marcos grew up along a river rising from a mammoth springs. The water made the air smell sweet and feel cooler than anywhere else south of the Hill Country. The mission lay close against a stand of cottonwoods a few miles to the east of the stage depot. As they neared, Molly realized calling the place a mission was a grand overstatement. It was little more than a few buildings huddled together. A temporary refuge from weather or attack.

An aging priest met them at a huge wooden door that looked like it hadn't been closed in years. He watched with hopeful eyes as she climbed from the wagon.

"You are here to help?" he asked in words flavored with foreign tones.

"I've come for my husband," Molly answered, unable to miss the disappointment in his eyes. "I was told Captain Hayward is here."

The priest nodded and seemed to accept the load he hoped might be lifted from his shoulders.

Molly asked Early if she would wait with Callie Ann until she knew the extent of Wolf's injuries. Now that she was near, fear rose to the surface. Molly fought it down with determination.

Early tied the reins and helped Callie Ann from the wagon. As Molly entered the mission, she glanced back. The two were walking toward the shade of nearby trees. The few clouds that had darkened the land this morning had disappeared, leaving the air still and dry.

Following the priest through the door, Molly felt the walls of the mission close in around her. The dark and airless building had been constructed as a fortress against attacks. Narrow windows hugged the roofline, offering no view.

Within a few feet, a familiar smell greeted her. Thick as cobwebs, blood and death hung in the air. How many hundreds of times had she walked into a building or tent behind her father, with the odor of rotting flesh and dried blood bombarding them like an invisible tidal wave?

Instinct told her to run. Training told her there was far more than one man injured in this place.

She followed the priest through shadows to a main room no larger than Granny's dining room. "What happened?"

"Raids two nights ago." The old priest shuffled among cots so close together their occupants could easily touch. "Farms west of here were hit. A few were killed, but the Comanche wanted horses more than blood."

He shook his head. "We were already full before folks wandered in here after the raid. Our mission provides a home for the elderly and those who have no family to take care of them. We're not equipped to handle this many injured."

He stared at her, his broken heart showing in his eyes. "All I can do is pray for them. Father Michael was our doctor of sorts, but he died of a fever six months ago. The mission in San Antonio promised us help."

As her gaze moved from cot to cot, Molly's mind raced. Some of the occupants were old, crippled by life, their eyes vacant and unaware. A few could have been broken soldiers with no family to take care of them after the war. Placed in between them were temporary beds soaked in blood. Children in too much pain to cry, a few adults with open wounds seeping, a woman who cradled a child with bloody hands.

If medical help didn't arrive soon, there would be few alive to doctor. She'd seen field hospitals better organized an hour after battle. These people had been suffering for two days.

"Where's my husband?" Molly asked as she passed the beds. She wanted desperately to stop and help them, but she had to see Wolf first.

"He's in the storage room. I put a bandage across his head and wrote the sheriff in Austin. I thought he might know what to do with a Texas Ranger."

Molly hurried into a dark cramped place where Wolf

lay stretched out on a table like a fallen warrior lying in state. Taking his face in her hands, she called his name, her heart aching at the sight of him. She didn't care that he was covered in mud and blood. All that mattered was that he was still alive. "Come on," she prayed. "Wake up, Captain."

Slowly, he groaned and opened his eyes. "Morning, Molly, my girl." His words were low, pushed through gritted teeth. He tried to smile as she unwrapped the filthy bandage and checked his wound, but his efforts failed.

Her fingers moved lightly over the wound, checking for infection, making sure the bullet had passed across and not lodged. Despite the dirt, the wound showed signs of healing.

"Wolf, I have to know, can you hang on a few hours? There are . . ."

"I know," he answered gritting his teeth once more as she covered his injury. "I've heard them crying. Do what you can for them." His voice faded. "I'll just sleep awhile."

Molly hesitated. She was here to help Wolf, but she couldn't turn her back on the others. His wound was deep but he wasn't losing enough blood for it to be life-threatening. From his few words and clear eyes she guessed there was no brain damage.

She kissed Wolf's cheek and whispered, "I'll be back as soon as I can."

She looked up at the priest. "I've never practiced medicine, but I do know how to help. Have you someone who can unload boxes from my wagon? I'll be glad to share my supplies."

The priest smiled as if his prayers had been answered. "I have a boy who can help. And Brother Luke. His mind is weak, but his back's strong. I'll get them both."

"Good." Molly pulled off her traveling jacket and rolled up her sleeves. "I'll need water, lots of water, boiled and cooled to warm if possible. And light—all the lamps you have."

The priest hurried out. She moved into the room where the injured waited. There was no time to think. No time to hesitate. Quickly, as her father had done many times, Molly surveyed the people. She tried to guess who needed to be treated first. After two days of suffering, it was more a guess than a decision. By the time Brother Luke arrived with the water, Molly was hard at work.

She asked that all the elderly and crippled who were not part of the raids be helped outside in the shade so that she'd have room to move. The boy didn't want to get close to blood, but he was willing to tote and stay with the aged.

The priest rolled up his sleeves, as well, and followed her directions. Like many of his day, he'd thought leaving the blood around the wound was nature's way. When Molly ordered him to start washing, he hesitated.

Her voice hardened with authority, and he began cleaning.

Again and again, she checked on Wolf. She put a

cool, damp cloth on his wound to soften the scab that had started forming and catch blood that still seeped out. He seemed to be resting quietly.

The priest delivered word that Early and Callie Ann were in the kitchen. They kept a constant stream of water coming and made soup for everyone. Early told the priest to say she was sorry she couldn't be there to help with the injured, but she didn't want Callie Ann catching anything.

Molly smiled and wiped the sweat from her forehead. Bullet wounds were seldom contagious, but she understood Early's desire to stay away. Some folks didn't have the stomach for the work; others thought trouble was catching. Early was obviously trying to do her part.

The priest proved more helpful than she first thought he might be. He held the children in his arms while she doctored them. His low, caring voice was as soothing as medicine. Most of them were cut or scraped from falls when they'd run from the raid. One had a broken arm.

Two men needed bullets removed. One from his chest, not an inch away from his heart. The other had a gut wound. Molly did her best with both patients but knew their chances were slim.

The woman with a baby had only scratches and cuts from falling. Reluctantly, she allowed Molly to examine the tiny child in her arms.

Molly fought to whisper her words only to the priest. "The baby's dead," she said. "There's nothing I can do."

For the first time, she saw the strength of the old man. "I can," he answered. "This time I know what has to be done."

As Molly moved away, she heard the woman's cries and the priest's soft words. No mixture of medicine could take away the mother's pain.

It was almost dark when Molly treated the last patient, a little boy with scratches and a cut along his arm. He couldn't be more than five and didn't know the whereabouts of his parents. But he didn't cry.

The grieving mother, who'd just finished washing her baby and dressing him for burial, looked over as Molly worked on the boy. "I know your ma and pa," she said in a deep Southern accent. "You can stay with me until we find them."

Molly lifted the boy and sat him beside her. The young mother set aside her sorrow long enough to comfort the child. Molly couldn't stop her tears. She moved close to the now-empty boxes she'd brought so that no one would hear her crying.

As she pulled her emotions under control, she realized most of the medical supplies were gone.

The priest offered her a cup of soup, but she had one more injured to attend to first. Wolf. The nagging thought that she risked his life to save the others had been in her mind all afternoon. He would have wanted it that way, she knew. But what would she tell herself if she'd waited too long to treat him, or if his wound needed medicine she'd already handed out?

She entered the small room that reminded her of a cell in some dark, ancient prison. Wolf hadn't moved since she'd checked on him an hour before. He looked like a giant spread across the table with his arms hanging off the sides. The priest had removed his boots and gun belt. They lay, covered in mud, next to him.

"Wolf?" she whispered, realizing how few times she'd said his name. It seemed strange to call him anything except Captain Hayward, but that didn't sound right now that they were married.

She placed the lantern a few feet from his head. Light fell across clutter piled in every corner of the room. She thought she could smell onions and earthy potatoes. "Wolf?" she whispered again.

He moaned.

"I'm here." Molly let her hand slide along his arm. "I'll try to make it better."

When she removed the blood-stained cloth and cleaned the wound, he didn't open his eyes. As she'd thought, the bullet must have caught him at the temple and slid along the skull. She knew immediately the danger would be infection.

As she cleaned, he called her name once—a haunting cry as though he'd said it a thousand times. The cut was deep, and even with stitches, there would be a scar at the hairline.

"I'm here," she whispered and was surprised when her voice calmed the giant.

While warm water dripped along his face and shoulders from a cloth moving in gentle strokes, Wolf relaxed. Unsure if he was asleep or unconscious, Molly worked as quickly as possible.

By the time he moaned again, she was bandaging

his forehead. The cotton strip banded across his tan skin and dark hair. She knew pain now gripped him. She could see it in the clench of his jaw. There was nothing more she could do. Except fight the fever—the fever that might kill him when the bullet didn't.

To settle him, Molly slowly rubbed a rag over his chest and arms, washing away layers of dirt. His strong chest reminded her of the dream she'd had of Benjamin. The two men must be near the same size, she guessed, only Benjamin had stayed young, not hardened to life like Wolf.

Benjamin was a dream, she reminded herself. Wolf was reality. Her reality. Their marriage might have been in name only, but from this point on, it would be more. She was bound to this man, not by a piece of paper he'd tucked away in his metal box, but by a promise. The preacher's words came back to her. In sickness and in health. At the time she'd added, For six months, no more. But now, with Wolf hurt, the words might truly mean for the rest of his life. Until death.

He caught her hand suddenly, stopping her daydream.

"Molly." His eyes stared directly at her. Feverish, but clear. "Get me out of this place."

Most women would have asked why, or tried to talk him into staying. Any doctor would have advised against moving a man so ill. But Molly heard the desperation in his voice. He wasn't asking. He was demanding.

She called for Brother Luke and the priest, who were

busy helping the elderly in from where they'd enjoyed an afternoon outside. The two men braced Wolf's weight as he shuffled into the night air.

For a long moment, Wolf closed his eyes and breathed. Brother Luke returned to his duties, leaving Wolf resting heavy against Molly's shoulders. "If I am to die," he whispered more to himself than to her, "then let me breathe fresh air until my last."

They stumbled, nearly falling with his weight several times. Finally, Molly and the priest got him to the river's edge. The boy ran ahead of them and spread a blanket beside Molly's wagon. Callie Ann and Early slept inside the wagon, too tired to wake when they passed by.

Wolf sank onto the blanketed grass, exhausted by his journey.

Molly knelt beside him and glanced up at the priest. "I'll check on the others in an hour. Call me if you need me, Father. Otherwise I'd like to stay beside my husband."

The priest nodded. "You've done your work this day, my child. Rest."

Until that moment, Molly hadn't thought about how exhausted she felt. She'd gone the night before without sleep, then ridden a stage all morning and worked into evening. She was so weary she felt her bones might shatter if the wind blew.

Looking up at the stars, she realized it had to be almost midnight. There was still much to do. She covered Wolf with a thin blanket and brought water from the stream to wipe his face and shoulders. Above all else, she had to keep him cool but not chilled.

The night was alive with sounds, and the air stirred slowly around her, too gentle to be a breeze. Wolf's skin felt warm. The heat passed up her arm into her entire body as she touched him.

This was her man. The only husband she would probably ever have. He wasn't what she would've chosen, or dreamed of, but for all the world, he was hers.

He wasn't a gentleman who'd been a dashing officer. He wasn't rich. But he was kind and good. He'd been there when she needed him. In the end, maybe that was the most important thing.

Molly curled beside him and placed her arm across his chest. The real world is where I belong, she decided. The real world.

But as she dreamed, Benjamin came back to her. She felt him beside her, keeping her warm, protecting her from harm. She slept soundly to the rhythm of his breathing, so close against her ear.

When she awoke he was gone, as before, leaving only the memory of his heartbeat next to hers. "Benjamin," she whispered, wishing for more of the dream.

It took Molly a moment to remember where she was. The forest, the stream, all looked foreign to her. Then she saw the mission and remembered. It hadn't been Benjamin beside her, but Wolf. His arm had protected her. His heartbeat had pounded next to her. Not Benjamin, but Wolf.

She stood, hoping that he might be much recovered. Logic told her otherwise. A man who couldn't walk alone the night before would not travel far at dawn.

She glanced in the direction of the mission. Nothing. The woods. Nothing. But when she turned to the river, she saw his dark form close to the water. The white bandage across his forehead shone bright in the dawn light.

Molly ran to him, kneeling on the wet grass only a foot from the water. She lifted his head and supported it on her lap, feeling the fever even through the bandage.

"If I could get in the water," he mumbled, "I could cool off."

"You'd catch pneumonia."

"I can't take it any longer. I'm going in the water!" He tried to raise his head.

"You are not!" She put her hands on his shoulders and held tightly. He was talking out of his head and she had to protect him. "I'll not have you dying on me, Wolf Hayward."

Anger fired Wolf's strength. With one mighty effort, he pushed her away and rose to one knee.

She landed in the mud. Rage rumbled through her body unlike she'd ever known. She clawed her way to her feet and faced him, preparing to ram him with her entire body if she had to, in order to keep him down.

But just before she jumped, she saw the pain in his eyes. He was fighting to stay conscious. When she stepped toward him, he crumbled in her arms and she sank to the ground.

For a while, she just held him, having no idea what to do. Finally, she pulled him back to the blanket and bathed his face with cool water.

As the day aged and warmed, so did Wolf. The fever raged no matter what she did. The air was dry and hot, pressing against the skin as if one were standing too close to a fire.

Molly left him twice to check on other patients.

On the noon stage, two priests arrived with more supplies and word that a young woman was missing. Her mother claimed she must have fallen off the top of the stage between San Marcos and San Antonio, but they'd seen no body on the road. Molly and Early promised to keep an eye out for her.

The capable priests took over the other patients but offered only an herb called feverfew for Wolf's fever. Molly knew the powder was made from chrysanthemum flowers. Early brewed him willow tea, swearing it would help but Molly could get only a few drops down him.

Wolf mumbled, out of his head. One moment he would be at a battle from long ago, the next he called her name as though she were the one lost and he had to find her.

"Help me," Molly finally called to Early. "We have to do something. Maybe he was right. Maybe we should take him to the water. I have to try. I can't just watch him die."

She cried as Early helped her drag him, blanket and all, to the river. They slipped him into the shallow water a few inches at a time. When he shivered suddenly Molly went fully clothed in beside him, holding him as he shook.

Cool, but not cold, the water lapped over him.

Molly cradled his head and waited. It seemed forever before he opened his eyes. "Better," he whispered, hugging her. "Stay close, my Molly."

She moved her hands gently across his shoulders and along his back. Over the hours she'd grown used to the feel of him. "Of course I will. I'm right here."

As the sun lowered, Brother Luke helped Molly carry Wolf from the stream to the wagon. They removed his wet clothes and dressed him in a clean set she'd found in his saddlebags. His fever had lessened, and he slept peacefully. Molly took down the sideboards so he could feel the breeze off the water. Then she helped Early and Callie Ann stack hay for a bed several feet away near the trees.

When all were asleep, Molly pulled a change of clothes from her bag and undressed in the relative privacy between the wagon and the river. She knew she was out of sight of the mission and hoped anyone walking past didn't have great night vision.

Her clothes had dried all afternoon on her body, chafing her flesh at the shoulders and waist. After she stripped, she carefully rubbed into her skin a powder made of lycopodium, oxide zinc, and carbolic acid she'd learned to carry during hot months. The mixture would ease her discomfort and prevent any further chafing.

As she dusted the excess powder off with a clean undergarment, Molly smiled. All she needed was a few more ingredients, and she'd smell like an apothecary. The fine powder made her body ghost-white against the night.

She slipped the thin cotton of her camisole over her head, then glanced in the direction of the wagon and froze.

Like a silent animal in the woods, Wolf's alert eyes stared back at her.

EIGHTEEN

THE THROBBING IN WOLF'S HEAD FELT LIKE A CAN-non shot reverberating to his heartbeat. The pain moved down his body in echoes of agony, making his stomach churn. However, the fever had passed, and for that, he was thankful.

He struggled to remain still to lessen the pain, but even his breathing disturbed the balance. He tried to sleep, but that proved impossible. So he waited and fought the urge to swear to high heaven. Wolf was not a man who took kindly to his own illness.

After he saw her dressing, Molly disappeared into the night. She hadn't said a word when she caught him watching—*watching,* hell, he was staring. She just turned her back to him and walked away into the night as though he'd been no more than the man in the moon looking at her.

By now she was probably digging up a gun to put him out of his misery. He couldn't picture her remaining calm and asking him if he enjoyed the view over breakfast in the morning.

The moon had drifted halfway across the sky when he heard her moving about the wagon. He didn't open his eyes. If she were mad at him, he was in no shape to face a fight. He tried to build an argument that watching could fall on either side of the "in name only" fence standing between them.

But as she crawled into the back of the wagon and stretched out beside him, she didn't seem angry, only tired. Carefully, she covered them both with his blanket, then felt his cheek for fever.

He didn't move. He figured shooting stars were more predictable than this woman. Outguessing her would only drive him mad, and right now, the way his head felt, it would be a short trip.

She cuddled against him as if he hadn't seen her standing bare-naked in the moonlight. She acted as though it didn't matter. Like he'd seen a hundred women without anything on, and she wouldn't stand out in his memory.

Or maybe she was just tired. More tired than embarrassed.

Wolf realized he'd forgotten his pain, but the fever seemed to be returning. He grew warmer with every moment that passed with her at his side.

She must have felt him heat up, for her fingers stroked his cheek. "Are you all right?" she whispered. "Would a cool cloth help?"

"No," he answered, thinking she'd probably not like where he'd need to put a cloth to cool off.

"Does your head still pound?" She moved her fingers into his hair above the bandage.

"Yes," he managed to say. She was so close. Wolf could feel her body along the length of him as she stroked her fingers through his hair. He could smell her, too, the rosewater wash she used on her hair, the perfumed cream he'd seen her smooth over her hands, even the powder he'd watched her sprinkle along her waist. Her bare waist.

"Try to sleep," she ordered, her words brushing against his face. "You'll feel better in the morning."

"Will you stay beside me?"

"I've nowhere else to sleep." She continued to comb through his hair. "We passed out the last blanket hours ago, and there is no room on the pallet Early and Callie Ann made."

His hand circled her middle. "Here is where you belong." The movement cost him dearly. His head pounded so fiercely he was surprised she couldn't hear it.

She must have sensed it, though. Molly closed the few inches between them and kissed his bandage. "Easy now. I'm right here."

Without loosening his grip, Wolf closed his eyes and drifted with the pain until he could bear it once more. By the time he could think clearly, she'd relaxed in sleep.

He floated in and out of consciousness, enjoying her nearness like a sweet dream when he awoke. He relaxed beside her as he slept, a part of him always aware of her. The feel of her fitting so perfectly at his side was like a rich wine washing through him, warming his soul, drugging his thoughts.

Just before dawn, when the sky was black, he woke once again to the bubbling sounds of the water. For a moment, he couldn't figure out what was different. The night was quiet, cool. The water lazy and pure-smelling. Molly slept beneath his arm, her hand spread protectively across his chest.

Then he knew what had changed. The pain was gone. She'd been right.

Molly moaned softly in her sleep, and he guessed she was dreaming. He wanted to enter the fantasy as he had weeks ago. Maybe she dreamed of him, of Benjamin, and he was right by her side. In the hours before, even through the fever, he'd noticed how comfortable she'd become with him. Touching him as casually as if they'd been together for a long time.

Wolf couldn't resist sliding his hand along her hip. He didn't know if the feel of her would ever become routine.

She didn't move as he caressed her.

His fingers glided lightly over her back. Though her blouse covered her, he had seen her body. He imagined he touched her flesh. He'd always liked the gentle curves of her slender body, but now the feel of them pleased him greatly.

She rolled onto her back, breathing deep and completely relaxed. He knew she'd worked hard all day and late into the night. Now, she slept as soundly as a child.

His hand grew bolder, brushing against the starched

cotton of her clothing, touching the silk of her hair, caressing the softness of her cheek.

She moaned again without waking, as though her pleasure in dreams was too great to keep inside.

He cupped her breast gently in his palm and rolled toward her, unable to resist the taste of her mouth. It was velvet and full in sleep. She made no resistance. He parted her lips with his tongue and kissed her soundly. As he felt her awakening beneath him, his grip closed tighter over her breast, wanting her to enjoy the expression as much as he did.

He relished the softness of her through the thin layers of clothing and savored every movement she made as she slipped from dreams to his arms. She twisted under him, and he showed his own desire by deepening the kiss.

Her hands shoved suddenly against his chest. It took his mind and body a moment to react.

She pounded her fist against him in rapid fire.

Startled, he pulled away, hating to allow room between them.

The moment Wolf released Molly, she rolled from the wagon and stumbled to her feet. She turned, staring at him in the velvet night as if she'd just fought her way, not from a dream, but from a nightmare.

Before he could react, she was running toward the river without uttering a word. But he'd seen all he needed to see in her stormy green eyes. He'd seen hurt. And hatred.

Wolf pulled himself up and tried to follow her. He must explain. But he felt weak, and the throbbing in his head returned like a low drumbeat. He tried to think but couldn't get his thoughts to make sense. He had to find her. He had to know if he'd gone too far.

Stumbling from the wagon, he forced his legs to move. What had he been thinking? To her, he was a man with whom she'd spent only a few days. He'd agreed to her terms of the marriage, and now, the first time she'd relaxed and felt comfortable near him, he'd advanced.

Daybreak lightened the horizon before he saw her huddled between two rocks at the water's edge. He moved slowly toward her, wondering if he should apologize or declare his love. Whichever he decided would probably be the wrong choice.

She didn't bother looking up at him when he neared, but he knew she heard him. He was making as much noise as a wounded bear, dragging his feet and grumbling as he moved. How could he ever explain that he wanted to get used to the feel of her as she had him? Was that the way it was supposed to be? he thought. She could touch him, but he couldn't touch her?

"Molly," he started, thinking he didn't have much of a speech, one word.

"Molly." Two words, and he was already repeating himself.

He moved closer. "Molly . . ."

Her stormy gaze stopped him. If this kept up, he'd never complete a sentence in front of her. She looked like a little girl, huddled with her arms around her knees. He thought of all he'd like to tell her. How much he loved her. How his very life started and ended with her. How he'd never hurt her, if she'd just let him near. But he couldn't say anything. He couldn't even think of where to start.

"I didn't mean to undress in front of you." She snapped so quickly the words slurred together as one. It took his pounding head a few minutes to sort them out.

He opened his mouth, but this time he didn't even get his one word out.

"I only crawled beside you because I wanted to be close if you needed me. I thought you understood that. I wasn't being forward. Or at least I didn't think I was, though I can see how it must have looked to you at the time."

Wolf rubbed his forehead. She was going to have to slow down. He couldn't hear as fast as she spoke. At this rate, there would be whole sentences left in the air between them.

"I came to help you. Until this trouble is over, you are my husband, and I'm trying to do what I think a wife, even in name only, should do."

She was apologizing, he thought. Hell, he'd been the one who'd acted like a fool. Here she was justifying herself as if she thought she'd somehow made him act the way he did. He was relieved and insulted at the same time.

Relieved because she wasn't angry at him but at herself, and insulted that she thought him so weak-minded or weak-bodied that he'd try to bed any woman who showed herself to him and cuddled against him. And whispered in his ear, he thought. And ran her fingers through his hair. And let her breasts rest against him.

Hell, he thought, sitting down beside her and lowering his head in his hands, he had no right to be insulted. Molly was right about him, he was weak-minded when it came to her. Maybe some of his brains splattered out when he got shot. He'd behaved like a fool. She had no business apologizing to him.

"So that's why I want you to know I don't consider it your fault, and I don't want you to think I'm doing this because of what just happened. I understand about men and their needs."

He'd jumped into the middle of one of her speeches and he wasn't sure he could catch up. But he wasn't about to interrupt her and tell her he hadn't been listening.

"But when we get back to Austin, I feel—"

"Stop." He finally found another word to say. "Just stop."

To his surprise, she did.

He took a moment to circle the wagons of his thoughts. He wasn't sure what she'd been about to say, but he was fairly certain he didn't want to hear her finish the sentence.

"I know you didn't mean to undress in front of me, and I didn't mean to look. So can we just call that even? As for crawling next to me, your reasons make perfect sense. Normally, I would have said you were putting yourself in the safest place you could sleep."

She opened her mouth to say something, but he held

up his hand. "I have to have twice the time as you, Molly. I only talk at half the rate.

"I'm not going to blame what I did on a fever or on just being a man wanting to touch someone. I knew what I was doing, Molly. I wanted to touch *you*. I have since the day we married. No, since the day we met. I should have been honest enough to say something, but I figured if all you wanted was a friend, I could be that." He had to be truthful about something. If she were going to kill him, he wanted to die for the truth, not for what she thought happened.

"Hell, Molly. It wasn't just because you were some woman lying next to me. It was you." He watched her closely. Now it was her turn to digest his words. "I have no right to touch you, if it's not what you want. It was my mistake thinking you wanted to be held, to be caressed the way a man touches a woman. *My* mistake, not yours. You set the rules from the beginning. I had no right to think they had changed."

The silence between them was thick and heavy. He'd said all he could today. He wasn't sure she'd listen to more. She might not believe him if he told her more.

"It won't happen again?" She lifted her chin.

"It won't happen again," he answered, knowing he'd cut off his arm before he'd touch her again if she was unwilling.

"And you'll forget seeing me nude?"

Wolf couldn't keep the corner of his mouth from lifting into a smile and only hoped his beard covered it. "I'll never forget seeing you, but I won't mention it to you or anyone. I swear."

She seemed satisfied with the agreement. "Friends?" she asked.

"Friends," he answered, knowing they were already so much more.

NINETEEN

BEFORE THE SUN GREW WARM, THEY RETURNED THE wagon to the livery and waited on a pine bench in front of the station for the stage from San Antonio to pick them up. It changed horses at the station and headed straight to Austin. With luck, they'd be home by noon.

The woman named Early, whom Molly introduced as someone traveling with them, seemed to jump every time Wolf looked at her. She was so shy, he wasn't sure she knew how to talk. But in her sad eyes he noticed a kindness when she looked at Callie Ann. If she wanted to tag along with them, it was all right with him.

"I wouldn't have minded driving the wagon," Molly said for the third time. "We'd planned to take you back so that you could rest while we traveled. Early and I are both good drivers. You could have slept the day away."

Wolf knew he'd upset her plan by insisting on the stage. He wasn't around women often enough to remember that they always had an order to their world worked out, and it usually wasn't worth the trouble a man would go through to change the plan. "I can rest in the stage," he tried to explain. "I don't want to enter Austin lying in the back of a wagon, and I'm not sure I'm clearheaded enough to sit a saddle."

Molly nodded, but he doubted she understood.

She didn't say another word about it. When the stage pulled up, she reached into her bag and handed him a roll of bills.

He raised an eyebrow.

"For the passage," she whispered.

"This is my money, not yours?" he questioned.

"Yes," she answered.

He guessed she was lying. He doubted there had been so much left in his account after he'd bought them the new clothes. But this was not the time or place for a husband and wife to have a discussion over money. He paid their fares and helped her into the stage.

Luckily, there were only two other passengers. Miss Early, as Callie Ann called her, and the child sat on one side with a sleeping cowhand who smelled of his trade. Wolf and Molly took the other seat next to a boy of about fourteen. He seemed happy to have someone to talk to.

"Mornin', folks." He smiled and tapped his hat. "Name's Riley."

"Morning," Wolf answered without offering his name.

"You folks traveling far?" The kid tried again.

"Only to Austin." Wolf wasn't sure he could keep

up conversation for long. He'd been awake for hours and looked forward to a nap.

Callie Ann scooted off her bench and folded down the extra side chair.

Wolf raised an eyebrow.

"For Uncle Orson," Molly answered.

Grinning, Wolf mumbled, "I thought he would want to ride up top."

The boy didn't understand about the chair, but he heard Wolf's comment. "Ain't no one riding up top, mister. A girl fell off a few days ago. Every driver's been asking people to keep an eye out for her. She couldn't have bounced far from the road."

"Maybe she never climbed up at the stop," Molly suggested.

"Oh, yes, she did, ma'am. Her mother swore to it. Said the girl was dumb as a box of rocks and probably didn't hold on."

Wolf saw the sadness turn liquid in Early's eyes. He didn't have to ask to know the truth about her. "Where you from, son?" Wolf changed the subject.

"San Antonio, but my cousins live in Abilene. I'm going to see them for a month or so. Their name's Haynes, Perry and Charlsa Haynes. Maybe you know them?"

The ranger shook his head. Folks newly arrived in Texas still thought it was a small enough place where everyone who'd been here awhile knew everyone else. "I don't get up that way much." He didn't want to tell the boy what he did for a living, or he knew he'd spend the entire ride answering questions. "If you don't mind,

I think I'll take a nap. I'll let you keep an eye out for the girl who bounced off, son."

The boy looked disappointed.

Lowering his hat over his bandaged forehead, Wolf crossed his arms over his chest. He fully intended to sleep, but as the stage rocked, he became aware of all the places he was touching Molly.

She didn't seem to notice. She was busy making notes in her journal.

The stage rolled back and forth. Her knee kept bumping his. Her elbow pushed against his side as she wrote. After trying to ignore her for several minutes, he finally shifted his shoulders to give her more room. In doing so, his leg now rested firmly against hers.

Molly thanked him for the elbow room and didn't seem to mind that their knees touched.

Wolf watched her through half-closed eyes. She was so beautiful this morning, she took his breath away. He didn't understand how no one else seemed to see it but him. The world was blind, he decided.

She wrote as fast as she could with a pencil no longer than her finger. By the way she frowned and bit the tip of her tongue, she looked like she was arguing with herself on paper about some great dilemma. He remembered her telling him that writing was how she worked things out when she had a problem to solve. He hoped *he* wasn't her topic for the day.

Sleep caught up to him, making the trip short. In what seemed only minutes, they pulled into Austin.

Charlie Filmore met them at the station with Noah's wagon.

"How'd you know we were coming?" Wolf asked Charlie in greeting as he offered his hand to Molly. When she took it, he didn't let go after she climbed out. To his surprise she didn't seem to mind.

"Didn't know you were on this one," Charlie answered as he collected the ladies' bags. "I've been meeting every stage. I figured you'd be on one if you were still alive. Miss Molly probably wouldn't let you ride with a head wound, and the only way you'd be traveling into town in the back of a wagon would be inside one of Miller's boxes."

"You know him better than I do," Molly said, then encouraged a shy Early to step forward. "Mr. Filmore, I'd like you to meet Miss Early. She'll be coming home with us for a visit if she can manage the time."

Early looked surprised by the invitation. Charlie appeared to be struck dumb at the sight of the young lady. He rarely got to meet respectable women.

He made the mistake of smiling as she glanced toward him, sending Miss Early hurrying behind Wolf in panic.

Charlie lowered his head and backed away. "I'm sorry, miss. I didn't mean to frighten you. I know I'm a sight. Most folks around these parts know better than to look me in the face."

"What happened?" she whispered from behind Wolf.

"Three bullets, three different battles. Each time, the doctors patched me up as best they could, but they didn't spend much time on me. Figured I'd die. Even left the death certificates signed before they moved on." He laughed. "But I fooled 'em. I lived even without much of a face left."

To her credit, the shy woman stepped out from behind Wolf and offered her hand to Charlie.

Wolf had never seen a man, much less a woman, offer to shake hands with Charlie. He decided Molly was right about the girl. She could stay with them as long as she wanted.

Charlie Filmore took her hand with no less honor than if he were shaking hands with the queen of England. He helped her and Callie Ann into the wagon while Wolf lifted Molly up with one effortless movement. When he climbed up beside her he let his arm slide easily along the back of the seat, bracing her against him.

Again, she didn't pull away.

"To Granny's?" Wolf asked, letting Charlie take the reins. "Surely she's still got room for us. I can almost smell the gravy now."

"Charlie?" Molly questioned.

Charlie smiled with pride. "It's home this time, Captain." He slapped the reins. "I moved your things over this morning." He glanced at Wolf. "Wasn't much of a move, a few books and a tin box."

They crossed town along the side streets. Shadows stretched from house to house, making evening come earlier. Wolf thought of asking where they were going, but he decided to wait and see. If Molly had found another place, he was sure it would be fine. After all, he'd probably only be here a few days a month, no more, and any place would be grand if Molly was there.

They pulled up beside a square two-story house painted white and trimmed in blue. Charlie jumped down, so excited he looked like he was dancing.

"The man said he'd meet you at the bank first morning you're back to sign the papers. Lease or buy, either way you like. He's headed back East and wants to travel light. The house has got furniture and everything." Charlie swallowed and lowered his head. "Including aunts."

"Ants? Red or sugar?" Wolf asked as he helped the women down.

"No." Charlie looked at Molly apologetically. "As in your father's sisters." He cheered slightly. "Or so they told me. Maybe you don't have any aunts, and I'll have to kick these two old bossy-biddies out on the street."

Molly shook her head. "If they're bossy-biddies, they're probably mine."

"There's four bedrooms upstairs." Charlie trailed Molly up the walk. "I told them the one with the fireplace in it is Wolf's and yours, and the one next to it is Callie Ann's. They had all kinds of questions about the fire and your marriage. I ain't known ordering around like that since the army. But I didn't answer them nothin'."

Molly reached the long porch that ran the length of the front of the house. She couldn't help but smile as Callie Ann squealed and ran to a swing.

"The aunts each took a bedroom. Where do you want

me to put Miss Early's things?" Charlie asked, seeming embarrassed he'd found such a small house.

"I'll bunk in with Callie Ann," Early offered. "If you still have room. If not, I'll understand."

"I'll need a friend desperately the next few days. Can you stay?" Molly asked. "It would give you time to look about the town without having to find something immediately."

Wolf could guess without asking that Miss Early had no other place to go and he'd bet she had little money.

Early lifted her head in pride at being asked and not told. "I'd be happy to stay and help."

Charlie shoved the blue door open. "I saw the aunts walking in town just before the stage came in, so you'll have time to settle before they get back. The house is a square. Four rooms down, four rooms up."

"I'd like to check the kitchen," Early whispered. "I could start lunch while you look around, if there's supplies. If I'm going to be a houseguest, I might as well make myself useful."

"Oh, the cupboards are full. The former owner had everything ready for his bride."

"Did she die?" Molly hesitated before entering. She could see pictures on the walls, rugs on the floors, even curtains.

"Nope. She killed the marriage at the altar. Sent him a note with the preacher."

Molly moved upstairs with Callie Ann as Charlie told Wolf the details.

The first door they opened had two beds with a doll

in the center of one. "This must be your room," Molly said as Callie ran inside.

Alone, Molly moved to the next door and opened it. A large room with a fireplace framed in colorfully painted tiles greeted her. It was airy and friendly, as if it had been ordered from a catalog. Molly put her one bag of belongings down and clapped her hands together. This would do fine. Just fine.

Charlie had found a house that was right for her. She'd felt it welcome her the minute she'd crossed the threshold and from the entry she could see the four rooms downstairs. They consisted of a parlor, a kitchen, a dining room with windows overlooking the street, and a small study. Upstairs, there were enough bedrooms for both Early and Wolf as soon as the aunts left.

"I guess I bunk in here." Wolf clambered from behind her. He had his bedroll and the tin box Charlie had moved over from Granny's. "We can sleep in shifts."

Molly whirled, ready to argue, then realized he had no choice. He wasn't being bold, he was being practical. There were no other rooms. If he went to Granny's house, the town would know it within the hour. If he bunked downstairs, the aunts were sure to notice. She'd promised him a room as part of the bargain.

"Would you mind sharing?" she asked.

He lowered his gear slowly to the floor and placed the box atop a dresser.

Molly hurried to explain. "I wrote my aunts that I

was married, without bothering with the details. I thought if they ever did visit, you'd probably be off somewhere. Believe me, once you meet them, you'll understand why. But they're here and you're here. You can't very well stay at a boardinghouse. They seem to have settled in already, so I can't ask them to find a hotel."

"It's all right." Wolf brushed her arm lightly. "We'll work something out."

Molly swallowed hard and jumped as always into a decision. "No, it's not all right." She'd been debating this very thing in her notebook all morning. It was time to make up her mind before she got so old she had no mind left to make up.

Wolf frowned. "You want me to leave?"

"No." She lifted her hand and covered his heart. He was trying to do what she wanted. The problem was she couldn't decide herself.

"What exactly are you asking me, Molly?" Wolf raised an eyebrow, as if he wouldn't have been surprised to hear her say she wanted him to carry the aunts out bodily. "We can split the room down the middle if you like."

Molly took a deep breath and tried to say what she'd written. "Shifts would never work. Splitting the room wouldn't work." The thought that had been haunting her for days jumped to life. "I'm asking you to be my husband, which you already are, but be my real husband, at least while they're here. Share this room with me."

Molly closed her eyes. There, she'd said it as bold as you please.

Wolf was not a man who liked playing games. He'd played enough of them during the war and promised himself he'd stick with the simple truth. "I'm not sure I can stay in this room with you all night and not touch you. I may be your friend, but I'm also a man. Molly, you're asking the impossible."

"Then touch me, Wolf. You've been doing it all morning and I haven't backed away. I don't find your touch unpleasant, I never have. Watch me like you do already when you think I'm not looking. I think it's time we shared a room and a bed."

There she went again, changing the rules. Why was it he felt like their entire relationship had been a series of games? About the time he learned one, she switched to another.

She stared at him as though she thought the problem lay in his lack of understanding rather than with her rules. "Be my husband, at least until my aunts leave."

"Molly, you can't pretend marriage. You can't slice a piece of it off like it's a pie. Make up your mind what you want."

"I think I want a husband."

He could see the uncertainty in her eyes. And something else. A need. She was in uncharted water now.

"Are you sure?" He tried to show no sign of the storm his feelings were whirling into.

"No. But I like being married," she answered him. "I like being your wife. I like not being alone. I don't want to pretend anymore. I want you to stay in this room with me as my husband."

"I don't know," he mumbled. After last night, he'd never expected this. But here she was, blindsiding his heart again. "I'll probably get drunk and shoot myself for saying this, but I don't want to play marriage with you, Molly. I might be able to do it in separate rooms, but not under close quarters. I failed that test last night. It'd be more than touching."

Molly swallowed hard, fighting back tears. He was turning her down. For the rest of her life, she'd have nothing but a dream lover to hold her. Her make-believe husband didn't want to play make-believe marriage anymore.

Turning to the window, she lifted her chin and fought back a sob. "I thought you wanted me," she whispered, knowing she wasn't being fair. He'd offered to be her friend, he'd never offered more. Betting on his needs as a man wasn't right. But he'd said no. Even the need he had for her wasn't strong enough to make him stay. No man in her life had ever been strong or real enough to stay.

He moved behind her, so near she could feel the warmth of his body through her clothes. "Are you offering what I think you are?"

"I am," she said without turning. This was her one hand. She might as well bet it all. "If we're to have a marriage, then let it be a real marriage. I'll sleep with you. I'll not run away again. I promise."

Wolf would have sworn a month ago that this day, hearing her asking—begging—for a real marriage, would have been the happiest day of his life. But it wasn't. He wanted his Molly to come to him, not surrender.

Gently, he placed his hands on her shoulders.

If she'd been any stiller, he would have thought her made of stone. He felt like a warden handing out punishment. If he said no, he'd break her heart. If he said yes, he was sure his own would take a tumble.

"Are you sure, Molly?" He pulled her back against the wall of his chest. No matter what she said, he wanted to feel her against him when the blow hit.

"Yes," she whispered. "I want to live in the real world with a real husband. With a real marriage."

She couldn't know he understood what she meant. Molly was telling him she had to give up her dreams. She had to settle for him. His wife now delivered a double blow to his heart—saying good-bye to Benjamin and their perfect love—and accepting a loveless marriage with Wolf.

He wanted to yell at her and hold her at the same time. Couldn't she see that he was the lover she wanted so dearly and the friend she needed? She'd chosen Wolf over Benjamin, not out of love, but out of loneliness.

His head and his heart were at war. Part of him could never walk away. Part of him knew she was asking him to stay for the wrong reasons. But deep down he knew that even if he left right now, his heart would stay. And this time he wasn't sure he could leave her without dying inside.

"I'll be your husband," he whispered against her ear. "I'll be your real husband."

She twisted without leaving the circle of his arms and hugged him tightly, as if holding on for life. "Thank you," she mumbled.

He felt a tear as his cheek touched her face and wasn't sure if it was hers or his.

TWENTY

"WELL, ISN'T THAT THE SWEETEST THING YOU EVER saw, Henrietta?"

Molly pulled away from Wolf at the sound of her aunt's voice. She shoved a tear from her cheek and faced the two women, who, after sixty years of living together, resembled salt and pepper shakers. They were short, stout, and almost twins, except Alvina's hair was snow white and Henrietta's still held a touch of mousy brown.

As always, it was Aunt Alvina who headed toward her with open arms. The hug was too brief to be real and the kiss an inch short of touching Molly's cheek. Alvina's world revolved totally around Alvina and her way of proving herself perfect was to constantly point out flaws in others. "You look so thin, child. I'm sure you haven't been eating properly."

"It's nice to see you, too, Aunt Alvina." Molly wanted to laugh. In a strange way, her aunt never let her down with her criticism.

"I hoped you would be, child, after all we've been through to get here." Alvina absently straightened Molly's hair.

Another flaw Molly decided she'd almost forgotten was that Alvina still considered her a child. To Alvina Donivan, Molly would always be her brother's poor motherless child in need of help.

"I'm sorry the trip was trying. Maybe you should have let me make the journey to see you." Molly knew she was hoping, or maybe wishing, since they were already there. The aunts would do what they wanted, no matter what she said.

"The trip wasn't all that terrible," Aunt Henrietta said from the doorway. "It would have been passable if we'd run into competent help. From the conductor to the baggage men, we were surrounded by idiots."

Molly knew better than to try and hug Henrietta. The woman hadn't been touched in forty years, as near as Molly could figure. She'd been in love once, but the man, a farmer named Herbert Aldmen, hadn't measured up to her father or her brother. No one had measured up since.

Henrietta folded her hands at her waist like a choir member making a grand performance. "And who is this giant you're hugging? I hope to goodness it is your husband."

Molly had the feeling she'd be in for a lecture if it weren't, so she quickly announced, "Aunt Henrietta, Aunt Alvina, I'd like you to meet my husband, Captain Wolf Hayward."

Wolf stepped forward and politely took Aunt Alvina's hand. "A pleasure," he managed to say before Aunt Henrietta interrupted.

"You were a captain in the war, sir?" Henrietta wasn't about to draw near enough for the man to touch even her hand.

"With the Texas Rangers," Wolf corrected, showing no sign of being intimidated by the woman. "We're a group of lawmen who do everything from patrolling the border to protecting the frontier settlements. After the Union Army pulled out in 'sixty-one, the Rangers were just about the only law left in the state."

"How interesting." Alvina said the words so slowly it was obvious she was lying.

Wolf took Molly's hand in his. "Welcome to our house, ladies. We hope you enjoy your stay."

Henrietta grumbled about the heat and Alvina complained about how small their rooms were.

Wolf tightened his grip on Molly's hand. He'd tried, but now he was at a loss on what to say.

Molly squeezed his fingers and decided to save him. "Please, ladies, join me downstairs. I'd like to hear all about your trip."

They hurried out, but Henrietta paused at the door. "Do you always dress like that, Captain?"

"I'm afraid so," Wolf answered without a hint of apology in his voice.

Molly poked him in the ribs and laughed. The aunts who'd driven her crazy for years actually seemed funny with Wolf around.

He knew better than to stay. As soon as they reached the ground level, he informed them all that he had to go into work for a few hours and not to wait supper on him. Before Molly could react, he pulled her into his arms in full view of both aunts.

"Good-bye, darlin'. I'll be back as soon as I can." He kissed her on the mouth. She felt his lips spread into a smile as both aunts gasped.

Despite the aunts, Molly spent the day making the house her own. She had Charlie find the owner, then signed the papers before Wolf returned. He questioned why Wolf wasn't there, but she explained that he was busy. The cash convinced him all was in order, and he asked no more questions.

The aunts tolerated Callie Ann without truly under-standing why the child lived with Molly. They treated Early like hired help, which she didn't seem to mind. It would have been far more disturbing to the girl if the aunts had insisted on talking to her. Charlie fright-ened Alvina into such a state, she carried her smelling salts in her pocket in case she ran into him. Henrietta watched him as if fearing he might go mad and kill them all.

Despite Molly's father having been a doctor and a general, the aunts had seen very little of hospitals or war. They always approached the idea that Molly trav-eled with her father as weakness in Molly's mind. At first, they'd say things like "poor thing, thinks she has to go with him." Later, when the habit continued, they'd just shake their heads as though she were an alcoholic too far gone to pull the bottle away.

Charlie didn't take offense at their dislike of him. He started calling out from the porch instead of enter-

ing the house, though. When Molly asked him to stay
for supper, Alvina melted onto the parlor couch in a
faint. Charlie thanked Molly kindly and asked if he
could eat on the porch.

A moment later, Molly thought of taking a whiff of
the salts herself when Early offered to join him for
dinner.

Wolf didn't make it back home until late, and when
he did, Molly could see by the pain in his eyes that his
head ached. He was a powerful man, but she'd seen
him weak with fever and somehow felt closer to him
because of it. Once, if only for a few hours, he'd
needed her.

She set the meal she'd kept warm for him on the
table while he washed.

Henrietta stormed into the kitchen. "I thought I heard
you come in, Captain. Do you always come in so late?"

"No," Wolf answered politely. "Some nights I don't
come in at all."

She looked at Molly. "And you put up with this?"

"I'm afraid so." Molly smiled. "He's worth it, you
see."

Henrietta huffed. "Well, I would never tolerate such
disregard." She walked out of the room without so
much as a good-night.

"She'd have us divorced in a week," Wolf said.

"Less," Molly answered.

Alvina strolled through as though the kitchen were
on the way to her bedroom. She complained about several discomforts. When no one seemed to be listening,
she also disappeared upstairs.

"Where's the sad-eyed girl?" Wolf asked, accounting for each houseguest. Hoping they were finally alone.

"She's on the back porch with Charlie. I asked her to take him a blanket after she put Callie Ann to bed. When I checked, they were sitting in the dark, talking." Molly brushed against his shoulder as she poured milk.

"That's the best way to talk to Charlie." Wolf thanked her for the meal with a slight touch along her arm. "The aunts get used to him yet?"

"No. Henrietta told me they'll cut their first visit to Texas short. I suspect he has something to do with it."

Wolf looked hopeful. "Short, as in they are leaving tomorrow or the next day?"

Molly shrugged. "I've only known them to come for a 'short' visit once before."

"How long did they stay that time?"

"They came to my father's farm in 'forty-three, and they haven't officially left yet, so I'm not sure."

Molly laughed, but Wolf didn't catch the humor. She thought he looked too tired to eat, though he tried a few bites while watching her every movement.

"I'll be right back," Molly said, already running upstairs. She didn't have to glance back; she knew he stared at her.

A few minutes later, she returned, wearing her robe and carrying a strip of cotton. She'd thought it wise to change clothes before he shared the bedroom with her. Though she guessed it wouldn't matter after what he'd seen the night before.

Her hands began to shake at the thought that it was almost time for them to go upstairs. Together. She twisted the cotton in her fingers and moved toward him. "I'd like to put a clean dressing on that wound."

He studied her as if he thought she might like to twist the strip around his throat, but he didn't move.

She waited while he drank the last of his milk, then cut the bandage away with kitchen scissors.

As she patted the stitches clean of a few drops of dried blood, she felt his breathing change and knew he was aware of how close she stood above him. Almost touching, almost embracing.

"You smell wonderful," he said, trying to stay still while she worked. "Like all the good things that ever happened to me rolled up together and made into a perfume."

"You're healing nicely." She moved her fingers through his hair to push it back, not knowing how to respond to his words. "Does the wound still give you pain?"

"Some," he answered. "But right now I can't say I'm giving it much thought." He moved his hand along her waist to the center of her back.

"I could mix up something over at Dr. Washburn's office that would help with headaches."

"It'll ease," he mumbled, then closed his eyes and smiled as she continued to move her fingers through his hair. "I've been ordered to stay in town and rest for the next few days."

"That's for the best, dear." She used the endearment because that's what she should do. He was her husband, and if she were to be his wife she had to act the part.

"Why do you do that?" he asked, without opening his eyes.

"Do what?"

"Move your fingers through my hair."

Molly shrugged. "I don't know. It feels good."

Suddenly, he drew her close and buried his face into the fabric of her robe. "You feel good, so good to me, Molly."

As she'd promised, she didn't pull away.

"There is so much that needs saying." He guided her into his lap. "So much I'd like to tell you, but I don't know the words."

Molly tried to relax. "Maybe you should just say them. I'm a good listener."

He leaned close. "I like you being near. I like being able to touch you and hold you like this." He was lost for a moment in his thoughts. "After all the years of war and fighting, I need the peace I find when you're at my side."

She felt as if he'd given her a gift. She knew he was not a man of words, but somehow he'd managed. She wasn't sure she could answer. She did like the way his thick hair felt between her fingers, and she was growing used to the length. His beard was much shorter than when they'd met, and she was surprised to find it soft. She liked how she felt protected in his arms.

But what else could she tell this man? She didn't love him. She wasn't sure she ever would. But he was good and kind. It would only hurt his feelings if she told him that she'd wanted to be a real wife because she didn't want to end up like her aunts, living on yesterdays, dried up on life. He'd been a good friend. He'd be a good husband. But never the love of her heart.

Without a word, he stood and lifted her in his arms. He carried her upstairs and into their room as quietly as he could.

The bed had been turned back on one side and a lamp burned brightly on the nightstand. Wolf laid her down and touched her lips, silently asking her not to speak.

He closed the door and stripped to the waist. He could feel her watching him as he washed at the stand near the windows. Her things were on one side of the stand. She'd laid his on the other, including the razor and strop he carried but never used.

If he'd had a nightshirt, he would have worn one for the first time. He pulled off his gun belt and boots, but left his trousers on. He wasn't sure how much she'd want to see of him.

When he turned the lamp down, the last flicker of light caught in her eyes, bright and frightened.

"Are you sure you want this, Molly?" He couldn't touch her unless he was sure she was willing. "You don't have to do this to keep me here. I'll stick to our original bargain. The aunts need never know."

"I'm not doing this because of the aunts or anyone else in this town. I want you to touch me the way a man touches a woman."

He wanted to cry out, "Why?" But he wasn't sure he could bear to hear the answer. Sitting beside her, he tugged at her robe until it opened to reveal a plain white nightgown. She was so still, he couldn't tell if she breathed.

"Don't be afraid." He smoothed the robe away.

"I'm not," she lied.

"I would never hurt you."

"I know." A tear slipped from the corner of her eye and rolled into her hair.

He moved the back of his hand over her cheek. "Would you mind if I kissed you?"

"Will you shave?"

"No." He laughed as he lowered his mouth to hers. Ever so lightly, he kissed her lips. "But I'll be careful."

Molly moved an inch away. "Your beard tickles."

He gently pulled her mouth back to his. "You'll get used to it, darlin'." This time when he kissed her, she didn't turn away.

She'd expected to feel nothing, to offer only accep- tance, but when he kissed her a warmth spread through her. His lips were gentle, tender, not demanding as she'd felt before when he'd pulled her onto his horse to kiss her good-bye.

For a long while, he just kissed her, letting her grow used to him. She gripped handfuls of covers, preparing for what was to come. But nothing happened. He didn't touch her except with the kiss.

Finally, he rolled away. "Good night, Molly," he said with his back to her.

"Aren't you going to do more?" She could have been no more shocked if he'd slapped her. "I thought you wanted me."

Twisting onto his back, he lay beside her so long

she didn't think he was going to answer. Finally, he said, "I do want you, but it's no good unless you want me."

"I want you." She tried to sound convincing.

"No, you don't." He met her lie straight on. "You want to be married. Maybe you want to know what you missed by never marrying. Maybe you just don't want to die an old maid. I don't know, but one thing I do know is you don't want me."

"Yes, I do." She resented the accusation that she was just using him, even if he had voiced the very thoughts she'd written in her journal.

"I could be any man." His words were low and blended in anger and hurt. "Why don't you go get Charlie Filmore out on the porch? Anyone will do."

"No. I married *you.* I will sleep with you."

"Do you love me?" The words seemed to cut in his throat as he tried to get them out.

"I can learn." She tried, but she couldn't lie about that. "You are the man I want to spend the rest of my life with. Have children with. Grow old with."

She knew he didn't believe her and she called herself a hundred kinds of fool for trying to pretend a "real marriage." This marriage was no more real than her dreams of Benjamin had been.

"Molly?" he finally asked in a voice that sounded low and sad. "What color are my eyes?"

Tears flooded her view as she tried to see him through the shadows. She'd looked at him dozens of times. They'd eaten across from one another. She'd treated his wound only inches from his eyes. She'd seen him stare at her and felt him watching her. But if her life depended on it, she couldn't have sworn to the color of his eyes.

"What color are my eyes?" he said again.

She couldn't guess. What if she were wrong?

Wolf stretched across her and turned up the lamp. Warm brown eyes stared down at her with pain no wound to his body could cause.

"Brown," she whispered and closed her own eyes tight. *Brown!* she screamed inside. Brown, the same color as Benjamin's.

TWENTY-ONE

Wolf wasn't sure, but he thought neither he nor Molly slept all night. He fought the urge to comfort her as he lay only inches away. Several times, he thought of reaching out to Molly, pulling her into his arms and just holding her until dawn. But he couldn't. He knew if he did, he'd make love to her. He'd make her his forever.

He could see the washstand outlined against the window light. His razor and strop rested by the bowl. All he had to do was get out of bed and shave. She wanted Benjamin. She loved Benjamin. He could give her the man she waited for. He could play the role if it made her happy.

Or could he? She didn't love *him*. It was clear from her inability to answer about the color of his eyes, she didn't even look at him. How could he make love to her, or hold her, or even give her the part of him that was Benjamin, when she was willing to give herself to a man she didn't love? Him.

About dawn, Wolf decided she was mad, and it was contagious. If he had an ounce of sense left in his battered brain, he would've made love to her. Hell, he imagined it so often, the act should've been routine.

Only nothing had been routine since the day he found her in Austin. Why should the new day be any different? He rolled out of bed.

He knew she watched him. She was no more asleep than he had been all night. But he acted as if he were trying carefully not to wake her. He even picked up his jacket and boots and backed from the room without a sound, so she wouldn't guess he knew.

Aunt Henrietta sat in the hall chair like a guard. Wolf glanced up, and the surprise of seeing her so close almost made him drop his belongings.

"Do you always tiptoe out of a room at dawn, Captain Hayward?" Henrietta had a way of asking questions that reminded him of an interrogation.

"Old habits are hard to break." He winked.

She fought it, but a smile cracked her face into a thousand tiny wrinkles. "I guess it's none of my business, is it?"

"I'd say you're a very wise woman." On a good morning he woke up grumpy. This morning, without sleep, he was downright irritable.

Henrietta, however, seemed to be enjoying herself for the first time since she arrived. "I always have a respect for someone more blunt than me."

"I would guess, madam, you respect very few people."

This time she laughed out loud. "Truer words were

never spoken. The world is made up of fools and nit-wits. It's my job to point out the differences."

He groaned. He had to make an effort with Molly's aunts no matter how crotchety they were. After all, they were her only kin. "Care to accompany me down the street where we can have some breakfast?"

Her smile widened. "It's been a long time—a very long time—since a gentleman has asked me out. We might as well, Captain. It appears everyone else in this house plans to sleep 'til noon. A habit I find deplorable."

Wolf pulled on his boots without comment.

"You *are* planning to change clothes, sir?" She raised an eyebrow so high it almost disappeared into her hairline.

"I am not," he answered. "They wouldn't recognize me at the cafe if I dressed any differently."

"Then you'll shave," she responded. "A clean-shaven man is an honest man."

"Why do people keep asking me to shave?" Wolf mumbled. "No, Miss Henrietta, I do not plan to shave or change my habits to please anyone in this household. Do you wish to decline my invitation?"

"No." She glared at him as if he'd challenged her.

He wouldn't put it past her to sneak into his room one night and try to shave him to teach him a lesson.

He offered his arm and they marched down the stairs in silence. Ten minutes later they were eating at Noma's. Wolf ordered a half-dozen eggs and a pound of bacon with all the trimmings, including cinnamon rolls. Henrietta ordered one boiled egg and dry toast.

She was from the era when ladies ate like birds. Wolf noticed that when his basket of biscuits was delivered, she reluctantly took one after he insisted, then two, then one with gravy just to try Noma's cooking, then one with just butter and jam to be polite because he was still eating.

By the time the cinnamon rolls arrived, the bird appetite had flown. They split the basket.

An hour later, they walked home with a plate of rolls for the sleeping household. Henrietta took his arm but didn't try to make conversation. Wolf couldn't help but wonder what she'd be like if he took her to a saloon one night. But he figured even if he could get her to go, Molly would probably kill him.

For a moment, he saw the girl beneath the years. He could almost picture what she must've been like with her young lover. Wolf thought he saw sadness still etched into her eyes from the day she had to give up her Herbert.

As they reached the house, a thought rolled around in his mind. If he could charm Henrietta, surely he could do the same to Molly. He was older and wiser than he'd been on that train platform all those years ago. If he tried, he could make her love him and forget all about Benjamin.

Molly awoke gradually, feeling the warmth of the noonday sun in the shadowy bedroom. Someone had drawn the curtains and let her sleep.

She jumped out of bed as if she'd been caught in a

crime. Minutes later, she desperately tried to tie up her hair as she ran down the stairs.

"Good morning, Molly," Aunt Alvina's voice sang from the parlor where she sat surrounded by quilt squares.

"Good afternoon," Henrietta added.

"I'm sorry." Molly felt like a child again, facing her aunts. "I overslept."

"It's quite all right," Alvina assured her. "Your husband said you needed rest." The way she said the word *rest* seemed to be asking a question. "He told us to help Early look after Callie Ann."

"Told us, mind you. Ordered us to 'keep it down'— as if we were drunken troops and not two ladies. How much noise does he think we'll make piecing quilt squares?" Henrietta snapped. "And Alvina, stop hinting about Molly resting. It's too early in the marriage for that kind of thing to happen."

"The first one can come anytime, I've heard. It's the second one that takes nine months."

Molly couldn't believe they were talking about her as if she weren't standing in the room.

"Besides, it's the woman who has mood changes, not the husband."

"His mood hasn't changed," Henrietta retorted. "He's the bossiest man I've ever seen. Ordering us around."

"He did?" No one had dared give the aunts an order since her father died.

"He left you a note." Henrietta handed her a sealed envelope. "Didn't mention what was in it."

Molly slowly opened the note, almost expecting words of farewell. She wouldn't blame him. What kind of wife doesn't even know the color of her husband's eyes?

"What does it say?" Henrietta asked. "That is, if you don't mind us knowing."

Alvina frowned. "It wouldn't be proper for us to know, if it's a love letter."

Henrietta shook her head. "Why would a man who just left the woman two hours ago write her a love letter?"

"Why would he write one at all when he knew we'd be standing right here to tell her anything that needs telling?"

"Excuse me," Molly whispered as she turned back to the stairs. "I'll only be a minute."

She hurried to her room and closed the door. She would read no further with her aunts watching her. If he were ending their relationship, her aunts would be able to see it in her face. She couldn't bear that.

Wolf's handwriting was as bold and powerful as the man. "Dear Molly," he started. There were several lines where he began sentences and stopped, crossing out words. Halfway down the page a note read, "If either of us is to survive this marriage, we have to talk, alone. You said you can drive a team. I am counting on that being the truth. Follow the directions closely, and *be alone.*" The rest of the note contained carefully laid out instructions.

When Molly returned downstairs, the aunts bombarded her with questions, but she only said that all was in order and she had to meet Wolf concerning business. For once, they didn't push.

She stepped onto the porch, putting on her gloves. Charlie waited beside a borrowed buggy. Since the fire, she'd noticed him slowly sobering up, as if it took weeks to dry out after all the years of drinking. People respected what he'd done, saving her life. With that respect came responsibility. Folks even spoke to him on the street, and he was expected to answer. A man who's a hero has to act the part.

He told her Wolf had asked him to have a wagon or buggy ready for her when she came outside.

Molly climbed in and headed west toward a place called Barton Springs. The horse pulling the buggy was an old nag. She had to keep a firm grip on the reins to turn. Molly guessed Charlie chose the horse because there was no question of such an ancient animal running away with the buggy.

On the road to the springs, she passed wagonloads of folks who'd spent the noontime enjoying a swim. She barely glanced at them. Wolf wouldn't be in the crowd. Whatever he planned to say, he wanted to say in private, or he wouldn't have struggled over the note.

Finally, the road became little more than a trail winding between trees with branches that touched the ground in heavy summer growth. She spotted Wolf standing alone on a rise a quarter mile past the springs. His hands rested on his hips, his feet wide apart. He looked like a giant facing her as if about to go to battle. He wore black trousers covered to the knees with the strange moccasins and a white shirt that made his shoulders seem even broader than usual.

Molly pulled the buggy into the shade and walked slowly toward him. She'd face what he had to say head-on. It was long past time they talked.

The warm breeze caught loose curls around her face. She could hear people splashing in the water. She was too far away to understand words, but their laughter drifted on the air.

He waited until she was within a few feet of him before he spoke. "I thought we could talk here." He sounded almost gruff. "There are things that need saying between us. I tried to write them, but I couldn't find the words."

"I agree," she answered, wondering if he could say the words any easier than he could write them. "But could we move to the shade?"

He nodded and apologized for not thinking of it.

To her surprise, he took her hand and led her slowly into the shadows, as if they were on a Sunday walk and not about to decide their futures. A fallen trunk offered a natural bench beneath a canopy of green. She sat down, thinking of how the shade softened everything around her. Maybe it would soften his words.

He straddled the log and waited as though she was the one who'd called the meeting. He looked tired and she guessed his head must still pound. Instinctively, she brushed her hand across his hair. "Are you feeling all right?"

"Yes." He closed his eyes, not wanting her to see how much he enjoyed her simple touch.

"Where do we begin?" she asked.

Wolf watched her. He didn't want to begin at all. He only wanted to hold her, but they had to talk. "I'll be thirty next year."

"I'll be twenty-seven. But don't tell the aunts I'm out giving away my age. If twenty marks old-maid status, I must be considered more dead than alive." She continued to move her fingers through his hair.

"We're not kids, Molly. Too old to be making fools of ourselves."

"I agree."

"Do you want this marriage to end?" He could barely make himself say the words.

Molly lifted her chin. "No," she said simply.

Wolf relaxed at her side. "Neither do I," he admitted. "But, after last night, I wasn't sure."

"I know," Molly whispered. "Wolf, I need to talk to my friend."

Wolf watched her closely. "Who?" As far as he knew, she had no close friends in town.

"You," she answered. "I need to talk to my honest and true friend about . . ."

"About anything," he promised.

"About my husband." She smiled.

"All right. Let's talk about the scoundrel."

"He's not a scoundrel, he's a good man. The best man I may have ever met. Only he doesn't want to sleep with me."

Wolf heard the sadness in her voice and it shattered his heart.

She stared at her hands as she continued, "He thinks

I don't love him, but I respect him. Doesn't that count for something?"

Wolf's hand covered hers. "But why him?" He spread his fingers wide as she threaded her hands through his. He couldn't help but wonder if she liked touching him as dearly as he loved her touch.

"He makes me feel alive. All my life I've day-dreamed about life. He makes me want to experience it. He takes big bites out of life." She looked up. "How do I make him want me?"

She met his eyes, his brown eyes. How could she have not noticed them a thousand times before?

"You wouldn't have been making love to me last night, Molly, but to just someone."

His words stung. Suddenly, she wished there were somewhere to go, something to do other than stare at him. Maybe it was better to miss life. To be an old maid. To never have a lover. It couldn't be more pain-ful than what she was going through. "You said you wanted me, but you didn't." The memory of the way he'd turned away from her still hurt. "When it came time and I said yes, you didn't touch me."

She stood. She couldn't bear to relive the rejection all over. The one time she'd offered herself to a man and he'd turned her down.

Wolf caught her arm and pulled her back so quickly, a cry escaped from her. She landed across his legs, locked in his arms.

"I wanted you!" he said as he stopped her protest with a powerful grip. "I still want you. I need you so badly my entire body aches for you, Molly."

"Don't lie to me." No man had ever made her feel less wanted.

His mouth closed down on hers so quickly, she didn't have time to say more. His kiss was hard and demanding, as though he planned to prove his point with actions and not words.

She struggled against him, fighting his advance, but he grew more determined. He held her hair in a tight fist, while his other hand roamed over her body, branding her with his touch as no man ever dared.

Anger fired her protest. She tried to jerk away, more furious than frightened. This wasn't the way she wanted to be loved. This wasn't the way Benjamin would have done it. Wolf had it all wrong.

Wolf didn't bother to hold her arms. The hits she pounded over him hardly registered. When she kicked at his leg, he shifted and her shoe only struck the log.

He'd prove his passion to her. He pulled her tight against him so that she could feel his need for her. His kiss was wild and hungry, demanding, leaving no doubt of his desire.

She jerked suddenly and pulled her mouth free. "Stop!" she yelled as her slap landed hard against the side of his face. "Stop!"

It took a moment for her cry to register. Wolf let her go so fast she tumbled backward. His arm caught her before she hit the ground. Gently, he lifted her up.

She shoved his hands away. "What do you think you're doing?"

"I was kissing you with passion. I thought that's what you wanted."

"I might have wanted to be kissed, but not attacked."

He sat on the log and stared at his hands, wondering if he should try again or stop while he was behind. She was telling him she wanted him as she shoved him away. "I'm not real practiced at lovemaking, Molly. The few times I've paid for a woman's company I found the experience hollow. I must be reading the signs wrong."

She swallowed and tried to straighten her clothes as she only half listened. Her blouse front was hopelessly torn and her hair had tumbled. "Practiced. Practiced! I'd say you never made it through the first grade." Her anger built like a summer storm. "If you'd held me any tighter, I'd be dead right now. My cheeks feel sunburned from having your whiskered face rubbing against them. My ribs are bruised. I don't own enough clothes to have you ripping them off me."

Wolf looked up at the sparkling light filtering through the branches. Surely, he could do better. If she'd ever give him another chance. The way she was yelling didn't sound like she was falling in love with him.

She tried to pull her hair in order. "I want to be made love to, not ravished. I feel like I've wrestled a bear."

"Why?" he interrupted her tantrum.

"Why what?" she answered.

"You still haven't explained why you want *me* to make love to you. You don't love me. I'm not even sure you like me most of the time, so why me? Surely there were men who suited you better back home."

Molly was too angry to hesitate. "No! Wolf Hay-

ward, you're the best I could find. Which doesn't speak
well of the male race. I picked you because I want to
live in the real world. I've spent my whole life dreaming, waiting for a man who didn't come back for me.
Well, I'm through waiting. I want someone to hold me
in more than my fantasies."

He finally lowered his gaze and glared at her with a
mixture of determination and rage. "I can be the man
you want me to be, but only if you can love *me.*"

The walls of Jericho tumbled in Molly's mind, and
for the first time she saw Wolf clearly. She'd been so
busy looking for a substitute for Benjamin, a fill-in for
the lover she'd never have, that she hadn't seen the
man before her.

She'd tried all her life to be the daughter her father
wanted, the niece her aunts insisted she be. None of it
had made her happy. She felt suffocated and a disappointment to all. When she'd finally broken free and
come to Texas, she'd found peace. Being a failure here
was better than being a success at what other people
wanted her to be.

Molly took a step toward him and touched his hair
as she sat beside him. When he stared at her, she saw
frustration fill his eyes. "You don't have to be anything,
or anyone, for me, Wolf. You're a fine man just as you
are."

"Are you saying you could learn to love me?"

Molly couldn't lie. She'd loved foolishly once. She
didn't want to step out again. The fall was too great.
She opened her mouth to answer, but didn't know how
to tell him that she'd given up on love altogether.

"I guess you just gave me your answer." Wolf hardened before her eyes. "I'll be your husband, Molly, but I'll not sleep beside you until you can say you love me. A mating between us wouldn't work otherwise. We've proved that last night and just now."

"Why can't you just love me?" she asked.

"Why can't you say the words?" he answered.

She saw something in his eyes that made her wonder if he'd ever heard a woman tell him she loved him. How could three words hold such importance?

Her hands slowly raked through his dark curls. "Maybe we could just start over, like we just met."

He shook his head. "I've been a loner too long. I, apparently, don't know the first thing about what a woman wants, and I'm not sure I have the days left in this lifetime to understand you."

She heard his every word, but she also noticed he didn't pull away from her touch. "I probably know less than you do."

Wolf laughed. "A fine pair we are." He brushed her cheek with his knuckle. "I didn't hurt you before, did I? You have to believe that was not my intent."

"No," she lied, thinking she'd be breathing shallow for a week.

He gently put her hand in his.

Molly accepted his silent apology and leaned closer, touching her lips to his. He didn't respond, but he didn't move back.

"Come on." She smiled and pulled him with her as she stood. "Let's go home."

"I meant what I said, Molly," Wolf repeated.

She didn't answer. She just kept walking and smiling, thinking of an old saying she'd heard once: It takes a lot of practice to teach a bear to dance. Wolf could say anything he wanted to, but she planned to start practicing. If he wanted her, she'd make him forget about her having to promise love. She never planned to love again, but she aimed to have Wolf Hayward in her bed.

TWENTY-TWO

By the time Molly returned the buggy to Charlie, she'd made up her mind. She didn't care what Wolf Hayward said. She wasn't going to lie about love to get him in bed. And she *was* going to sleep with him if she had to tie him down in order to do so.

The only problem was she had no idea how she might accomplish such a goal. But she had until dark to come up with a plan. He was willing; he just didn't know it yet.

As soon as Molly got home, she knew the aunts were in a tizzy. Aunt Henrietta had made Miss Early cry by criticizing the meals, and Aunt Alvina was running around like a madwoman because she'd decided to have a dinner party. She'd invited the banker she'd met an hour before, his wife, the preacher who'd married Molly, and, of course, his wife.

"How can I plan a menu with Early crying?" Alvina whined before Molly could pull off her gloves. "She won't even talk to me about the courses to be served."

Molly brushed Callie Ann's blond curls as the little princess tugged on her skirt for attention. "Early is a guest in this house, Aunt Alvina, not a cook. I can help with the cooking."

Alvina frowned. "I've tasted your cooking. Your offer to help only makes matters worse."

If Molly hoped to calm Alvina, she was greatly disappointed. The little woman started circling like a medicine man in a rain dance.

"I have guests coming to dinner and no cook," she kept chanting. "I'll have my hands full finding flowers and setting the table, but a lot of good it will do without anything to eat."

"Well, it can't be helped," Aunt Henrietta announced matter-of-factly. "I can cook better with one finger than that girl can with both hands. Someone had to tell her she's no chef. We couldn't go on letting her believe we enjoyed what she served. I had to inform her that her meals were better suited for a trough."

Callie Ann tugged again at Molly's skirts. Early's sniffling sounded from behind the kitchen door.

Molly patted Callie Ann's hand gently.

Her aunts suddenly turned and glared at Molly.

Henrietta raised her eyebrow. "This is your house, dear. You're the one who has to do something."

"All right," Molly answered, wondering why it was her house when there was a problem but not when the decision to have a dinner party was made. "Early, would you take Callie Ann to eat at Noma's tonight? My treat."

Early poked her head around the door and smiled,

spotting the light at the end of the tunnel. "I'd love to. But I never ate at a cafe. I don't know if I'll know how to act."

"Callie Ann will show you." Molly looked down at the girl still trying to get her attention. "Won't you, dear?"

The little girl nodded as she tried to pull Molly to her level.

"But—" both aunts began in unison.

"Aunt Henrietta"—Molly faced them both, thinking how frightened she used to be of displeasing them— "I'm sure you'll cook a grand meal, and Alvina's guests will enjoy it."

On rare months there's a double full moon. Once in a million times a calf is born with two heads. Now, for the first time in her life, Molly saw her aunts turn on one another.

Molly grabbed Callie Ann and backed from the room. Early pulled her head into the kitchen like a turtle hearing thunder. Molly could still detect rumblings from their battle when she and Callie Ann reached the porch swing. The princess climbed into her lap as they swayed.

"What is it?" Molly gave the child her full attention.

"I think Uncle Orson wants to move to the barn, but we haven't got a barn. He says he's darn tired of listening to the hens."

Molly laughed, knowing Callie repeated something she'd heard an adult say. "I don't blame him. Would he like to go with us to see how my store is coming along?"

Callie leaned her head over. "Can we stop by and see Mr. Wolf?"

"If you like," Molly answered. They jumped off the swing and hopped down the steps without a backward glance toward the house.

The afternoon was warm but cloudy enough to offer some relief from the sun's glare. They took their time shopping and visiting with Miller about the construction. When they reached the Ranger office, both were ready to sit for a spell.

"Captain!" a young ranger shouted when Molly and Callie Ann stepped inside the main room. "Your wife is here!" His words held a hint of alarm.

For a moment, Molly thought the aunts' troubles might have reached the office. If so, she wouldn't blame Wolf for hiding. Then she saw the frowns on the men's faces as they stood around the main room. Something was seriously wrong. A gun case near the door had been unlocked, the rifles lined a table. The sound of a gun being loaded clicked behind her.

"What is it?" she asked, looking from face to face. Rangers were a solemn lot to start with, but today they seemed to have turned to stone.

Someone behind Molly whispered, "Thank God, she has the child."

Molly kept her hand on Callie Ann's shoulder and moved closer to Wolf's office door. "What's happened?" she asked when she spotted him coming toward her.

Wolf lifted Callie Ann in his arms as he shook his head slightly at Molly. "Hello, Princess. How are things at the castle? Have the dragons taken over yet?" His voice was deceptively calm, unhurried.

"The aunts are fighting something terrible," Callie Ann answered. "We may have to throw water on them. Uncle Orson wants to move someplace where there's less noise. He says he can't take it." She obviously liked having the adults' attention. "Aunt Henrietta said she didn't believe in him, but that's okay 'cause Uncle Orson doesn't believe in her, either."

Several of the rangers muffled their chuckles.

Wolf tossed Callie Ann's curls. "Would you and Uncle Orson do me a great favor? I don't have any more cookies in my jar, and Josh doesn't know which ones to buy at Noma's. You know, though, don't you?"

Callie Ann nodded as Wolf handed her the jar.

"Would you go with Josh to get some more cookies? I'll keep an eye on Molly while you're gone. You can pick a cookie to eat when you get back."

"Two," she bargained.

"All right, two." Wolf laughed, thinking she'd been around Charlie Filmore too long.

Callie Ann stared at Josh. "You have to carry me. I'm too tired to walk. But I have to carry the jar."

Josh stepped forward, looking very much like a man who was about to be bossed around by a five-year-old. He glanced at Wolf for help, but Wolf simply thanked him.

Josh lifted Callie Ann awkwardly onto his arm and grabbed his hat. Two other rangers decided they could do with a walk to Noma's as well and followed Josh.

When they disappeared, Molly faced Wolf. She

knew there was trouble but was afraid to ask again.

Without a word, Wolf took her arm and led her to his office. He tried not to look in her eyes. He wanted to keep what he had to say official before rage, greater than he'd ever known, broke out inside him.

"We uncovered something about the fire at your place," he said in low tones as he offered her a seat.

Molly's back was rod straight as she sat down. "Yes?" she breathed the word. This wasn't going to be good news.

"It was set, as we figured. The door had been blocked from the outside and no one could have run through the front to safety the way it caught fire within seconds. Whoever did it knew what they were doing and planned to kill."

"Me?" Molly tried to think of anyone who would want her dead. "Someone's trying to kill me?"

"No," Wolf answered, forcing his words out slowly. "Someone wanted Callie Ann dead."

Molly was on her feet and in front of him before he could add more. "No! You're wrong! No one would want to kill her." She fought down a scream—*It was me, someone wanted to kill me, not her*. The idea that someone would burn a child alive was too horrible even to imagine.

Wolf gently placed his hands just above her elbows. "We've got two witnesses who overheard a conversation earlier that night. A stranger in town, who called himself Black, was offered quite a bit of money to see that a little girl went up in flames. You just happened to be in the way when he went to work."

"Did you find this man? Did he admit to such a thing? It doesn't make sense." She shook her head. The witness had to be lying. No one! No one could burn a child.

Wolf pulled her against him and held her as he spoke. "They found Black dead the day after the fire. His throat slit from ear to ear. He'd been strung up like a hog to bleed out. It took two days dragging every barmaid and prostitute in town to see the body, but finally someone recognized him and related the story. A saloon girl over at Tandy's and a gambler were sitting nearby when the deal was made over several rounds of drinks. An argument over price drew their attention, so they listened in. They both swore they thought 'the little girl' was some kind of code for a bank job or a stage robbery. They didn't believe the men really plotted to kill a child."

"The man who paid to have Callie Ann killed is still alive?"

"That's right, darlin'. The saloon girl said the man with Black was bone thin with a face weathered and tanned. He kept referring to his 'bosses,' like he worked for more than one man. He was just a middleman hiring the killer. He paid Black the first half in silver that night. I can think of only two men who might have a strongbox full of silver."

Molly looked up and waited.

"The Digger brothers." He said the names as if they were swear words. "The stage they robbed a few months ago was carrying silver. When we found Black's body, his pockets were empty except for a handful of matches. The Diggers don't give away their money easily. Or maybe they figure he failed and deserved to die."

"But why would they want to kill their own kin? She couldn't hurt anybody. Callie Ann doesn't even know about them."

"I can't say, but I aim to find out. We've had word that since they think they got me off their trail for good, the brothers are headed this way to finish the job themselves this time. I figure they'll come after me first, as soon as word gets out that I'm still alive. Then Callie Ann. Anyone standing near her will be killed. The Diggers don't like leaving witnesses."

He kissed her forehead. "I have to get you and Callie Ann hidden away somewhere safe."

"No." Molly shook her head. "They could be watching the roads. Someone might be watching us right now and reporting back. If we leave, we'll be sitting ducks."

Wolf had to admit she might be right. Someone had helped the Diggers escape the night of the fire. That same someone could be following Molly and Callie Ann's movements right now, waiting for a chance to catch them alone. If Wolf sent them by stage, half the town would know it. In a buggy, they'd face all kinds of threats on the open road. "I agree," he finally decided. "You're safer here, for now."

Molly hugged him tightly. "We'll be safest beside you. I know it."

"Behind me," he corrected, for if the Diggers got past him to Molly or the girl, he'd be dead.

By the time Callie Ann returned with the cookies,

plans were made. Two rangers would be stationed outside Molly's house at all times. Another would sleep
in the parlor. If the outlaws were true to form, they'd
strike at night. Wolf would go to work each morning
as usual, then double back and watch the house. Molly
and Callie Ann were to stay inside and away from the
windows until the Diggers made their move.

"When do you think they'll come after us?" Molly
whispered to Wolf as they watched Callie Ann passing
out cookies to everyone in the main room.

"The soonest we figure will be tonight, about dinnertime. But don't worry, I'll have you home by then."

"Dinnertime!" Molly jumped to her feet. "I forgot.
The aunts! What are we going to do about the aunts?"

Wolf didn't answer. There was no easy answer.

Josh looked up from where he sat cleaning his Colt.
"Red or sugar?" he asked casually.

Molly rolled her eyes and sat back down. She almost
felt sorry for the brothers if they bothered the aunts.
Somehow two bloodthirsty outlaws and her two aunts
didn't seem like a fair fight. The outlaws would need
reinforcements.

TWENTY-THREE

Wolf stormed and shouted and raged, but Aunt Alvina stood her ground. She'd never canceled a dinner party in her life, and she wasn't about to now. The fact that the drapes were covered, an armed ranger sat in the parlor, and Charlie Filmore was making his bed in the kitchen didn't deter her.

Henrietta wasn't surprised at the troubling news. Most people were low-life outlaws to her way of thinking, anyway. What difference did two more in this world make? Henrietta was practical, however. She loaded every chamber in her pocket sidehammer, made by a family friend, Mr. Samuel Colt. Then she calmly told her sister not to worry, she'd take care of anyone who barged in on their party.

Miss Early finally stopped crying and helped with dinner, with the understanding that she and Callie Ann could eat at the little table in the kitchen with Charlie. Molly had feared she might run when trouble came, but Early proved to be a true friend.

Wolf, on the other hand, became a bear. He grumbled and stomped around the house, refusing to cooperate in any way with even the idea of having a party. As the dinner hour grew near, Alvina decorated and Wolf fortified.

By the time everyone sat down to the charred remains of Henrietta's cooking, Wolf wasn't even speaking a language any longer. He watched the window and listened for every sound, paying no attention to the dinner conversation. He ate nothing but kept his hand ready near his weapons.

Molly tried to keep the peace. She answered for him when the preacher or the banker asked questions and complimented both her aunts repeatedly.

The preacher didn't seem to notice anything amiss. After meeting Wolf when he performed their wedding, he wouldn't have been surprised by anything the giant did. The banker, however, had a great respect for the legendary Wolf Hayward and tried to draw him into conversation. He would have loved to go home with a Captain Hayward story to tell his friends.

The aunts made up for Wolf's silence. They volleyed small talk between them with practiced ease. By the time the guests left, everyone was exhausted. The aunts mumbled a good-night and left the dishes on the table. Something Molly had never seen them do.

Callie Ann had already been put to bed, and Miss Early was in the kitchen drinking coffee with Charlie.

Molly watched Wolf check the locks for the fifth time, then take up his post at the top of the stairs where a window overlooked the back of the house. Wolf propped a rifle on either side of it and placed a chair so that he could see out without being seen.

She changed into her nightgown and robe, then joined him. "Everything's finally quiet," she whispered as she moved to his side.

Wolf didn't turn from the window. "Mmmm," he mumbled.

She leaned against his shoulder. "Are you angry?"

"No." He slipped his arm around her waist, hungry for her nearness. "I'm just trying to keep you, and everyone else in this house, safe. I've seen what the Diggers can do. If they plan anything in town, it'll be after dark."

Molly touched his hair lightly. "My father and his father were both military men. We Donivan women are used to taking care of ourselves."

Wolf caught her hand and held it. "I can't take that chance." He said the words more to himself than to her. "I'd give my life for you."

Molly knelt beside his chair. "I know," she whispered. "That's what frightens me." How could she tell him she didn't deserve the kind of love and devotion he offered? She had the feeling if she gave him all her love, it would only be a drop in the ocean compared to what he would give her in return.

As she rested her head against his leg, his hand spread over her hair. "I like your hair down," he said without looking at her.

Molly closed her eyes. It seemed they'd had so little time to talk. "Wolf, why do you watch me so closely? I feel your gaze whenever we're in the same room.

Even at dinner tonight, you stared at me like I was the only one there."

"You *were* the only one there," he answered.

He brushed his fingers along the side of her face. "I know we have this unspoken agreement not to talk about the war."

Molly nodded. She knew, as a Southerner, he must have fought for the Confederacy. She didn't want to know more. What if he'd been at the battle where her father had been killed? She couldn't face knowing.

Wolf continued, "But during the war, I saw so many horrible things. Scenes that I won't live long enough to forget."

He paused, his hand caressing her face, his eyes fixed on the thin sliver of an opening between the curtains.

"It wasn't just the death and dying, but the senseless destruction. I saw Atlanta burn and miles of farmland stained with blood. I saw families torn apart and a way of life destroyed. Men whose ancestors fought in the American Revolution were left crippled and homeless overnight. Thousands who'd never owned a slave returned to watch their land sold for taxes and the right to vote taken away from them."

Molly pressed her cheek against his palm. She hadn't really thought about what it must have been like for the Southern soldier returning home. In her town, there had been bands to meet each train and parties to welcome them home. She'd heard Rebel supplies had dwindled toward the end of the war and that soldiers sometimes fought barefooted.

"I'm telling you this not to make you sad, Molly, but to let you know that when I look at you—every time I look at you—for a moment I forget."

Molly kissed his hand. "That's the most wonderful thing anyone has ever said to me."

He looked down at her and cupped her face. "Don't you know, Molly? If something happened to you, there would be no beauty left in the world."

His palm caught her tear. She had no idea he cherished her so. She rose to her knees beside him.

"Go to bed, darlin'."

"Come with me."

He closed his eyes slowly, as though he couldn't say the words looking at her. "I can't."

"Then kiss me good night."

His free arm encircled her, and he drew her gently against him. His kiss was tender with longing. When he pulled away, Molly didn't move.

"Good night," he whispered and stared back at the window, mentally returning to his job.

Molly swallowed, trying to make herself stand. She wanted to ask, even beg, for him to kiss her again, but he'd already turned away.

She stood slowly and walked to their room. One of these nights he wasn't going to turn away, she thought, and what would she do with him then?

The clock downstairs chimed half past the hour as she crawled into bed. She left the door open so she could see him guarding her. Wolf propped his foot on the windowsill and leaned back in the chair. A rifle rested across his lap. He'd give his life for her, she thought. His life.

Molly closed her eyes and dreamed of dancing, not with Benjamin, but with Wolf. They waltzed across a marbled floor while all the other dancers circled the fringes, watching. The candlelight blurred into streaks as Wolf lifted her off her feet, and they whirled. The women wore flowing dresses made from yards and yards of silk, as they had been before the war effort. The men were polished and regal in their blue uniforms.

In her dream, Molly looked down at Wolf as he lifted her higher and higher. His brown hair barely touched his collar, his beard was cut close against his strong jaw, the bars on his uniform reflected the light, twinkling like gold stars.

She couldn't help but smile down at him. He stared at her as though she were the only woman in the world and this night was the only night he'd lived.

Like faraway thunder, the stomping of advancing troops invaded her dream, drowning out the music. Wolf lowered her to the marble and ran as the beat of marching soldiers became deafening. Molly called to him as a single shot rang across the dance floor. A scream pulled the air from her lungs. The bullet hit him, and he crumbled. With her terror, the dream turned foggy. She ran to him, crying so much she could hardly see his body curled on the floor. A circle of blood stained the marble.

As she knelt to roll him over to see his face, her fingers touched the torn, dirty gray uniform he wore.

Hands from all directions reached for her, pulling her away. Molly fought and struggled, trying to stay close to Wolf. She screamed, but still they tugged at her. Her fingers felt the fabric give way as her cries echoed around the great hall.

"Darlin'?" a low Southern voice whispered into her dream. "Darlin'?" He made the single word sound musical.

Molly opened her eyes wide and stared up at Wolf leaning over her. For a moment, reality mixed with her dream.

"I heard you crying out. Are you having a nightmare?" Wolf asked as though he knew nothing of her terror, as though he hadn't been there.

"You've left your post." She pulled herself up on her elbows.

"Yes, but it's all right. Josh stomped up the stairs a few minutes ago. I'm surprised he didn't wake you. He's taking over for a while."

She stared at him, forcing the dream into the shadows of her mind.

"If you've no objection, I'll stretch out here and get a few hours of sleep before dawn." He lay back, but she could tell his body wasn't relaxed.

Molly rolled close to him, surprised that he hadn't removed his Colts. "I dreamed we were dancing."

"I don't know how to dance," Wolf mumbled, already half asleep.

"Then I'll teach you." Smiling, Molly placed her hand over his heart.

His hand covered hers, and she felt him relax.

"Sleep," she whispered. "I'll watch over you."

The aunts were packed and ready to leave when Molly awoke the next morning. Henrietta had decided this Texas was too wild a place for her. She missed her teas and garden parties.

By the time Molly sat down to breakfast with the two of them, the lecture was well under way. "You must come back with us," Henrietta stated, "and that's all there is to it. No one in her right mind would stay in a state where she's been burned out, threatened, and kept prisoner in her own home."

Molly tried not to listen. She'd learned years ago that arguing with her aunt was a waste of time. Henrietta's ears only worked when she was the one talking.

"This child, Callie Ann, isn't even yours, you know. She got along just fine before you came, and she'll get along when you leave."

Pouring herself a cup of coffee, Molly was thankful Callie Ann still slept.

"Your mother left you enough money and a fine house," Alvina added as if they were simply having a chat and it was her turn. "Henrietta and I won't always be around to take care of it for you. There is no need for you to work."

Molly guessed long ago that the aunts had nowhere else to go. They'd often said their parents had left them enough money to live on, so they didn't have to accept some inferior offer of marriage. But Molly knew it wasn't enough to live in the style they enjoyed now.

Her father always referred to Allen Farm as Molly's house. For as long as she could remember, he'd told her that her mother had gone to Heaven early, but she'd left Molly a home that would always be hers. The rambling three-story was large enough to offer each aunt a suite of private quarters. Though it was called Allen Farm, it had never been a working farm. As far as Molly was concerned, it was no longer her home.

"Molly!" Aunt Henrietta shouted. "You must give up this impossible dreaming and come back home with us. You can't seriously consider living in this place"— Henrietta waved her arm as if pointing at a slum— "with a man who doesn't even know how to dress for dinner."

She strutted and gestured like a tour guide. "There's an armed stranger in the parlor and a horrible creature sleeping in the kitchen."

"We're safe enough now that it's daylight." Molly hoped her words would reassure the aunts, but they weren't listening.

"Henrietta, don't forget to mention a cook who can't cook," Alvina added. "And no housekeeper at all."

Molly heard Wolf moving down the stairs almost without a sound. Both aunts jumped when he suddenly appeared in the doorway.

"Coffee?" Molly asked Wolf, as if she weren't in the middle of a debate.

Wolf took a chair at the dining table, pushing aside the dessert plates from last night.

When Molly handed him a mug, he set it down carefully before pulling her gently onto his lap. "Morning." He smiled.

She liked the way he touched her so easily. No one had ever dared. She knew he was getting used to the nearness of her, just as she was of him. He looked even more rugged than he had last night. His eyes were warm as they watched her. His arm protected her from the world as it rested around her waist. Maybe he didn't know how to dress for dinner, but he knew how to make her feel safe and cherished.

"Are you two aware there are other people in the room?" Henrietta snapped.

"No," Wolf answered. He leaned slightly and kissed Molly on the lips.

Molly laughed, knowing he teased the aunts. If he hadn't come to the table so well armed, she might have thought of warning him. "Want breakfast?"

He nodded as she stood.

Henrietta cleared her throat. "We've decided Molly will be returning with us, Captain, so you will need to purchase three tickets on the stage leaving this afternoon." She turned back to Molly. "We'll be happy to help you pack. Though I doubt you have anything worth taking back since the fire. The clothes you've been wearing couldn't have been made for you."

Wolf never took his gaze off his wife. "And what did Molly decide?"

"I'm staying," she answered. "Someone has to watch over you."

He winked at her. "Then I guess my wife is staying, ladies."

"I don't think that will be the case, Captain," Henrietta started. "We've—"

Wolf gulped down a drink of coffee. "End of discussion," he said, as he watched Molly move toward the kitchen.

The aunts had never been addressed in such a manner and complained all the way to the stagecoach station. Wolf helped them both embark as Molly stood a few feet away, waving. She couldn't believe she'd won so easily and half feared they might try to pull her in if she stepped within an arm's reach of the coach.

Just before the stage rocked into action, Wolf patted it twice, the way a man would a horse. Molly watched the action curiously. A memory stirred from years ago. The gesture would have gone unnoticed if Wolf had been on horseback, but somehow it seemed strange now. And somehow familiar.

TWENTY-FOUR

M OLLY WATCHED THE STAGE DISAPPEAR FROM VIEW. She felt like a part of her life was gone forever. She might see her aunts again, maybe even visit Allen Farm, but it wouldn't be the same. Her years of daydreaming were over. There was much to be done.

"We'd better get back." Wolf offered his arm as the wind kicked up dustdevils in the street and distant thunder rumbled like gunfire.

"They're really not so bad," she whispered.

"Really?"

Molly laughed. "Okay, they are so bad, but they mean well. I think I'm finally starting to understand something my father once said. 'Happiness in life comes in the production, not the consumption.' My aunts have always been consumers; they'll never understand my need to work. They only want what's best for me."

"I know," Wolf said with all seriousness. "That's why I didn't kill them."

For a second, Molly almost believed him. He looked like a man who could carry out any threat he made. She shoved him hard with her elbow when she recognized his lousy attempt at humor.

To her surprise, he pushed her back, though his hand steadied her so there was no chance she would fall.

They walked down the street like two drunks locked arm in arm as they elbowed one another off the walk. She was playing with the bear again, she thought, only she wasn't sure who was teaching whom.

As they turned the corner and headed home, huge raindrops plopped around them, creating tiny individual puddles. Clouds moved in fast, shoving morning into shadows. Wolf quickened his pace and offered his arm as shelter.

Molly noticed Charlie Filmore sitting on the front porch a second before Wolf did. The little man held his head with bloody hands as he yelled for help.

Molly started running first, but Wolf passed her in only a few steps. When he reached Charlie, his Colts were drawn. While Molly knelt by the little man, Wolf circled into the house, his keen gaze missing nothing.

"Charlie!" Molly tried to get him to release his head so she could see the damage. "Charlie! What happened? Let me help you." She'd feared from the beginning that his wobbly walk would cause him to fall and injure himself.

"No," he cried. "I wanta die!" Blood oozed between his fingers at the side of his head.

"Charlie! Let me see," she asked again, realizing the

blood was pulsing out to the rhythm of Charlie's heart-beat.

Wolf appeared behind him, his guns still drawn.

Molly glanced up at him for help, but his gaze scanned the street.

Wolf's words came hard but not cruel. "Where is she, Charlie? Where's the girl?"

Molly stood and took a step toward the house. "Callie Ann!" Logic registered that the child couldn't be inside, or Wolf wouldn't have asked.

Charlie cried out in a heartbreaking gulp. "Early was upstairs when one fellow jumped Josh in the parlor and another grabbed me in the hallway. I screamed for the kid to run. She was halfway up the stairs when we heard a round of gunfire from above.

"Callie turned to run back down toward me as a man stepped out of one of the bedrooms and shouted, 'One dead.' "

Charlie's cries made his words come in a rush. "The fellow holding me yelled, 'Grab the kid and let's get out of here!' Then he hit me with the butt of his gun."

The little man pulled himself together enough to continue, "As I tumbled, I saw them start beating on Josh. It was the Digger brothers and their men. I'd swear to it. Callie Ann screamed and cried and kicked to get away from one of them. I must have blacked out, 'cause the next thing I remember, they were gone."

Molly looked up. The yard was full of neighbors and rangers, all standing in the rain listening to Charlie.

Before she could react, Wolf shouted orders in rapid fire. No one questioned a word, everyone acted. The only time he lowered his voice was when he looked at Molly. "I need your help," he said, staring straight into her eyes. "Can you help?"

Molly nodded, fighting down her fears.

"I've sent someone for Washburn, but we have three injured. Charlie, Josh in the parlor, and Early upstairs."

"Early's still alive?"

"Barely." Wolf's expression gave her little hope. "Can you take care of them? I need every man to go after Callie Ann."

Molly was already moving. Two men helped Charlie inside while two others followed her. Her body shook all over. All she wanted to do was cry and hide. But she had to help. She had to do her part.

First, she'd do what she could for the wounded, then she'd go after the Digger brothers herself. All her life she'd thought of helping people, but if they'd hurt Callie Ann, she'd shoot them and leave their bodies to the buzzards.

Josh attempted to stand when she entered the house. He looked like he'd been run over by a herd of buffalo, but he was alive. Another ranger was already helping him.

Molly ran upstairs. Early's body lay on the rug beside a half-made bed. Carefully, Molly rolled her over and met her worst fear. Early had been shot in the chest. Blood was everywhere.

Molly leaned close and heard the young woman's shallow breathing.

She glanced at the two men at the door. "Get her downstairs to the dining table. Fast!"

She ran ahead of them and cleared the table of dishes with one sweep. She spread a white tablecloth as the men reached the bottom of the stairs.

There was no time to waste moving from room to room. "Put her on one side," Molly ordered, "and Charlie on the other."

Charlie still sobbed when men helped him onto the table. "I wanta die," he cried. "I just want to die."

As the men hurried to get the supplies Molly asked for, she grabbed Charlie's hands and pulled them away from his eyes. "Listen, Charlie. Listen! Miss Early's still alive, but I don't know for how long. You've got to lie very still and talk to her. She likes to talk to you. If she can hear your voice, maybe she'll stay with us long enough for me to sew her up."

He stopped crying and looked beside him.

When she saw the pain in his eyes, she shouted, "Don't you even think about losing control! We need you now." Molly moved around the table to Early's side. "I have to help her. I don't have time to treat you. So lie still so you don't bleed to death while I work on her."

Charlie's eyes widened with panic, but he did what she said. He held a rag to his head wound while he talked to Early, telling her how she was going to make it and how she wasn't to give one thought to dying.

Callie Ann was never out of Molly's thoughts, as her hands worked with lightning speed. Early's wound was so severe, Molly didn't see how she was still breathing. There was no time to hesitate or wait for Washburn. She had to act and act fast.

As supplies filled the room, Molly pressed against Early's chest in an effort to slow the bleeding enough to have a closer look.

Dr. Washburn appeared next to her, soaked with rain and out of breath. "What do we have here?" Washburn asked, without trying to take charge.

"We've got to get the bullet out and the bleeding stopped."

Washburn nodded and spread his instruments on the table. But instead of moving Molly out of the way, he handed her the first tool.

"I can't," she started. She'd watched others, but she'd never done anything like this. "I haven't . . ."

"Neither have I," the young doctor answered. "We've got more help on the way, but it may take an hour. Do we have that much time to wait?"

He asked her. Her! How would she know? She'd never wanted to be a doctor. She wasn't even a nurse. But no cream or powder would help Early. "I don't think we do," she whispered.

"I agree," he answered.

Together they worked, trying to stop the bleeding, trying again and again to pull out the bullet. Trying with bloody hands to thread a needle to sew her together.

Molly kept telling herself she had to do what she could. They were Early's only hope.

Charlie's voice drifted around the room, soothing the panic that hung in the air thicker than the humidity. He talked of all the times he'd been shot and what he'd thought about each time and how he'd never let his mind think of dying.

Early never moved. Maybe she was too near death to fight anymore. Maybe she could hear Charlie fighting with words harder than he'd ever fought in his life.

A few times, Molly heard Wolf shouting orders just outside the window, but the thunder rattled the panes as if echoing his rage.

Washburn's assistant reported the ranger named Josh had two broken ribs, several cuts and bruises, but he had already insisted on returning to duty. The assistant said, short of hitting the man again, he couldn't think of any way to stop him.

Molly's fingers seemed slippery and clumsy, but Washburn's were no better. About the time they had Early sewn up, two doctors appeared from the state hospital. They were older and experienced. Their eyes showed no sign of shock at the amount of blood flowing across the table.

"Fine job," one man said. "I couldn't have done better myself." His hair and beard were white, and he reminded Molly of her father.

The other doctor slowly pulled the rag from Charlie's head. "This man almost bled to death waiting."

Charlie's eyes were closed, and Molly wasn't sure how long ago he had quit talking.

Both doctors removed their coats and rolled up their sleeves. The white-haired one looked straight at Molly as if sizing her up. "You finish with the woman," he said as more a question than a statement. "We'll take care of her man."

Molly started to correct him. Charlie wasn't Miss Early's man. But then she glanced at the center of the table where their blood had mixed. Charlie's hand held Miss Early's tightly. If either knocked on death's door this night, Molly knew they'd walk in together.

TWENTY-FIVE

WOLF WATCHED MOLLY WORK AND FELT A GREAT pride growing inside him. How many times had she told him she didn't want to be a doctor? How many times would she prove herself wrong before she accepted the truth? From the very beginning, he'd seen the intelligence in her green eyes and the caring in her touch. Maybe that was what made him love her at first sight at the train station all those years ago. Maybe that was part of what made him love her now.

She reminded him of a newborn, tasting life for the first time, taking both the good and the bad with a mixture of curiosity and caution. Handling it all in stride. And for some reason, she'd decided she wanted him. Molly didn't know yet that he was already hers and always had been.

He longed to talk to her, but there was no time. She had her job, and he had his. Only, the storm was making his hell right now. He had men on every outbound trail wide enough for a horse to travel. They worked in pairs, so one man could report back every few hours. They'd seen nothing. The town's law enforcement combed Austin, looking for places where the Diggers might hide with a child. Nothing. The gang appeared to have left Molly's house with a screaming captive and completely vanished.

"Captain?" The white-haired doctor held up his bloodstained hands as he approached Wolf. "We're doing what we can for the little fellow. Someone said a ranger was down. *He's* not a ranger, is he?"

"Yes," Wolf answered without hesitation.

The man Washburn called Doc Harley nodded. "We're finding bone fragments that need to be removed."

"He was shot three times during the war," Wolf announced.

Harley shook his head. "He must have been very young at the time, because the skull has grown back. I think we can help him out a little and relieve some of his pain. Whoever patched him up during the war did a lousy job. I'm surprised he hasn't gone mad from the agony he's endured."

"Do what you can." Wolf had never thought much about Charlie's age. With his deformed face and crippled legs, he'd seemed old, but Wolf hadn't taken the time to look closely. "How's the woman?" Wolf asked before the doctor turned away.

"She's alive, that's about all I can say. The lady doc is doing a grand job, but it will be hours, maybe days, before we'll know. For every breath that woman takes she's one breath closer to making it."

Wolf thanked the man and moved away. As he stepped onto the porch, he filled his lungs with damp air to remove the smell of blood. For a moment, he stood watching the sky. The storm wasn't letting up. They would be tracking in mud. He stepped into the downpour, unaware of his own discomfort. Josh said he'd heard Callie Ann screaming that her Wolf was going to get all the mean men.

If she were his little princess, he guessed that made him her knight. He planned to search until he found her. And she was right, he would get those men who took her.

He rode until midnight, following every hint of a lead. He changed horses every few hours, unwilling to push an animal the way he pushed himself. Several folks came forward reporting that they'd seen men with a tiny blond girl. If they were right, the good news was Callie Ann was alive and yelling. The bad news, all the trails had disappeared.

Wolf spoke to the undertaker, Miller, twice. The man was too nervous not to know something, but he wasn't talking. Callie Ann had told Wolf about seeing Miller take the extra drugstore key the day before the fire. Wolf planned to keep a close eye on Miller, guessing he'd eventually lead Wolf to some kind of crime. That it would be the Digger boys was little more than a hunch Wolf had.

As if to add to his problems, the rain continued, finally driving him back home. There was nothing to do but get a few hours' sleep and start again at first light. The storm prevented him from recognizing his own men five feet away. The brothers were holed up some-where and would crawl out when the storm passed.

Wolf took care of his horse then walked the few blocks to Molly's house through streets that were now rivers. Her place shone like a beacon in the rain. Every room downstairs was fully lit while all other homes around Molly's slept.

When he stepped onto the porch, he pulled off his hat, slinging water in every direction. Wolf hesitated, not wanting to face Molly and tell her they hadn't found Callie Ann. He'd promised to protect them, but in the end, Early might already be dead and Callie Ann was kidnapped.

Finally, Wolf opened the door. Frank Washburn sat on the stairs, cradling a mug of coffee in his hands. "Evening, Captain," he mumbled. "Any luck?"

Wolf shook his head. "How about you?"

Washburn shrugged. "Well, they're both still alive. We moved them up to the child's room, where there were two beds. A nurse is sitting with them in case there's a change. Old Doc Harley is in the parlor snor-ing. He told the nurse to wake him if she needed him." The young doctor took a long breath. "Right now, it looks like Miss Early and Charlie Filmore are in a race to the grave."

Wolf pulled off his rain slicker and hung it on a peg by the door.

The doctor stood slowly. "I'm building my courage to step into the rain and head home. There's nothing more to do here." Frank Washburn had aged years in one day.

"Captain?"

"Yes?" Wolf waited.

"You were in the war, right?"

"Right."

"What we went through today, was it anything like how the field hospitals operated?"

The captain smiled. The war had only been over for four years, and it was already starting to be stories, not memories. "It was worse, Frank, far worse."

The young doctor nodded. "I was afraid of that."

"Where's my wife?"

"Last time I saw her, she was headed toward the back porch with a bar of soap and a towel. She said she was going to wash up in the rain."

Wolf offered the doctor his slicker before saying good night and heading into the kitchen. Food lined the counters, making Wolf grin. It was the Southern way, he thought. Whenever there was trouble, folks brought food.

As he stepped onto the back porch, Molly's outline blinked in the lightning. She'd removed her blouse and was scrubbing her arms with soap then leaning into a waterfall of rain cascading off the roof. Her hair hung in wet curls down her back, and her camisole clung to her like a second skin.

He watched her lean into the rain three times before he realized she wasn't planning on stopping. Slowly, he moved behind her.

When she felt him at her back, she jolted, then relaxed into his arms.

Wolf took the soap from her hand and set it aside.

Then he stretched her hands into the rain, moving his over them to wash away the last of the lye. As he folded Molly into his embrace, Wolf realized she was soaked to the bone.

For a while, he held her without saying a word, loving the way she felt against him, needing the home of her arms to retreat to, if only for a little while.

There were no games or rules between them now. The horror of what they'd both been through today had washed all that away. He needed her, and he knew she needed him just as desperately. In the world of his arms lay the only peace either of them would know this night.

Without a word, he lifted her and carried her inside. She leaned her head against his shoulder as he moved carefully up the stairs. They passed Callie Ann's room. Charlie, his head and face a mass of bandages, lay on one bed, Early on the other. The nurse sitting between them smiled up at Wolf as he slowly walked by. She nodded that all was quiet.

Wolf closed the bedroom door and gently stood Molly in front of the fireplace. She didn't move as he lit the wood. The painted tiles flickered to life as they reflected the flames in warm welcome. He pulled several towels from the stack by the washstand and returned to her side without lighting any lamps. He undressed her by the firelight.

Molly watched him closely as his awkward fingers worked the buttons at her waist. Her skirt tumbled to the floor. There was no need for her to ask about Callie Ann. If anything had changed, he would have told her.

Even in the dim light, she could see the exhaustion and sorrow in his eyes.

His big hands calmed her as they moved over her body, pulling layers of clothing away. Her emotions were raw, brittle to the point of breaking. He handled her with great care, as though he knew how near the edge she walked.

When she was fully nude before him, he knelt and began drying her with a towel. She moved when he directed. The warmth of the towel soothed over her, along with the warmth of his hands. He dried and caressed every part of her until, finally, he stood and moved his fingers into her hair. Gently, Wolf leaned her back, bracing her with his arm so her hair fell free in the warm air drifting from the fire. He swayed gently in a slow rhythm while her hair dried.

When he finished, he wrapped her with one of Aunt Alvina's handmade quilts and sat her close to the fire while he undressed.

Wolf unbuckled his gun belt slowly, as if with the weapon went the weight of his job. When he hung the Colts over the bedpost, she knew his responsibilities were never far away. She'd expected him to stop before he removed his trousers, but he didn't. As if he were unaware that she watched, he removed all his clothes and dried before the fire.

The flickering firelight reflected off his body, the powerful muscles, the slim planes, the scars. Lightning flashed across the windows. Like a wild animal in his prime, he was frightening and beautiful.

When he finally turned back to her, Wolf raked his

hands over his damp hair and closed the distance between them.

Pulling her to her feet, he let the quilt fall away and drew her to him.

The completeness of holding him engulfed her senses. She could feel not only their skin touching, but their very hearts. Raising her arms, she melted into him, keeping nothing back from this man who'd somehow become a part of her.

For a long while, they held one another. All that she breathed was him. All that she felt was him. The sound of his heart pounding was the only sound in the world. No dream could ever touch this reality.

After a while, she became aware of his hands moving over her, the action so natural she couldn't have said when it began. His gentle touch spread across her hips and moved up her back and sides.

Molly leaned back, knowing his arm would hold her. Closing her eyes, she let the warmth of his hands flow over her. He caressed her so gently, so completely.

When she straightened, she rested against the solid wall of his chest, feeling as if she'd come home. He didn't kiss her, though they were near enough to feel one another's breath. He pushed her hair away from her shoulder and lowered his face against her throat, breathing in her scent as if it were more vital than air.

Molly felt his mouth open over her flesh, and she tilted her head to offer him all he wanted of the taste of her. The pleasure of the tip of his tongue sliding over her neck made her weak with need. She would have fallen if he hadn't held her to him. Finally, when she was lost in warm sensations flowing like wine through her veins, he raised his head.

His brown eyes smoldered with desire and a need so great it took her breath away. Lifting her in his arms, he carried her to the bed. With gentle hands, he lowered her onto her stomach.

She'd expected him to stretch out beside her, but he vanished. For a moment, she panicked, thinking what she'd just experienced had been a dream, thinking she'd have to give this heaven up for reality.

Then he was back, standing beside the bed with the powder she'd used the night he'd seen her undress. Without a word, he shook some in his hand and began slowly smoothing it into her skin. His callused hands stroked from her shoulder to her knee, smoothing the powder into her flesh. Relaxing tired muscles along with broken dreams with his gentle caress.

She rolled over and let him continue. His fingers circled her breasts. She kept her gaze on his eyes as he explored her body. The pleasure she saw there made her believe she was beautiful, desirable, and desperately needed.

And explore her he did, like a man starved for the feel of her. He drew her into his world, his real world, of touch. His hands molded over her again and again until she accepted his embrace without hesitance or shyness. Each time she relaxed fully, he became bolder. He was making her his and she willingly took the journey.

Slowly, the warmth in his hands spread a fire within her like she'd never known. She moved with his touch, responding, loving, feeling. When his mouth finally lowered to hers, she was hungry for him. Sighing, she lifted her arms, aware of how much she'd longed for his kiss.

Wolf lowered his body above her. The joy of feeling him covering her made her shake with urgency. She wrapped her arms around him and brought him closer, wanting all he offered.

His kiss was tender, hesitant; hers wild and demanding. Each pleasure he gave her made her long for more.

When he rolled to his side, she cried out softly in disappointment, but then his hands moved over her and she understood. The kiss deepened as his touch grew bolder. He slipped his hand between her legs and pulled them apart, meeting no resistance. Without breaking the kiss, he rolled on top of her once more, pressing her deep into the covers.

When he entered her, she would have cried out in pain, but his mouth covered hers. As he moved inside her, she broke the kiss, frantically trying not to scream. She heard him whispering something in her ear, but couldn't understand the words. Sensations washed over her in waves, blocking out all the world but him and what he was doing.

The pain eased and the warmth of him above her seemed to dissolve into her. As when he'd touched her, she moved with him, riding the wave of excitement that surged through her body.

A longing for more raced through her. She held to him, afraid that he might leave her alone with the fire inside her. Afraid she'd die from the agony, the need, the desire for more.

Then, suddenly, he pushed deep inside her, and the need exploded into ecstasy. She held to him as pleasure washed through her with such a raging flood that she shook.

He carried her gently back to shore in his arms. Tenderly, he settled her with his touch and soft kisses over her body.

Molly relaxed, too exhausted even to try to understand what had happened to her.

As she moved into a deep sleep, she heard him whisper in his low Southern tone, "I'll love you forever, Molly."

TWENTY-SIX

"Molly," wolf whispered against her ear.

She stirred, reaching for him in the darkness. The fire had died down, and the room had grown cold. She heard the pounding rain against the windows, but she was cuddled warm in his arms.

"Hmmm," she mumbled, brushing her hand across his heart.

"Molly?" He lifted his arm, moving her to a sitting position, demanding she wake. "We need to get under the covers." He lifted her off the bed without waiting for an answer.

She put her arms around him as he pulled back the blankets and lowered her into place. Her sleepy body wanted him near.

When she would have slipped back into sleep, he whispered against her ear, "Are you awake?" He shook her shoulder gently. "Molly? Are you awake?"

"Why?" she yawned. "It couldn't possibly be morning yet."

"Because I want my wife awake when I make love to her again." His hand boldly cupped her breast. "I want her *fully* awake."

She rubbed her eyes and tried to see him in the shadows. "Again?" she whispered as he pulled her close. Her bare body moved against him naturally.

"Again." He laughed and lowered his mouth to the breast he'd just claimed.

Molly opened her eyes wide as a jolt of pleasure shot through her. "Wolf!" she cried when she realized what he was doing. "Wolf," she pleaded, fearing he might stop.

He explored her body as if for the first time, while she tried to hold to an ounce of control. "No matter what you do, Wolf Hayward, I'm not going to tell you I love you."

He seemed far more interested in the way her body moved to his touch than in what she said. Finally, he mumbled, "Fine, I'm not going to tell you I love you either."

In the warmth beneath the covers, he taught her more of heaven. This time, there was no pain, only sweet pleasure. He made love to her slowly. He wanted her so deep inside his senses that he'd never get the taste or feel or smell of her out of the core of his being.

Finally, when she lay exhausted in his arms, Wolf smiled as he pushed her hair away from her damp flesh. He couldn't resist spreading his hand wide and moving down her body. He circled over her abdomen, knowing someday his child would grow inside her.

Almost back to sleep, Molly still responded to his

touch. He pressed his hand lightly along her flesh. "I love you, Molly." He said the words he'd promised himself he wouldn't say again unless she answered. "I love you, and I will until the day I die."

He lowered his face to where their child would grow and kissed her there. She let him do whatever he liked now. She was his in body.

The vision of her with child brought Callie Ann to mind. Slowly, he forced himself to leave Molly and stand. He would sleep no more tonight. He'd stolen a few hours away, but now it was time to return. When he'd seen Molly on the porch, he hadn't planned to love her, only to hold her, protect her.

As Wolf dressed, he watched her. She looked even more beautiful now that she'd tasted passion fully. He felt more lost than Callie Ann. He was in love with a woman who was only playing at marriage. Not only in love with her, but dumb enough to tell her so.

He'd seen men make fools of themselves over love and swore he'd never be one. But he had to fight to keep from crawling back in bed with her right now. She was just a woman, he thought. Just flesh and blood. She was stubborn, with a loose lasso around reality. She was one of the best doctors around, but thought of herself as a druggist. She wanted to be married and was willing to offer her body, but she didn't want to give her heart.

Wolf reached for his gun belt and strapped it on. He might as well shoot himself in the leg, he decided. Nothing would stop him from being a fool, but a limp might slow him down. It was only a matter of time until he went mad and started begging for drinks and sleeping in the streets. Wolf laughed. Liquor wouldn't wash Molly out of his system.

He thought of waking her to say good-bye, but he wasn't sure he could get that close to her without touching her again.

Silently, he moved from the room.

The house was still. He checked on Charlie and Early. They slept quietly, as did the nurse. Charlie's hand twitched slightly, as if he were reaching for something. Early's face looked almost as white as the sheet, but she still breathed.

In the kitchen, Wolf noticed a pot of coffee left over low coals. The beans had boiled so long in the pot he almost had to chew before he could swallow, but it was hot enough to kick him full awake. He stood and watched the rain out the kitchen window while he ate half a pound cake he'd found wrapped in a tea towel.

Something had been gnawing at the back of his mind since before dark yesterday. The Diggers were good at getting away, but they weren't that good. The rain might have cloaked them somewhat, but most rangers could have tracked fresh trails. If they didn't get away, there was only one answer. The Digger brothers and Callie Ann were still in town. And, he guessed, they wouldn't dare kill her here. It would be too obvious. If they wanted to murder her, they could have done that yesterday and left her body in the house with Charlie and Early. For some reason, they needed Callie Ann alive, or at least they needed not to be marked as her killers. All he had to figure out was why.

"Wolf," Molly whispered from behind him.

He whirled around, taking the impact of her beauty full against his senses. She took his breath away. Her hair was a mass of tangles and curls. Her bare feet stuck out from beneath her robe. A robe beneath which, he imagined, she wore nothing else.

"Yes?" He gripped the counter to keep from moving to her.

"I thought you'd gone."

"I will be in a few minutes."

She didn't meet his eyes, but crossed the room to stand in front of him. He could still smell the powder he'd rubbed across her skin. Her lips looked slightly swollen, exactly as if they'd been kissed thoroughly during the night.

"You'll be careful?" she asked.

"I'll be careful," Wolf answered, knowing that wasn't what she'd rushed down to tell him. If she moved a step closer, she'd be in his arms. He'd like to hear her confess her love while he touched her.

She hesitated then began, "I just wanted to say thank you for last night."

The smile vanished from his face. Wolf's muscles hardened, taking the blow. He grabbed her so quickly, she didn't even have time to react. He pulled her against him and kissed her on the mouth with none of the tenderness or gentleness he'd shown an hour before.

Just as quickly, he shoved her away and moved to the door. As he crammed on his hat, he looked back. Hurt and anger burned in his brown eyes. "Don't ever

thank me again, madam. I wasn't performing a service."

Before Molly could react, he was gone.

It took several attempts for her to control her
breathing. She collapsed into the kitchen chair, trying
to figure out what she'd said that had been so terrible.
How could a man be so loving, so caring, and turn into
such a bear at dawn?

The memories of the night drifted back to her. She
recalled standing on the back porch, letting the rain
wash over her, feeling broken and drained. And then,
he'd been there, holding her, caring for her, loving her.

Tears rolled down her cheeks without being checked.
"Loving me," she whispered, trying to understand the
words. He must have been as tired and frustrated as
she was last night, but his thoughts were for her.

She closed her eyes tightly, sending a waterfall down
her face. She knew what he wanted her to say. What
he'd thought she'd been about to say when she'd
rushed down before he left. He was a big strong man,
the bravest in town, many said, but he needed her to
tell him she loved him.

And she couldn't. He should understand. She'd told
him from the first that she'd never say the words. What
did they matter? She'd be his wife in every other way.

She wished she could make him understand. If she
said she loved him, she'd have to turn loose of Benjamin forever. Three words would shatter all the
dreams she'd had with Benjamin, and he'd be nothing
more than a man she'd met once on a platform. A man

who'd kissed her and gone away to war and never returned.

Benjamin had been in her thoughts and journals for years. She'd built a life for them in her mind. They'd grown together. They'd talked in her writing. He'd asked her to wait, and she'd sworn in her heart that she would.

Molly pushed the tears off her face and stood. Wolf wanted too much. She'd already lost all her writings in the fire. Did she have to give up her dreams as well?

Halfway up the stairs, Molly caught her breath, suddenly realizing that Benjamin's love was only a paper valentine compared to Wolf's real beating heart. One was a man, her man. The other only a memory.

By the time Dr. Washburn arrived, Molly was dressed. With the help of the nurse, she changed Early's bandages and managed to get a few swallows of water down Charlie. But there was little progress.

Washburn watched the patients from the bedroom door as he removed his coat. "If this rain doesn't let up, I'm going to quit medicine and start building an ark."

Molly smiled at him. Yesterday, although he was the least skilled of the doctors who'd arrived, he'd made up for it in caring. In a few years, he'd make a great doctor.

"I woke Doc Harley up when I came in. He said he'd be back this afternoon." Washburn moved to the bedside and studied Early carefully. "He said that since the stitches appear to be holding, Miss Early may have a chance of making it. A slight chance. Every hour that passes gives him more hope, though."

Molly nodded. "I wish her color were better."

"It'll come," Washburn said as if he'd seen patients like Early a hundred times before. "We need to be thankful there's no fever. Give her time to heal."

He moved to Charlie. "How's our ranger?" Washburn winked at Molly so the nurse didn't see. He'd played along with the comment Wolf had made to the other doctors about Charlie being a ranger.

"He's called for water and something for the pain now and then." Molly touched Charlie's arm. "He's tried to pull off the bandages a few times. I don't know what we'll do when he gets stronger. Harley said, no matter what, the bandages have to stay in place for a month."

"We'll tie him down," Washburn suggested. "We can't keep him drugged up for that long."

Molly didn't want to think of Charlie tied to the bed, but she had to agree with Washburn. Even now, with all the drugs, and weakness from loss of blood, Charlie's hand opened and closed as if reaching for something.

As the day passed, Molly and Washburn worked in shifts. The rain eased to a drizzle, making the world seem dark and depressed.

Josh Weston showed up in midafternoon, looking for Wolf. They'd finally received a letter from the sheriff back in Savannah about Callie Ann. It appeared he'd sent a letter with her and another one general delivery to a Francis Digger in Austin. The one traveling with

Callie Ann must have been lost. Callie Ann's grandmother had left her about a half million dollars and a farm. Should something happen to the child, the next in line to inherit would be Francis and Carrell Digger.

Molly's mind quickly sifted through the facts. That was why they hadn't killed Callie Ann outright. The murder would be traced to them too easily. But if they kidnapped the child, claiming she was their kin and they had a right, the Diggers could take their time doing away with her. If, somehow, they could beat the robbery charges in Texas, they could go back to Georgia and live as rich men. They just had to keep Callie Ann with them until it became more convenient for her to be eliminated. Then they could collect.

That had to be why they took her. They might even claim she had been held against her will and her uncles had had to save her. With a corrupt judge, the Diggers could step into a new life.

"I have to find Wolf." Molly tugged at Josh's sleeve as he sampled a plate of chicken Noma had sent over from her cafe.

He shrugged. "I thought he was here. He stormed in before dawn, giving every ranger standing orders, and then disappeared."

"What orders?" Molly asked.

"He wants every road out of here covered and every stage checked. We've got double guards, but nothing's moving." He took a bite and added, "I even heard Miller had to cancel a funeral. The ground is so wet, the casket would float right back up."

Molly offered the young ranger a plate and fork, but

he said he couldn't take the time. He didn't say any-thing, but Molly guessed that he believed the longer it took to find Callie Ann the less chance they'd find her alive.

She thought about what Josh said all afternoon. In the back of her mind, Molly felt as though she had all the pieces but couldn't fit them together. Somewhere in all the muddle of facts lay a way to help Callie Ann.

About ten, Molly finally gave up waiting for Wolf and ate alone at the kitchen table. Everyone had gone home but one nurse. Charlie and Early suffered ups and downs all day but were resting now. Strange how we live from crisis to crisis, she thought, when someone is so ill. The hours didn't matter, only the condition.

Molly tried to finish her meal, but she didn't have the energy. It felt like weeks since she'd slept. She checked on the patients one last time and went to her room.

The bed was unmade, as they'd left it this morning. Her aunts would have been shocked, but there was no time for housekeeping. Without removing her clothes, Molly curled into the wrinkled sheets and rested her head on Wolf's pillow.

She could smell a hint of him and wished his arms were around her. She closed her eyes and remembered the night before. For a man who'd claimed to know little of loving, he'd done a fine job, to her way of thinking.

A few minutes later, she smiled just before she fell asleep, thinking memories were far better than dreams.

Long after midnight, Molly heard the nurse calling

her name. For a moment, she couldn't get her bearings. She stumbled from the covers like a drunk and hurried down the hall.

"I can't get him to be still," the nurse complained. "I've tried everything."

Molly moved to the side of Charlie's bed and placed her hands on his arm. The nurse did the same on the other side. "Charlie," Molly said as calmly as she could. "Charlie, you have to settle down. You'll only hurt yourself if you keep thrashing."

He mumbled beneath the layers of bandages.

"Charlie, please lie still." Molly could feel him growing stronger and more agitated. Soon, they would have to strap him down like some wild animal. "Settle down, now. Everything's going to be all right. Settle down and try to sleep."

He struggled again, increasing his efforts to break free of their grasp.

Molly leaned close. "Charlie, you've got to be still. Your head will only hurt worse if you move. Please be still." Harley had warned her how dangerous it would be if Charlie pulled his stitches loose or bumped his head.

This time, when he mumbled she could hear his words. "Early," he whispered. "Is Early still alive?"

Molly's heart jumped to her throat and blocked her cry. He wasn't asking for medicine or going mad with pain. He only needed to know about Early. "Yes," Molly whispered. "She's right beside you."

"Early!" His voice was hoarse with fear. "Early," he cried as if he didn't believe Molly's words. As though

Early could answer him if he could force the words through his bandages.

Molly glanced up at the nurse. "Move the bed!"

"What?" The nurse didn't understand.

"Get out of the way, and help me move the beds closer together."

The nurse shook her head. "I don't think that would be wise. Then we couldn't get around each one. It would cause trouble. Both these people are very near death."

"Move the bed!" Molly shouted. "Or, get out of my way and I'll do it myself. Stop acting as if they might catch a disease from one another."

The nurse finally stepped from between the two beds. Molly slowly pushed with all her strength until Charlie's bed was within six inches of Early's.

Then she leaned over and brought Charlie's hand to Early's side. "You see, Charlie, she's still alive. She's sleeping next to you."

He stopped thrashing as his fingers brushed along Early's arm.

Molly leaned a few inches from Charlie's bandaged face. "She has to lie very still, Charlie, but she's alive. If you're to stay this close, do you think you could fight the pain and be very still also? Do you understand?"

Charlie cupped his hand around Early's elbow. "Will she live?" he asked.

"I don't know," Molly answered.

He was silent so long, she feared he'd passed out

once again. Finally, he begged, "Can I stay right beside her?"

Molly patted his arm. "We may have to move you to change her bandages, but I think she'd want you nearby."

Charlie didn't say another word. His fingers rested lightly on Early's arm. He didn't move again, except to pat her as though silently telling Early he was close.

Glancing up at the nurse, Molly was surprised to find her crying.

"I'll put a quilt under Mr. Charlie's bed in the morning so we can shift it when we have to. That way, it won't cause him any more pain than necessary." She stared at his hand resting on Early's arm. "Do you think he can take the hurting in his head and stay still?"

Molly looked down at the little man who had sounded so young and so afraid only seconds ago. "I think he can," she said loud enough for Charlie to hear. "He's very brave, you know."

She left the room and went downstairs, too awake now to sleep. The rain finally stopped. She pulled her jacket from the peg by the door and slipped outside.

She needed to walk.

TWENTY-SEVEN

MOLLY WALKED THE DESERTED STREETS TOWARD HER half-finished store. The dream she'd thought was her destiny when she came to Texas seemed of little importance now. All the sorrow of the past few days had brought her life into perspective. Wolf's love had balanced it.

She had no idea of the time. Long after midnight, she guessed. She wasn't afraid. With her black coat, she'd see anyone long before they'd see her. If she could find Wolf, she'd apologize and ask him to come home. But she doubted he would. By thanking him this morning, she'd hurt him. It was strange. He couldn't stop saying he loved her, and she couldn't start saying she loved him.

Her store loomed like a skeleton before her. For a while, she stood in the shadows and stared at it, thinking of how important it seemed only a month ago.

A yellow glow shone from Miller's furniture and casket store, lighting the front part of the new drugstore's frame. He'd worked hard, as he'd promised, to rebuild her place.

She moved a few feet closer to the light. Surely he wasn't building something this late. How could the man work all day on her store and all night in his shop? He was money hungry, but not fool enough to kill himself by pushing too hard.

The curtains of his shop were pulled, but she could see shadows moving about inside. Maybe there had been several deaths, and he was building caskets. Without Charlie to help, it might take all night.

But she'd remembered hearing the faint tap of a hammer even from inside her store when he'd been working. Now, with only a glass window separating them, she heard nothing. A carpenter wouldn't be practicing his trade this late.

She slipped along the side of the building, listening. There was no use wasting time telling herself to mind her own business. Something didn't feel right, and she planned to take a closer look.

Voices drifted from inside the shop. Molly moved along in the shadows between stores so she could get close enough to hear.

A board in the walk creaked. She paused to make sure all was quiet then continued to inch closer to the building.

"Well, how long do you think it's going to take?" an angry man shouted from inside. "We have to be on our way by dawn."

Molly jumped back a step at the sudden sound, then

slipped silently into place in the darkness so she could listen.

Miller mumbled something Molly didn't understand. She leaned her ear against the wood, trying to hear through the wall.

"I don't have that long. I've got to get the kid out fast without losing my own hide in the process. You said you'd do this, Miller, and we're paying you twice the money. If you even think about backing out, you'll be building your own casket."

Molly tiptoed into the total blackness beside the window, so she wouldn't be seen by anyone from the street. She had to hear more.

She reached the shadows. Before she could take a breath, a hand closed over her mouth, and a punishing grip encircled her waist. Panic hit her like a lightning bolt. She fought wildly, but the grip only tightened, allowing no movement. Her foot hit the wall with a tap before she was jerked backward.

The smell of her attacker's filthy hand almost made Molly faint. She could tell he was tall and thin but strong.

"Come along," he hissed in her ear. "And don't say a word if you want to be alive when we get to the little girl."

Molly nodded that she'd cooperate, but he didn't lessen his hold on her as he dragged her through the night to the back door of Miller's shop. Her captor slammed her against the building so hard the air left her lungs. He opened the door and grabbed her before she could breathe or think of running.

When he shoved her into the light of the back room, she took a step, but he caught her by the hair and twisted it around his fingers. "Come along," he mumbled again, dragging her down the narrow hallway lined with lumber. "The Diggers'll want to see you."

Molly had seen Francis Digger briefly when he'd flown through her store window, but she was unprepared for the sight of him now. Then, he'd been handcuffed and unarmed. Now he looked like a walking arsenal. Gun belts crossed his chest. Long Colts were strapped to his legs, and a rifle dangled from his hand like an appendage. Yet, as frightening as the guns were, his eyes were what made Molly's blood freeze. Cold, heartless gray eyes, the exact color of a headstone.

Standing next to him was a man almost his twin, only more frightening.

"Where'd you find her?" Francis asked the lean man who yanked Molly along with him. Francis had a grin that twitched across his face as he glared at her.

"In the alley," the thin man answered as he shoved Molly toward Carrell Digger. "She was hiding between them buildings trying to hear what was going on in here."

The older Digger closed his fist around the material of her coat and pulled her within an inch of his face. She could feel his foul breath as well as smell it. The odor of rotting teeth and bad whiskey made her gag.

Then, just as suddenly, he let her go, shoving her toward the center of the room. "You know who she is, don't you, Fran?"

Francis laughed. "She's the captain's woman. You

know, killing him is too easy. How about we just take her along with us? He's caused us nothing but trouble for years. It's time we paid him back."

Molly's anger kept her from fainting. She'd been a fool to go out alone. A fool for not bringing a weapon. She had no way of defending herself, and she knew if she tried screaming, she'd be dead in a heartbeat. The three men watched her like coyotes inspecting a trapped rabbit.

She had no choice but to attack. "Where's the child?" she demanded, as if a hundred armed guards stood behind her. "You better not have harmed Callie Ann."

Francis seemed surprised by her tirade. It took him a moment to recover, then he slapped his brother on the back so hard Carrell staggered forward several feet. "Take her to the child." He motioned with his rifle. "And tie her up. I'll tell Miller we need another box."

Carrell Digger's hand closed around Molly's arm with bruising force. He jerked her hard, first one direction, then the other, as if making sure she understood and would follow without trouble.

Molly wasn't about to fight. He was taking her to the very place she wanted to be, with Callie Ann.

But Digger didn't seem to care that she offered no resistance. He continued to shove her down a narrow hallway. Several times, she fought to keep standing. And twice, he knocked her into the wall, laughing as she yelped in sudden pain. By the time they reached the door at the end of what looked to be a storage hall, Molly was barely able to stand.

He opened the door and pushed her onto a pile of fabric that might once have been a wagon cover. "Wanta cause a ruckus, lady?" he asked, raising his hand above his head. "I'd love it if you wanta be trouble."

Molly knew, if she moved, she'd give him the excuse he looked for. She'd once heard Wolf say that Carrell was Francis's older and meaner brother.

He seemed disappointed when she didn't answer. "Sit up and hold your arms together, toward me."

Molly followed instructions.

He tied her hands together with one end of a rope and looped the other end around a support beam. "Jerk on this and the place will come down around you. The way Miller builds, we're lucky it's standing as it is." He checked his tie job. "If I come back and you've messed with these ropes, I'll beat you so bad, you'll be begging me to kill you. Understand?"

Molly nodded. "Where's the child?"

The back of Digger's hand slammed against the side of her face so hard Molly tumbled backward. The rope cut into her wrists as she fell.

"I didn't tell you to say anything." He laughed. "You'd better learn fast 'cause we're keeping you with us. You're ours now, just like the kid is. It'll drive Hayward crazy, knowing we got both you and the girl, and he can't get to you. If you don't cooperate, he won't recognize you even if we turn you loose."

Blood dripped from Molly's lip, but she didn't move.

Digger crossed to the door. "Don't worry, the brat's

there with you. She cried herself to sleep an hour ago."

The moment he was gone, Molly rolled to her knees and searched for Callie Ann. Another rope was tied to the same beam. She followed it, and beneath a layer of dust and fabric Callie Ann slept, curled into a tiny ball.

Molly fought down horror. Tied around the child's neck like a noose was the other end of the rope she'd followed. She wanted to lift Callie Ann into her arms, but Molly's hands were bound. Molly was also afraid of waking her. Maybe the best thing would be to let the child sleep while she figured out a way to escape.

Wolf had been standing in the shadows across the street from Miller's place since just before dark. He'd heard shuffling in the alley a few hours ago and seen shadows moving across the window shades. Someone else had entered the shop, but he wasn't sure if it was friend or foe. To his best guess, there were three men, maybe four. Two of them had to be the Diggers.

He didn't dare leave his post. The brothers could make their move at any moment, and he had to be ready. While he waited, Wolf figured out what they planned. Miller had been building caskets all night. They were going out of town in boxes and, simple as the idea was, Wolf doubted the men he'd posted on the roads would check coffins.

A wagon pulled up in front of the store. Wolf watched as a tall, lean-faced man climbed down. He tapped twice on the door, and Miller let him in. A few minutes later, they started hauling out caskets with the lids loose on top. The two men were so lazy, they were planning on having the Diggers climb into the boxes inside the wagon. One coffin was loaded, then two.

Wolf could do nothing but watch. If he fired a shot, he'd have help. But before anyone could cover him, the Diggers would be out the back door of Miller's place and gone again. He couldn't risk charging in with his Colts drawn, Callie Ann might get hurt.

He waited.

Just before dawn, Josh walked down the street toward the Ranger office, as Wolf knew he would. With a quick whistle, Wolf pulled him into the shadows.

When Josh saw Wolf, he didn't waste time on greetings, he simply explained about the letter from the sheriff in Savannah and waited for orders. The plan was simple. Josh would go get help, if any could be found. They'd need a couple of men to cover the back door, three more on each end of the street in case the Diggers tried to make a run for it. Each man was to carry a rope. The less gunfire used, the better chance they could get Callie Ann back alive. Most of the rangers had served time herding cattle. They should be able to swing a loop over either the Diggers or a wagon wheel.

Josh disappeared. Wolf checked his weapons. He knew all was in place, but the habit was like an itch. Every so often, he had to scratch. Wolf glanced around. The street was deserted.

Miller stepped out with a third box, half the size of the others. He tossed it in the wagon and Wolf cringed, guessing who that casket was for.

All but one light inside Miller's place went out. The

door slowly opened. Wolf expected to see the Diggers, but instead, Miller and the lean-faced man shuffled out with another box.

A fourth box? Why would they need four boxes? Wolf had a feeling he wouldn't like the answer.

They took a chance loading up on the front street, even if it was before dawn. But the Diggers loved taking chances. Wolf had heard of them robbing stages almost within shouting distance of a town, when they could've just as easily waited until they were five miles down the road.

Francis Digger hurried out with a sleepy Callie Ann in his arms. Wolf could see the rope around her neck even in the darkness. Carrell Digger was right behind his brother with a woman in tow.

It took Wolf only a second to recognize the woman. Molly! Forgetting his plan, he stepped into the street.

"Stop!" Wolf lifted his hands up, hoping the Diggers would talk before firing.

Francis drew his weapon and pointed it toward Wolf as he twisted slightly to use the child as a shield. Carrell pushed his revolver against Molly's side and moved her in front of him.

Wolf stepped closer. In the darkness, he could see Molly was hurt by the way she stood, but she didn't say a word or cry out to him.

"What do you want, Captain?" Francis laughed, knowing he held all the cards. "Don't try to stop us, or we'll fire."

Carrell poked the barrel of his Colt hard enough against Molly to make her yell. "Your woman decided she's tired of you and wants to go with us."

"Give up, boys. You're surrounded," Wolf lied. "If you lay your guns down, I'll see that you live 'til the hanging."

"Some choice," Francis yelled. "How about you step aside and we leave? If you let us go, we'll drop the woman, still breathing, on the road somewhere for you to find."

"And the child?" Wolf took another step.

"We need the child!"

"No, you don't. If you try going to Savannah with her, I'll see that the sheriff will be waiting for you. She's no use to you. Let her go. If you have any hope of getting away this time, you'll need to travel fast."

The brothers looked at one another. Wolf could see their dream of being rich vanishing between them. Survival was all that remained.

Francis shook his head in disappointment. "You maybe can spoil our plan to get the kid's money, but we still need her and your wife to make sure we get out of Texas. Not a man will fire on us if he thinks he might hit your wife."

"Take me instead!" Wolf shouted, switching strategies. "I'll come unarmed."

The Diggers moved closer together to discuss the offer. Only one thing would be better than having Hayward's wife and that would be having the captain himself.

"Captain?" Josh whispered from a few feet behind Wolf. "Don't go. They'll torture you all the way to the border then kill you as soon as they think they're safe."

Wolf didn't waste time arguing. He knew Josh was right. "If they take the deal, open fire as soon as Molly and the child are safely out of range. Don't give them the pleasure of even getting me out of town."

"But—"

"Open fire." Wolf's whispered command left no room for discussion.

"Captain!" Francis yelled. He couldn't resist the chance to have Wolf at his mercy. Wolf was betting Molly's and Callie Ann's lives on it. "Put down your guns and walk slowly toward us. You got yourself a trade."

Wolf dropped his gun belt behind him, knowing Josh could make use of it in a battle. "Release my wife and the child," he yelled as he stepped into the center of the street.

"Try anything, Hayward, and you're all dead." Francis handed Callie Ann to Molly. "Meet your wife halfway."

He pushed Molly and she stumbled forward, almost dropping Callie Ann.

"When you're on the steps with us," Francis yelled, "Carrell can let the other ends of the ropes go. If she or the kid tries to run before you're to us, I'll pull the ropes. Your wife will only be dragged through the street, but the kid'll strangle before anyone can reach her."

Wolf nodded and took a step as Molly moved off the front of the porch and into the road. She walked very slowly, holding Callie Ann tightly in her bound arms while she tried not to trip over the ropes.

When they reached one another, Molly stared up at Wolf, her beautiful green eyes brimming over with emotions.

"Your life for theirs!" Francis teased, his rifle ready to fire if Wolf made a wrong move.

Wolf slowly raised his hand and touched Callie Ann's curls. "You all right, Princess?"

She smiled. "I knew you'd come."

His fingers brushed the side of Molly's face. "They didn't hurt you, did they?"

She shook her head. He could see her lie in the bruises along her chin, even in the shadows of dawn.

He leaned and kissed her bloody lip, lightly. "Take care of the princess," he whispered as if he were leaving for a day of work and not marching to his death. "Wait for me, Molly. For I'll love you until my heart beats no more."

She choked her tears back. "I love you," she whispered.

"I know." He smiled. "You always have."

He moved away toward the Diggers. She waited for Carrell to drop the ropes that bound her hands and Callie Ann's throat so she could run to safety. A sob escaped from her very soul as she realized Wolf had said the same words Benjamin had all those years ago.

"Don't worry, Miss Molly, he'll be all right." Callie Ann kissed both sides of Molly's face. "Uncle Orson stayed behind to help him."

TWENTY-EIGHT

W OLF GLARED AT CARRELL DIGGER. THE KILLER HELD
the other ends of the ropes that were tied to Molly and
Callie Ann. "Let them go," Wolf said as he stepped
onto the walk in front of Miller's store.

Carrell played with the ropes, taunting Wolf.

"Inside first," Francis snapped. "I think we should
have a little talk with you, Captain, before we leave.
Miller! Unload the wagons. We won't be needing the
boxes now. We're traveling with the famous Wolf Hayward. They'll let us through any blockade."

Wolf noticed Miller standing behind the door, shaking so badly his body knocked against both the wall
and the door. He almost felt sorry for the man. If Wolf
were guessing, he'd say Miller probably got involved
with the Diggers a little at a time. Doing things for
them that were not quite legal, but no great crime. Now
he was in way over his head, and fear kept him their
slave.

"Miller! Get the boxes out of the wagon." Francis

guided Wolf into the shop with the rifle barrel. "We're gonna take the captain down a few notches before we leave. If he's bleeding a bit here and there, he won't be near the trouble. It'll show his men we mean business."

Carrell Digger smiled like it was Christmas morning and he had presents. "Can I use my knife on him, Fran? I'd like to keep his ear." He dropped the ropes and hurried inside behind his brother.

The moment Molly felt the ends of the ropes fall, she held Callie Ann firmly and ran.

Josh stepped from his hiding place and welcomed her with open arms. He hugged them both tightly as he pulled them to cover, then stepped back, a little embarrassed by his boldness.

"Are you all right?" he asked, trying to sound all official.

"Get these ropes off, please," Molly answered. "Where are all the other men?"

Josh shrugged. "There are no other men. I sent word, but it may be a while before they get here."

"But I thought Wolf said the Diggers were surrounded?"

Josh pulled the rope free from her wrists. "He may have exaggerated a bit."

Molly was near panic. "A bit! A bit! You mean he went in there, traded his life for ours, with no one to back him up?"

Josh looked insulted. "I'm here."

Molly wasn't comforted. "What do we do? I can help. I know how to use a gun. Do we go in firing?"

She knew she was rattling, but Wolf was too close to death for her to worry about remaining calm.

Josh shook his head. "We wait here. Wolf can handle it. If they try to make a run for it in the wagon, I'll open fire."

"But Wolf might be hit." If she'd known Wolf was truly offering his life for hers she'd never have let him do it. "If they used us as a shield, they'll use him as one."

Josh didn't blink. "Those are his orders."

Molly looped Wolf's gun belt over her shoulder and waited. Callie Ann stood beside her, watching from the safety of the folds in her skirt.

Dawn crept up the street. Miller rushed out of his store and began pulling the hurriedly made coffins from the wagon. He didn't bother carrying them inside, but let them crash to the ground.

As soon as they were out of the wagon, he glanced back toward his store. In a sudden burst of panic, he ran for freedom.

"Miller!" one of the Diggers shouted. A rifle barrel slid out a crack in the door opening.

Miller didn't glance back. He made it to the center of the street before a shot rang out. When the bullet hit him, he stopped and raised his hands.

Molly thought he might be surrendering, but a second later, he crumbled. Blood poured from the center of his back.

She folded Callie Ann behind her skirt. The shot drew early risers. Another shot rang from inside the store, and Molly screamed. "Wolf's in there alone and unarmed with three killers!"

Josh didn't move.

A body crashed through the window. The man had been propelled so hard, he flew for several feet before landing in the street.

Josh and Molly stared at the lean-faced man lying like a broken toy in the dirt. "Two killers," Josh corrected.

They could hear the fight now. It sounded like ten men were inside Miller's place slugging it out. The dull thud of blows against flesh. The sickening sound of cries cut short by newly landed strikes. The slamming sound of bodies hitting walls.

"We have to help him!" Molly tried to pass Josh. She couldn't stand by and let Wolf die.

The young ranger held her back. "No, we can't. It's dangerous. You could get hurt in the fight and then the captain would kill me. Plus, I don't want to insult him. He can handle them alone."

Molly glanced at Josh as if she were certain he'd lost his mind.

Carrell Digger staggered out the door moaning in pain. He tried to make it to the wagon but crumpled before he could climb up. The horses spooked, dragging him several yards down the street before someone stepped out to stop the team.

When Molly turned back to the open door of Miller's store, she realized all was silent. She couldn't breathe. "Wolf's not dead!" she told herself over and over. *He's not dead.*

Several people hid behind doorways and buildings. All watched the store. All waited.

A huge man stepped into the breaking sunlight. For a moment, Molly could only stare as Wolf moved into the open, dragging the body of Francis Digger behind him.

Josh and several others ran forward before Molly could make herself move. She stood there, staring at the man she loved, watching his eyes narrow as he searched from face to face.

Their gazes met. He'd found what he looked for. Though he was surrounded by men, Wolf stared only at her. He smiled and nodded slightly, telling her everything was all right.

Molly lifted Callie Ann and walked slowly toward her husband.

People seemed to be everywhere asking questions, wanting to see, talking about what must've happened. Wolf didn't say a word. When Molly reached him, he put his arm around her and held her close.

She couldn't keep from brushing her hand over his chest, making sure there was no injuries. "Are you hurt?" she asked quietly amid the chaos.

"No," he answered. "Funny thing, I feel like I'm the luckiest man alive. Francis fired right at me from five feet away and missed me completely. He was so shocked, I had two blows on him before he realized I wasn't dead."

Callie Ann moved from Molly's arms to Wolf's. As she always did, she stroked his whiskers as if petting a cat. "Uncle Orson said to tell you, you're welcome," she whispered in Wolf's ear then laid her head on his shoulder.

Wolf glanced at Molly and raised a questioning eyebrow. He shook his head. "Come along, ladies. I'll take you home."

Hours later, Molly had had a bath and a nap. Callie Ann slept soundly in one of the extra bedrooms. As Molly headed downstairs, old Dr. Harley met her coming up for his turn on watch.

"How are the patients today?" he asked in his usual monotone.

"I just checked on them. Better, I think. Charlie drank half a cup of broth, and Early's dressing was almost free of blood when I changed it."

Harley smiled. "They're going to make it, thanks to you, Doctor."

"I only helped."

Harley protested then put his hand on Molly's shoulder. "You're a fine doctor, even if you think of yourself as a druggist. We've been talking. If you'd like a job at the state hospital, there's one waiting for you."

Molly was flattered. "I'll think about it."

Harley accepted her answer. "I heard what happened at dawn. You're a very brave woman, Mrs. Hayward. Maybe a match for that husband of yours. You know, I heard a rumor once that he was the leader of a group of spies during the war. Saved hundreds of Rebs' lives by making sure they weren't in the wrong place when the Yanks came through."

"I didn't know that." Molly had a feeling that, if she had waited for Wolf to tell her, she'd never know.

Harley nodded. "Oh, sure. I heard a man say once that Wolf was a chameleon who could walk back and forth between the lines like they weren't even there. They say he could blend into Northern or Southern camps without notice. 'Course, he won't talk about it. Like most of them boys, he wants to forget the war."

Molly thanked the doctor for taking a shift and walked out onto the back porch. "Between the lines," she whispered as she sat in the swing. "Northern or Southern."

She was still sitting there an hour later when Wolf came home.

He trudged up the steps slowly.

She could see the exhaustion in his every movement.

When he noticed her on the swing, he smiled. "I'm home," he said simply.

She knew the words didn't have anything to do with the town or the house.

He lowered himself into the swing beside her and pulled her against him.

Molly waited, not knowing how to start what she needed to say to him. She simply let Wolf rock them back and forth. Finally, they slowed. She looked up to find him sound asleep beside her.

When Molly heard Callie Ann calling her name, she carefully slipped from his arms and moved inside.

She checked on him from time to time, but he didn't move all afternoon. Molly worried that he might not be comfortable, but there was no way she could carry him upstairs, and she didn't have the heart to wake him.

Callie Ann played wherever Molly worked. If Molly moved to another room, even for a minute, Callie Ann would follow. When it came time to put her to bed, the little princess insisted she sleep on the cushion in the windowsill of her own room since both her beds were taken. The space was just long enough for her and she could watch Early and Charlie from her spot.

The nurse wasn't too happy, but Molly allowed it. Callie Ann needed to feel she was home and, to her, Charlie and Early were part of the family.

Charlie talked without pain in his voice when he was awake, and he seemed to enjoy Callie Ann checking on him. He'd visit with her for as long as she wanted to stay, but his hand never left Early's arm.

When Callie Ann asked if Early was going to be all right, Charlie said, "Sure, she will, kid. I'm going to hold on and not let her go anywhere."

In truth, Early rested far easier today. She seemed in a deep sleep, letting her body heal.

When everyone else was asleep, Molly went downstairs, intending to wake Wolf. To her surprise, he sat at the kitchen table consuming half their store of food. Two pie pans were empty, and he'd eaten most of the leftover chicken.

"Have a nice nap?" Molly smiled as she neared.

He didn't look up.

"I said—"

He swept her onto his lap. "Say it again," he demanded.

"I said, did you have a nice—"

"Not that," Wolf interrupted. "Say you love me."

She didn't hesitate. "I love you."

"Again."

"I love you."

"Again."

"How many times do you want me to say it?"

"Every day for the rest of our lives," he answered.

"All right. I promise, every day for the rest of our lives. Now, if you're finished eating, I have a bath ready for you upstairs."

He followed her to their room. She made no excuse as she sat on the corner of the bed and watched him undress. They talked of little things, pulling all the pieces together of what had happened the night before. Carrell Digger was dead, as was Miller. The thin-faced man would live to go on trial. Francis would hang. The judge gave Wolf and Molly custody of Callie Ann until she came of age. Then, if she wanted to go back to her grandmother's house, it would be waiting for her.

"I'm so sorry," Molly commented. "She'll never find a man who'll have her now that she has money."

"Nonsense." Wolf raised an eyebrow. "Any man would be a fool to not love a woman just because she inherited a little money. I'd have a talk with Callie Ann's fellow myself."

"I'll remember that," she agreed with him.

Wolf asked about Charlie and Early, listening to every detail.

Molly smiled as she watched him dry his hair on a towel. She thought about how good it felt to be here with him like this. She felt warm and protected and loved. She also noticed he dripped water over half the floor space and he'd left his dirty clothes in a pile.

Molly laughed. He was real, all right. Dream lovers would never do such a thing. Dream lovers never got dirty or spilled things . . . or made love like the world was going to end any moment if he didn't hold her.

Wolf pulled the towel off his head and looked at her. "What are you laughing at, darlin'?"

"Nothing," she answered. "I was wondering if you were going to shave before you came to bed, Benjamin."

He froze. "What did you call me?"

"Benjamin," she answered as she stood and began undressing.

Her actions almost erased the conversation from his mind. "I'm Wolf, remember?" he tried to sound gruff, but it was hard when all he could do was stare as her blouse opened. She was so proper, with never a button undone, and here she stood, taking off her top in front of him like it was something she'd done a hundred times.

Wolf couldn't stop looking. She'd have to do it a few hundred times more before he'd get so used to seeing her that he'd even chance blinking.

She let her blouse drop and twisted to undo her skirt. "I know. You're Wolf, my husband. The man I love. The only man I've ever loved."

Wolf ran a hand through his hair. "I thought I heard you call me by another name." He must be hearing things, he decided.

"I did," she said as her skirt drifted to the floor, revealing the thin white cotton of her underwear. She moved a few feet closer, just out of his touch. "I called you by your first name . . . Benjamin." As she spoke, she pulled the ribbon on her camisole. The lace over her breasts parted, showing the curve of her flesh.

Wolf tried to keep his senses about him, but they were mutinying fast. He could smell the rose water of her hair and a perfume that seemed blended into her underthings. He could see the outline of her body clearly through the cotton covering.

"I'm not . . ." Dear God, he couldn't lie to her. Not now. Not when she stood so close, playing with the ribbon of her camisole that, any minute, would be tugged just a little harder to reveal her fully.

"It took me a while to figure it out. The night you lay next to me after the fire was so much more than I'd ever known. In my dreams, the two of you kept mixing. You patted the stage, just like you patted the train that day years ago. The way you say you'll always love me. No one else would put the words together in just that way." She smiled. "I thought of prying your box open. I have a feeling you signed Benjamin on the marriage license."

"Why didn't you?"

"I didn't have to. I know."

"But, who do you love?" Wolf strangled the towel, trying not to reach for her.

"I love you. I've always loved you, but never more than I do right now." She tugged at the ribbon. The lace fell away from her breasts.

Wolf was lost to words. He closed the distance between them and kissed her wildly as his hands caressed what she'd offered to his full view.

They made love as she knew they would. Like the end of the world would come any moment and there was nothing he wanted, needed but her. Part of him was wild and exciting, part so tender she almost cried when he caressed her. But all of him was hers, and all of her belonged to him.

When they finally lay beside one another too exhausted to do more than breathe, he whispered, "I thought you wouldn't love me if you knew who I really was." He wasn't making excuses or trying to explain, only telling her his thoughts.

Molly moved her hand slowly over his chest. "I've loved you in both times, the past and the present. I've loved you in two worlds, my dreams and reality. I was meant to love you, Benjamin Wolf Hayward."

He stopped her hand over his heart. "And I will love you until my heart beats no more, my Molly."

EPILOGUE

Winter blew through Austin, Texas, in cold blasts of icy rain. Wolf turned up his collar and pulled his hat low as he headed home. This was his last trip. Tomorrow, he'd be taking over as sheriff and leaving the Rangers, at least for a time. Being a ranger got in a man's blood. He knew if he were called up again, he'd serve, but only for a short time. Soon, Molly would be needing him home more.

He laughed. The men had been teasing him that he was getting old and wanted to sleep in his own bed every night. He didn't argue. He could think of nowhere else he'd rather be. They said he'd miss the excitement of this life, but they hadn't lived with Molly.

Wolf moved through the streets at twilight. No one expected him in until tomorrow, but he'd ridden hard. He didn't want to spend another night without Molly in his arms.

Only one man remained at the office to greet him. Wolf filed a quick report and checked his mail. One letter lay in his box. Wolf didn't have to guess from whom. Wes McLain's bold writing filled the front of the envelope.

He leaned against his desk and cut the letter open, expecting bad news. Wes wasn't a man who'd write just to pass the time. But, as Wolf read, he couldn't help but smile. The letter simply listed John Catlin's progress. The wild kid had spent several months at his grandmother's ranch. Somehow, the wide open spaces had eased his soul. The English he fought so hard against came back to him as smoothly as if he'd never stopped using it. Allie and Wes thought he should go to school. Maybe one of the new colleges in Texas. But his grandmother sided with her grandson, who she insisted on calling Jonathan. He was a man fully grown and wanted to travel, see the world. She felt he'd get his education from living, and she'd offered to fund the trip.

Wolf folded the letter. Jonathan. A handle he never thought would fit the wild kid. But, people change. Look at him. A year ago he'd have stopped by for a drink and already be thinking about his next ride. Now all he wanted to do was go home. Home to Molly.

Wolf only nodded at the ranger as he left. Suddenly he could wait no longer.

As he passed his house, he saw Molly and Callie Ann in the kitchen, but the rain kept him from smelling what they were burning for dinner. He moved to the newly finished barn behind the house and unsaddled his horse. Charlie had done a good job on the barn. It was completely dry inside and had an extra room for

Uncle Orson, who didn't visit as often as he once did.

When Wolf stepped onto the porch, he stopped for a few minutes to look inside. Early was sitting at the table, wrapped in one of Aunt Alvina's quilts. She must be feeling stronger if she was able to help cook. Her recovery was slow, but she was pampered so much by Charlie that she didn't seem to mind. They'd made her a room in the study so she wouldn't have to climb the stairs. By spring she'd be well.

Charlie was still hard to look at, but his face appeared more normal since the doctors had worked on him. He'd bought Miller's old place and had been working regularly. He was only a memory at the saloons, but he'd become a constant at Molly's table.

Callie Ann spotted Wolf and squealed, running to the door. "Daddy!" She flew into his arms.

Wolf held her close. He felt his heart roll over every time the child called him that. She'd decided it all on her own when she'd learned Molly was expecting. Someone had to teach the baby what to call everyone, and Callie Ann appointed herself.

Molly waited at the door for him. She kissed his whiskered face and whispered, "I love you," as she always did.

Wolf let his hand fan out over her swollen tummy, loving the feel of their child growing inside her. He knew tonight, long after she'd gone to sleep, he'd place his hands around her and almost be able to hold his son or daughter.

Early frowned at him. "I only made one pie," she said. "I didn't think you'd be in tonight."

Wolf winked at her. "I'll survive if you'll promise to bake more tomorrow."

Early still didn't look happy.

Wolf stepped into the kitchen and removed his coat and gun belt. "What's the matter? You not feeling well?"

He glanced at Molly. She had the same strange frown. Something was wrong.

"What is it?" He looked from one to the other.

"We have aunts." Molly sighed as if announcing the end of the world.

"Really?" Wolf laughed. "Sugar or red?" He was truly home.